THE BLOOMSBURY MURDER

By Mike Hollow

THE BLITZ DETECTIVE SERIES

The Blitz Detective
The Canning Town Murder
The Custom House Murder
The Stratford Murder
The Dockland Murder
The Pimlico Murder
The Camden Murder
The Covent Garden Murder
The Soho Murder
The Bloomsbury Murder

THE BLOOMSBURY MURDER

MIKE HOLLOW

Allison & Busby Limited
11 Wardour Mews
London W1F 8AN
allisonandbusby.com

First published in Great Britain by Allison & Busby in 2025.

Copyright © 2025 by MIKE HOLLOW

The moral right of the author is hereby asserted in accordance with
the Copyright, Designs and Patents Act 1988.

*All characters and events in this publication,
other than those clearly in the public domain,
are fictitious and any resemblance to actual persons,
living or dead, is purely coincidental.*

All rights reserved. No part of this publication may be reproduced,
stored in a retrieval system, or transmitted, in any form or by
any means without the prior written permission of the publisher,
nor be otherwise circulated in any form of binding or cover
other than that in which it is published and without a similar
condition being imposed on the subsequent buyer.
A CIP catalogue record for this book is available from
the British Library.

First Edition

ISBN 978-0-7490-3200-5

Typeset in 11/16 pt Sabon LT Pro by
Allison & Busby Ltd.

By choosing this product, you help take care of the world's forests. Learn
more: www.fsc.org

Printed and bound in Great Britain by Clays Ltd. Elcograf S.p.A

EU GPSR Authorised Representative
LOGOS EUROPE, 9 rue Nicolas Poussin, 17000, LA ROCHELLE, France
E-maill: Contact@logoseurope.eu

For Barbara, faithful and generous of heart

CHAPTER ONE

He stopped at the traffic lights and looked up at the sky, one foot on the pedal and the other on the road while he waited for them to change. It was dull and grey, just like the streets around him. It wasn't so long ago he'd wished he was up there, roaring around in a Spitfire, but the past year had taught him there was a world of difference between what you'd like to be and what you actually were. With this job, when his time came round for being called up they'd probably put him straight into the army as a regimental cook. Not quite the same as a dashing young fighter pilot, but what could you do about that?

Besides, glamour wasn't everything. Just yesterday he'd heard about a young Spitfire pilot who'd joined the RAF at eighteen a couple of weeks before the war started. He'd fought over France and then over London, got the DFC and all, then last week he got killed, still just nineteen. That wasn't what Joe fancied, so maybe the army cookhouse would be just fine – at least he might come through the war alive. In any case, by the time he was old enough to be called up the war would most likely be over. He might miss the whole thing and still be here working for Old Man Harris.

Harris – Mr Harris to his face, of course – had a butcher's shop in Lamb's Conduit Street, and Joe was his delivery boy. Probably everyone in Bloomsbury knew who he worked for, because the space under the crossbar on his bike was filled by a big metal nameplate with 'N. Harris & Co., High-Class Family Butchers' painted on it, together with the shop's address and phone number.

The lights turned to red and amber and then to green, and he stood on the pedals to get the bike going again. It was a Runwell, one of their special ones made for butchers' and bakers' deliveries, with a small front wheel to make room for the biggest possible wicker basket on the front. It was the kind of thing Harris would probably call 'sturdy', but to Joe it just meant hard graft. No luxuries like gears to make the going easier, and with forty or fifty pounds of meat in the basket he soon worked up a sweat. The only good thing was that it got lighter as you did the round, dropping off packages to the customers' homes. He was on the last leg of his Monday morning deliveries now, heading back to the shop and hoping Harris might allow him a cup of tea before he got on with the rest of his day's duties.

He pedalled his way across Brunswick Square and down Grenville Street until he came to a narrow turning on his right, identified by the single word 'Colonnade' carved into the stone lintel above it. This was what the old people called Colonnade Mews: a long row of two-storey buildings behind the houses on Guilford Street, put up in the days when people got around on horses, not bikes or cars. Back then, apparently, they had stables on the ground floor, and upstairs there were flats for the coachmen to live in. Then when motors came along and horses weren't needed any more they became slums that only very poor people would live in. Now, though, to Joe's eye at least, they looked quite smart – perhaps they'd been done up.

His bike rattled and bumped its way across the cobbles that formed the narrow lane stretching a couple of hundred yards ahead of him. He'd learnt to be careful here, because the uneven stones could play havoc with his steering, what with the front wheel being so small. His next delivery was about a third of the way along, so he kept his eyes focused on the road immediately ahead.

He didn't see the cat until it was almost under his wheel. He wobbled, and the startled creature skittered away across the road. From the corner of his left eye he glimpsed the open door from which it had shot, just in time to see a woman staggering out behind it. She was about his mum's age and had red hair – that was all he had time to notice. It was too late to manoeuvre the heavy bicycle out of her way, and she clattered into him. He stuck his right foot out onto the ground to stop the bike going over and dumping the contents of its basket onto the cobbles, then got off and kicked down the stand over the front wheel so he could make sure the woman wasn't hurt. She was leaning back against the wall, panting for breath. Her eyes scared him – she was staring straight ahead as though she'd seen a ghost.

'You all right, Mrs?' he said, approaching her cautiously. She shook her head, her faced etched with fear. 'No.'

'What's happened?'

'I can't—' she blurted out. 'She's . . . She's in there.' Her voice dropped to a terrified whisper. 'I think she's . . . dead.'

CHAPTER TWO

'Yes, sir,' said Jago.

He rarely found himself in agreement with Detective Superintendent Hardacre, but years of working in hierarchies of rank, first by conscription in the army and then by choice in the police, had taught him that dissent was generally best left unvoiced. Not that he actively sought a quiet life – he wouldn't be a detective in the Metropolitan Police if he did – but he'd also learnt in those years that wherever possible it was best to fight on your own terms and when the circumstances were most favourable. In Hardacre's case, Detective Inspector Jago was still finding his way.

The question he'd answered was an apparently simple one, albeit unexpected: 'Do you know anything about Canadians?'

It seemed prudent, however, to admit that his experience was limited. 'I met a few in the war, sir,' he said. 'They were there at our side and came a long way to fight for the King.'

'So they did,' said Hardacre. 'And now it looks like one of them's been murdered – in Bloomsbury.'

'A soldier?'

'No, a middle-aged woman, but Canadian, and that makes it a bit sensitive, what with the Canadian Army coming over here to help us with this war. They were quick off the mark, too – got stuck in as soon as it started. So it doesn't look good if one of their civilians gets murdered on our patch.'

'I see what you mean, sir. Those Canadian troops were fearsome men to have with us. Some of our best snipers too.'

'Yes – damn good fighters, those lads, if my memory serves me right. When a tough job needed doing, they were the men to do it. Remember what they did at Ypres, 1915?'

'No, sir – before my time. Were you there?'

Jago knew that asking this question was a calculated risk, but he was curious to know how Hardacre would respond. He was not to find out, however, as his superior officer ploughed on as if he hadn't heard it.

'The Germans used gas,' said the detective superintendent, 'and there was chaos, but the Canadians held the line. An impressive body of men – good generals, and fine foot soldiers who knew how to obey orders. An example to us all.'

'Absolutely,' Jago replied, in no doubt that Hardacre saw himself as the general in the room and his subordinates as the foot soldiers.

'Backbone,' Hardacre continued, warming to his theme, 'and dedication, that's what they had. Not like the miserable cheats and layabouts we have to contend with these days.'

He swivelled his eyes in the direction of Cradock, who instantly drew himself up to attention, staring straight ahead and not daring to breathe until the detective superintendent's gaze returned to Jago.

'I don't know what it is about this war,' he continued, 'but discipline seems to have gone to pot – everywhere you look there's grocers fiddling the rations, frauds claiming the dole when they're getting paid for a job, people conning gullible fools out of their life savings, confidence tricksters round every corner. I tell you, it beggars belief. There's a bloke living not two miles from me who's just been tried for bigamy – he was living with a woman he called his wife and had three kids by her, but it turned out he's been married to someone else since 1919. And on top of that he'd been posing as a copper so he could check up on what his so-called wife was getting up to with some other bloke. These people are shameless.'

'Was he convicted, sir?'

'Oh, yes, he was convicted all right – he's been sent down for eight months for bigamy, which is something, I suppose, and fined ten quid for impersonating a police officer, but I mean, what's the country coming to? Whatever happened to good old-fashioned honesty?'

Jago suspected that honesty was no rarer today than it was in the rosy past of the detective superintendent's imagination, but knew by now that expressing an alternative view when Mr Hardacre was in full flood was like trying to calm a runaway horse by stepping into its path. 'I suppose there's always going to be wrong 'uns out there pretending to be what they're not so they can trick some mug out of their money,' he said. 'We just have to try and nick as many of them as we can to spare the victims. Isn't that right, sir?'

'Well said, Jago,' said Hardacre, looking slightly surprised by such ready agreement. 'So you just keep your eyes peeled.'

'Will do, sir. So this Canadian woman who's been found dead in Bloomsbury – was she some kind of trickster?'

'Good Lord, no. She was a respectable woman by all accounts, highly thought of – a bit of a do-gooder, apparently. So mind your step. The powers that be don't want any complications to mess up our relationship with Canada, not now they've sent thousands of troops over here to fight for us. So you get over to Bloomsbury double-quick and find out who did it, and try not to tread on anyone's toes, especially Canadian ones.'

He turned to Cradock. 'And you, Detective Constable – what do you know about Bloomsbury?'

'Nothing, sir,' Cradock blurted out, instinctively taking the path of least resistance.

'Well, you mark my words – there's a lot of people there who think they're very clever. Been to university, friends in high places – people who've got ideas.' He pronounced the last word in a way that sounded to Jago's ear as though he was saying it with a capital *I*. 'Dangerous things, ideas – they can get you into a lot of trouble. Do you know what the sergeant said when I joined the army?'

Cradock twitched his head rapidly from side to side. 'No, sir.'

'He said, "If any of you lot've got ideas, leave 'em

behind where they belong. You just do as you're told and leave the ideas to the officers."' He cast a hostile glance in Jago's direction. 'And we know where that got us, don't we? Same with some of those characters in Bloomsbury – intellectuals and the like. Too clever for their own good, some of them. So don't let any of them run rings round you, Detective Constable. Just remember your job's not getting tangled up with their fancy ideas – your job's nicking villains. I don't want to hear of any tomfoolery by you. Is that understood?'

'Yes, sir,' said Cradock.

'I can assure you, sir, you won't,' Jago added.

Hardacre peered at him through his wire-rimmed spectacles, as if weighing the meaning of this assurance with a degree of scepticism. 'Right,' he said. 'Just watch your step – both of you.'

'Yes, sir. And the address?'

'It's Guilford Street, near Russell Square – number 85. But you have to go round the back, to a mews sort of alley called Colonnade – there's a back entrance to the property there, and that's where it happened. I've told the photographer to report to you at the scene, and I've left a message at St George's Hospital for Dr Gibson, asking him to get up there as soon as he can.'

'Thank you, sir. If that's all, we'll get over to Bloomsbury straight away.'

'Yes.' Hardacre looked thoughtful for a moment, and then fixed Cradock with a scowl that seemed designed to induce guilt in the young man. 'And by the way, Constable, those Canadian snipers your guv'nor mentioned – you could learn a thing or two from them. They were good at their job – farm boys and hunters, most of 'em, and they'd learnt their business by hard graft. That's what I want to see from you – hard graft. They didn't just go over the top, charging in with all guns blazing – they were too valuable for that. No, they were patient, stealthy, focused on their target, waiting for the moment when they had him squarely in their sights, and then bang, they got 'im. If you want to be a half-decent detective one day, think about them. Don't go in with your blunderbuss, shooting at everything and hitting nothing – bide your time, wait till you've got your man in the crosshairs, and then pounce.'

'Yes, sir,' said Cradock, 'thank you, sir.'

'Right, off you go, then – and try not to make a fool of yourself.'

Jago was surprised: his private estimation would have put Hardacre's approach to policing firmly in the blunderbuss category. Perhaps these remarks to Cradock about subtle preparation and patience were more a reflection of how the detective superintendent imagined himself to be than the reality of his character, but even so, it wasn't bad advice. And a reminder to young Peter not to make a fool of himself was as timely to him as it was to anyone, including, Jago inwardly conceded, himself.

CHAPTER THREE

There was a flurry of snow in the air as the two detectives approached Bloomsbury in Jago's Riley Lynx. Not the useful kind of snow that might capture criminal boot prints, but the irritating kind that blew down the collar of your overcoat if you didn't keep it well buttoned up. You couldn't blame Nature for wanting to snow, of course, but for Jago, one of life's other minor irritants that definitely could be blamed on someone was the fact that since war broke out, weather forecasts had completely disappeared from the newspapers and the BBC's airwaves. It was understandable: the traditional forecasts would be of great value to anyone living across the Channel who fancied coming over to bomb you. As a result, like most people, Jago had had to fall back on reading the sky – easy enough to spot the dull grey cloud cover that signalled an impending snowfall, but that didn't give you as much advance warning as the old forecasts on the wireless used to do.

Colonnade proved to be too insignificant a lane to be marked on Jago's *A to Z* map book, but when they arrived in Guilford Street, a helpful passer-by directed them to the entrance in Grenville Street through which the butcher's boy had cycled earlier that morning. The car rumbled over the cobblestones as Jago drove in, and he could immediately see a uniformed constable standing guard at a door to their left. He parked the car and got out, followed by Cradock, and identified himself to the officer.

'Morning, sir,' said the constable, acknowledging Jago's rank with a smart salute. 'The body's in there, sir, in the sitting room – up the stairs and it's on your left. The photographer's just arrived, so he's gone up to take a photo of it.'

'And no one's entered the building since you got here?'

'No, sir, and I got round here pretty sharpish as soon as it was reported – I'm at Gray's Inn Road station, so it's only about ten minutes' walk from here. We've got a man on the front door too.'

'Who was it who reported the body?'

'A young lad called Joe Thompson – butcher's delivery boy. He dialled 999. I've told him to wait in the kitchen. That's upstairs too – it's an old stable building, you see, with a flat upstairs. The housekeeper says that's where the deceased lady lived.'

'The housekeeper?'

'Yes, sir – a Mrs Annie McCready. She lives on the premises, and it was her who found the body. I've told her to wait for you too, but not in the kitchen with the lad, in case you didn't want them talking to each other before you'd seen them.'

'Good – so where do we find her?'

'She's got a room in the main house – she says there's a connecting door at the back of the flat, and her room's the first on your left after you go through it.'

'Does she know who the victim is?'

'Yes, sir. She says it's Mrs Rosemary Webster – she owns the property and lives in the flat here.'

'Very good. Right, we'll go in, but I want you to stay here and keep anyone else out. I'm expecting Dr Gibson to arrive, though – he's the pathologist – so send him up as soon as he gets here.'

'Will do, sir.'

Jago left him at his post and entered the building with Cradock. They went to the room at the top of the stairs that the constable had identified as the location of the body, and found Nisbet, the Scotland Yard photographer, already at work. The room was tidy, clean and uncluttered. It was simply furnished, with a pair of comfortable-looking armchairs, a gateleg dining table and two chairs, and a standard lamp. In one corner stood a small desk adorned with some framed photographs, a telephone and a potted plant, and in the opposite corner an equally small table bearing a wireless of modest proportions.

There were no signs of a disturbance, and everything seemed in its place. Everything, that is, except the body of a woman lying conspicuously in the centre of the room, dressed in a pair of dark green slacks and a thick woolly jumper, and sprawled on her back on a carpet stained with blood.

'See if you can find any useful prints before Dr Gibson gets here,' he said to Cradock, 'and I'll go and tell that lad who reported the body to hang on for a bit until we can speak to him.'

'Will do, sir,' said Cradock, beginning to unpack his equipment from the murder bag. He still felt a surge of pride to be entrusted with this job, and couldn't resist setting about it with the kind of flourish that a conjuror might use for a stage performance of a magic trick.

Jago stood back and took in the scene. The blackout curtains at the small window were drawn back, and the remains of a fire in the grate were grey and lifeless. Apart from the body, only one thing looked incongruous in this unremarkable setting: a brass poker of the kind one would expect to find in any living room as part of a fireside companion set, but not standing neatly beside the fireplace. Instead it was lying where dropped or thrown on the floor, and the end of it was stained with what he guessed might be blood. He would leave that for Dr Gibson to deal with.

He left the living room in search of the kitchen, but as he did so he heard energetic footsteps coming up the stairs. He turned round to find the pathologist, who greeted him heartily.

'Hello,' said Gibson. 'I hope I haven't kept you waiting. I came as quickly as I could, but the windscreen was getting steamed up, and it's difficult if you haven't got a passenger in the front who can keep it wiped clear for you. I didn't want to crash into anything on the way here – it would be too embarrassing to end up as a patient in my own hospital. But anyway, here I am. Where's the body?'

'Just through here,' said Jago, leading him into the sitting room. 'What do you make of it?'

Gibson knelt beside the body and checked for signs

of life. 'Well, she's certainly dead,' he said. 'As for how she died, you can probably see there's a small wound here above her left eye. Judging by that and the presence of the poker on the floor, my initial guess would be that she's been killed by a blow to her head. But I'll be able to give you a more considered opinion when I've carried out a proper post-mortem examination.'

'So are we looking at a case of murder?'

'I'd say it would be unlikely for a sane person to attempt suicide by beating themselves over the head with a poker, and equally unlikely for someone to deal themselves a fatal blow to the head with one accidentally, but one must keep an open mind – anything's possible, in theory at least.'

'But you'd agree that it's most likely someone else who dealt the blow?'

'On the face of it, yes. But what I can't tell you is whether such person did so with malice aforethought – you'll have to come to your own conclusions about that. And then it's for the court to decide whether it was murder or manslaughter. But for practical purposes I imagine it would be appropriate for you to treat it as suspected murder unless or until your findings persuade you otherwise.'

'Thanks,' said Jago. 'And you'll let me know your estimate of the time of death?'

'Certainly – I'll get onto that straight away.'

Jago judged that now would be a good time for him to have a word with the boy who'd reported the body, so he adjourned to the kitchen. It was a very small room, with basic equipment, much as he would have expected in a flat like this. A youth was wedged into the corner, sitting on a small chair and reading a newspaper.

'Joe Thompson?' said Jago.

'That's me,' the boy replied.

'I'm Detective Inspector Jago.'

'Right – the other policeman told me to wait here. He said you'd want to talk to me. It won't take long, will it? I don't want to get in trouble with my gaffer, and he doesn't like me being late.'

'Don't worry – we can explain it to him if necessary. I just want you to tell me what happened this morning. I understand you're a butcher's delivery boy.'

'That's right. I work for Mr Harris – he's got a shop in Lamb's Conduit Street, and I do local deliveries for him. I was running a bit late today, on account of the crazy stuff that's been going on with the rations.'

'What do you mean?'

'Well, today's the day, isn't it? The meat ration's been cut from one and tenpence each a week to one and sixpence, so from now on everyone's going to have to make do with less meat. The Ministry of Food's said most of the offals are on the ration from today too, so people won't be able to get as much liver and kidneys and suchlike as they used to. It's been chaos the last few days – housewives were queuing up to buy what they could before the ration went down, so all the butchers were running short and couldn't even give them the new ration's worth. Mr Harris could only let them buy a shilling's worth, and some of them were getting quite angry.'

Jago recalled seeing something in the newspaper about the impending change to the meat ration but hadn't paid it much attention. Since being transferred from West Ham on K Division to Scotland Yard, he'd been lodging above

Rochester Row police station and relying on the canteen for his meals, so buying meat from butchers' shops wasn't something he had to do. Meat might well get a bit scarcer in canteens too, he supposed, but apart from that a change in the ration didn't have much impact on his day-to-day life. For butchers and their customers, however, it had clearly been very significant.

'Even this morning,' the boy continued, 'I had customers asking me what it was all about when I did their delivery, so that made me late, and I've got other duties to do back at the shop. I want to get on in the job, see – you can't be a delivery boy all your life.'

'You're hoping to be a butcher one day?'

'That's right. At the moment I have to do things like sweeping the shop and putting the fresh sawdust down on the floor, but I'm learning about all the different cuts of meat and how to make sausages too – I like that. And that's the only bit of good news about the ration changing, by the way – they said sausages still aren't rationed, so you can buy as many of them as you like if you can find them.'

'I'm pleased to hear that.'

Thompson leaned a little bit closer. 'I'm even learning butcher's back slang.'

'What's that?'

'It's like a sort of secret language, so the customers don't know what we're saying to each other – saying all the words backwards, like "kayrop" instead of pork, and "bemal" instead of lamb. I don't know it well enough to chat in it yet, though.'

Jago tried to imagine the lad before him as a portly

middle-aged butcher in a long white apron, knife in hand and a sharpening steel dangling from his waist, ruling over his own shop, and thought the youngster still had a lot to learn. 'You'd better not give away any more of your trade secrets, then,' he said. 'Now, I'll try not to keep you much longer. I just want you to tell me what happened when you got here this morning. What time was it?'

'It was about eleven o'clock, and I'd done most of the round, so I was working my way back to the shop. I was riding my bike past here when this woman suddenly ran out in front of me, and I crashed into her. She was in a right state, and she said there was a lady in here, dead.'

'What did you do?'

'The first thing that came into my head – I ran off down the road to find a phone box and called 999. Then I rang the shop and told Mr Harris what had happened, in case he was wondering why I was late, and he said I should come back here and see if I was needed as a witness or something. So I came back, and then a policeman turned up in no time at all and took over. He told me to wait here until you came.'

'Did you go back to the room where the body was?'

'No – the policeman told me not to touch anything and to stay put here in the kitchen.'

'Good. Now, this lady who was dead – did you know her?'

'No – she wasn't one of our customers, so I've never done a delivery here. I was on my way to someone up the other end of the road.'

'Did you see anyone else leaving this property when you were approaching it?'

'No – only the woman I told you about.'

'And did you see or hear anything that might've had something to do with what happened here?'

'No, nothing at all. Is it all right if I go now? It's just that I'll be in trouble with Mr Harris if I don't get all those orders delivered pretty soon. He'll have my guts for garters.'

Jago smiled at the boy's inadvertently appropriate choice of phrase. 'OK. You'd better run along then, and finish that round of yours. But if you think of anything else, just let us know.'

'Will do,' said Thompson, and left immediately.

Jago returned to the sitting room. 'Right, Peter,' he said, 'any prints on that poker?'

'No, sir,' Cradock replied. 'I reckon if someone hit the lady on the head with it, either they gave it a wipe afterwards to make sure they hadn't left any, or more likely they had gloves on – I mean, it's taters outside, isn't it?'

'It is, yes, but if you find yourself giving evidence in court I'd advise you to say it was very cold outside, not taters – unless the magistrate's a cockney who speaks the same language as you, which is unlikely.'

'Yes, sir.'

'And if the assailant was wearing gloves, what else would that suggest to you? Apart from the weather outside being cold, I mean.'

Cradock thought for a moment. 'Well, I suppose it could mean it was someone who was just popping in for a moment, so didn't take them off – so maybe it was someone she knew.'

'Or a stranger who'd called, and she invited them to

come in out of the cold for a moment out of the kindness of her heart?'

'I suppose so, if she was that kind of person. But it could've been someone who turned up intending to do her in, so deliberately kept their gloves on.'

'Yes – although again, "harm her" might play better for you in court than "do her in".'

'Yes, sir. So you mean it doesn't really tell us anything?'

'Not in itself, perhaps, but we must see what else we can turn up. Speaking of which, let's see how Dr Gibson's getting on.'

Jago crossed the room to where the pathologist was putting some of the tools of his trade back into his bag. 'Well, Doctor,' he said. 'Do you have that estimated time of death for me?'

'Yes,' Gibson replied. 'You probably know by now that a dead body doesn't cool at a consistent rate, and a lot depends on the circumstances, but I've taken her temperature, and allowing for the fact that it's cold outside and the fire in here has been out for some time, and that she's fully dressed, I'd say she probably died between approximately two and four hours ago.'

Jago checked his watch. 'So between about eight and ten o'clock this morning?'

'That's right. And now I suggest that if you have any more questions you pop over to St George's Hospital later today. I've arranged to have the body picked up in a few minutes and taken there, so I'll head back now and get on with the post-mortem examination immediately.'

'Thank you,' said Jago. 'We'll see you later, and in the meantime we'll see what else we can find out here.'

Once Gibson had departed, Jago turned his attention to the woman's pockets. These yielded nothing except a handkerchief, but there was a handbag lying on the table. 'Let's take a look in here, Peter,' he said, picking it up.

Jago's acquaintance with women's handbags was based more on his experience in the line of duty than on any intimate personal relationship with their owners, but the specimen in his hands seemed in every respect unexceptional. It was of average size, its brown leather was scuffed on one side, and it held a miscellany of everyday items: a purse, a small hairbrush, a comb, a compact, a lipstick, a couple of keys on a ring and other oddments. A Lloyds bank-book recorded the usual small deposits and withdrawals, but no conspicuously large amounts. A national identity card was made out in the name of Rosemary Webster, with her address given as 85 Guilford Street, Bloomsbury, WC1, which bore out the facts they'd already established. It seemed that the dead woman had taken the advice given by the government the previous summer, because when he opened the identity card he found a folded slip of paper on which were handwritten the words 'Next of kin: Flying Officer J. H. Webster, RAF Northolt'. Jago recalled that the Minister of Home Security had advised everyone to carry such a note in case they became an air raid casualty. Understandably, the minister had not added that this would also be helpful to the police in the event that they were murdered, but it was undoubtedly true.

'So,' he said, showing the card to Cradock, 'we know who her next of kin is and where to find him. It's a pity these national identity cards only ask for your Christian name and surname, so you can't tell whether a woman's a Mrs or a Miss, but that constable said she was Mrs Webster, so I suppose this Flying Officer Webster's either her husband or her son, or failing that her brother-in-law. Not her father-in-law, though – if she's got one, I doubt whether he'd be young enough to be a junior officer in the RAF. We'll have to buzz over to Northolt and see if we can find him, assuming he's not up in the air somewhere.'

'And assuming he's alive, don't you think, sir?' said Cradock. 'I mean, we don't know when she wrote that note, do we, and there's blokes in the RAF getting killed every day.'

The untroubled expression on the young man's face suggested an indifference to the violent deaths of men of his own age. Jago couldn't tell whether this was because the boy had grown callous or whether it was simply the unfeeling response of ignorance. He guessed it was the latter, but still it pained him.

'Yes, well,' he replied, 'let's hope he's alive – and you be thankful you're down here on the ground with me and not up in the sky trying to dodge a Messerschmitt.'

Cradock must have picked up something from the tone of Jago's voice. 'Oh, yes, of course, sir. I didn't mean—'

'I know you didn't, Peter – but don't go saying things like that to this man Webster when we meet him.'

'Yes, sir,' said Cradock, looking chastened.

Jago continued his examination of the handbag's contents. The purse contained a single pound note and a handful of coins, but nothing else of interest. It was lying, however, on a folded silk scarf, and when he removed that from the bag it revealed something else. 'Ah,' he said. 'This might be a bit more interesting.'

Cradock moved closer as Jago took from the bottom of the bag a postcard. It wasn't the kind with a picture on one side that you might send home from a seaside holiday – it was a plain one, with Rosemary's name and address and a tuppenny stamp on one side and a message on the other. The handwriting was in pencil, and was smudged here and there, presumably by rain.

'I can't make out the date it was posted,' said Jago, peering at the postmark. 'But the message says this, "No one's going to bully me. Best thing is for you to keep quiet. These things have a nasty habit of blowing back in your face, and we don't want that, do we? I recommend you don't breathe a word. If you do, you'll regret it – trust me."' He passed the card to Cradock. 'What do you make of that?'

'I'm not sure,' said Cradock, studying it carefully. 'It depends how you read it.'

'It's ambiguous, you mean?'

'Yes, sir. I mean, "No one's going to bully me." That could mean the person who wrote it was being threatened by someone and was trying to reassure Mrs Webster that they wouldn't succeed. But if you read it with a different kind of voice in mind, they could just as easily be saying "Don't you dare try to bully me." And the rest of it too – you could read it as friendly advice in a gentle voice, but it could just as easily be someone making a nasty threat.'

'That's very perceptive, Peter – I think you're right.'

'Thank you, sir – I wonder what the postman made of it. Or the post lady – we've got them too now because of the war, haven't we?'

'Whoever it is, I don't imagine they have time to read every postcard they deliver. Especially when nine out of ten probably say "Weather fine, nice food, room OK. Wish you were here." But I do think it'd be interesting to know who wrote this, and why.'

Jago slipped the postcard into his pocket and scanned the rest of the room. It was neat and tidy, and nothing looked as though it had been disturbed during whatever incident had cost Mrs Webster her life. The only sign of activity was a half-empty cup of tea on the table, together with a folded newspaper that looked unopened and a plate on which were half a slice of toast and some crumbs. One chair had been pushed back from the table.

'What does that little scene say to you, Peter?' he said, gesturing towards it.

'It looks like she was having her breakfast, sir, but didn't finish it. Maybe she was interrupted by a ring at the door and got up to let someone in – and maybe that's when she was attacked. There's no way of knowing that's what actually happened, though, or what time it was if it did – she could've fancied a spot of toast any time.'

'Yes – annoying, isn't it? But it does at least suggest that something happened to interrupt her.'

'That newspaper, too – looks like she hadn't had time to read it.' Cradock moved towards the table. 'It's *The Times* – that's what posh people read, isn't it?'

'Yes, but it's also what's known as a serious newspaper, so it could just mean Mrs Webster took an interest in things like politics and foreign affairs and business.'

'Oh – yes, right.' Cradock picked the newspaper up to take a look, but stopped when his eye lighted upon what had been lying beneath it. 'Look, sir – there's an envelope. It's got an address written on it, but no stamp.'

'Let me see,' said Jago, taking it from him. 'That's interesting – it's addressed to ABC Introductions, Hadleigh Mansions, Museum Street, Bloomsbury. That sounds like what they call a matrimonial agency, doesn't it?'

'Do you reckon she was looking for a husband, then, sir?'

'She wouldn't be the first widowed woman to look in that direction for solace, would she? Let's see what's inside.' He took a couple of sheets of paper from the envelope. 'Hmm – looks like she's written two letters.' He began to read one, then switched to the other. 'That's curious – one starts "Dear Henry" and the other "Dear Brian", and she's signed them both at the bottom, but neither of them has her address at the top. Do you suppose that's because an agency like that sends letters to men who might be interested but holds their addresses back so they can't make direct contact with the woman?'

'Don't know, sir – I've never used one. Have you?'

'Don't be ridiculous. Let's see what they say.' Jago quickly scanned the letters. 'Curiouser and curiouser, as Alice in Wonderland said. In this one she says "I'm a young widow who longs to find an experienced and responsible man who I can rely on to take care of me. I have independent means but my tastes are simple, and I believe I would make a very loyal and dependable wife for the right man", and so on. This other one says, "I'm a fun-loving adventurer with my best years ahead of me and am looking for a similarly adventurous man to share my energetic life with. I love travelling to warmer climes and fortunately I'm blessed with the money to do it – my favourite destination is the South of France", and she goes on in the same vein.'

He passed them to Cradock. 'Have a look for yourself. I don't know whether either of them's an accurate description of her, but she can't be both of these women. I think we need to find out a bit more about this. If she was thinking of linking up with strange men looking for marriage, I'd like to know whether she confided in her housekeeper or that next of kin of hers – or anyone else for that matter.'

CHAPTER FOUR

'Right,' said Jago as soon as the body had been removed from the flat, 'let's start with the housekeeper and see if she can shed any light on all this.'

The connecting door that the constable had mentioned was shut, but it had a Yale lock on their side, so Jago only had to turn the handle to open it. He found himself looking down a short corridor with a couple of doors on his left. He knocked on the first, since this was where she reportedly had her room, and it was opened by a woman who looked to him in her late forties, with lank red hair and a weary expression, dressed in a heavy skirt and cardigan and what he believed would be described as 'sensible' shoes.

'Mrs McCready?' he said. 'We're police officers – I'm Detective Inspector Jago and this is Detective Constable Cradock. May we come in?'

'Of course,' she said, her voice sounding flat. 'That young policeman said you'd be wanting to talk to me –

sit down and make yourselves comfortable. Can I get you anything?'

'No, thank you very much. We'll try not to be too long – we just need to ask you a few questions about what happened to Mrs Webster.'

She closed her eyes and bowed her head briefly, then raised it again and faced him with a resolute expression. 'Yes, I suppose you have to, God rest her soul. Best to get it over with – what do you need to know?'

'I understand you're the housekeeper here – is that correct?'

'Yes. I came here getting on for ten years ago – I saw an advert in the paper. Mrs Webster's husband had died not long before, and she was looking for a live-in housekeeper for a pound a week. I'd not been long widowed myself – my husband was gassed in the war and struggled on, but it finally caught up with him in 1929. Things weren't easy for me financially after that, so a job that meant I could live in . . . well, it was a godsend, really.'

'So how did you get on?'

'We got on very well. She didn't actually advertise for what some of the wealthy ladies call a companion-housekeeper, but I think that's what she was really looking for – someone who'd be a companion. And that suited me too. So, perhaps it was because we'd both lost a husband, but whatever it was, we became more like friends. She was still my employer, of course, and I was her employee, but she always called me Annie and insisted that I call her Rosemary.'

'I see,' said Jago. 'Now, I'm sorry if this is distressing, but I understand it was you who found her this morning.'

'Yes. We'd sometimes have a cup of coffee together, and we'd arranged to today. I've always been a big coffee drinker, and I'm very thankful it's not been rationed yet. So anyway, I came through here just a bit before eleven to get a pot brewing, but when I called out hello there was no answer, and as soon as I went into the sitting room I saw her there, lying on the floor, with blood all over her face, and that poker next to her. At first I couldn't believe it, but she wasn't breathing, and I knew she must be dead. I ran out for help, and that's when I met the butcher's boy. I expect he's told you he ran off to fetch some help.'

'Yes, he has, thank you. So there was no one else in the flat when you arrived?'

'No – not unless they were hiding very quietly somewhere. They must have fled before I got there.'

'Do you have any idea who might've been responsible for this attack?'

'No. I can't imagine anyone wanting to hurt her – she was a friend to everyone. Do you think maybe she was mistaken for someone else? Killed by accident?'

'We don't know, I'm afraid. A friend to everyone, you say – can you tell me a bit more about what kind of person Mrs Webster was?'

'Certainly. I'd say she was someone who always wanted to help other people. She was very involved with Bloomsbury House, for example. Do you know what that is?'

'No, I don't.'

'It's not far from here. It's on Bloomsbury Street, at the far side of the British Museum from where we are now.

It used to be the Palace Hotel, but before this new war started it was turned into a kind of headquarters for about a dozen organisations helping refugees, and they call it the Central Office for Refugees. Rosemary said most of them arrive in this country homeless and penniless, with barely the clothes they stand up in, and Bloomsbury House finds shelter and support for them, mainly with private individuals. She did voluntary work there, and she took some of the refugees into her own home here. I thought it was very kind of her, but I don't think it went down too well with some of the neighbours. Probably thought it was "not quite the thing" for a respectable neighbourhood, but I don't suppose she cared too much about that.'

'She had strong convictions, then?'

'Oh, yes. That's why she was living in that flat instead of here in the house.'

'What do you mean?'

'Well, it was when the Blitz started and all those poor souls in the East End were being bombed out of their houses. Do you remember that big to-do there was about better-off people in the West End moving out to safer parts of the country and leaving their nice big houses locked up and empty?'

'I do – and then the government told the borough councils to start requisitioning those places to accommodate them.'

'Exactly. But Rosemary was one step ahead of all that. She was already taking in refugees, like I said, and she'd offered to let the local council use this place for billeting bombed-out people, so she actually volunteered to have it requisitioned. It's run by the council now.'

'So she moved out into the flat so they could use the house.'

'That's it.'

'But you're still her housekeeper?'

'Well, I suppose I'm not really. The thing is, when the councils take these places over, they put a woman in to run them, and to do communal cooking for the residents. So I'm still the housekeeper, but now I'm paid by the council, not by Rosemary. I still help her out, of course, but that's what you might call my own bit of voluntary work. It saved her a few bob too, not having to pay me, so that must have been a help.'

'Did Mrs Webster have any financial problems?'

'I couldn't say for sure, but I don't think she was too flush with money. People probably thought she was, because she had a big house and was generous, but neither of those things necessarily mean you're well off, do they?'

'Not necessarily, I suppose, no. So that flat of hers was effectively a separate residence from the rest of the house?'

'Yes, but all one building, connected by that door you came through. Rosemary once told me that when these houses were built, they all had stables and coach houses joined on at the back, but then the area got run down and the stables ended up as slums for poor people to live in. Eventually most of those bits at the back were knocked down and then rebuilt separate from the house, but this one kept the two connected. So this is all one building, but two homes – the council controls the house, but Rosemary kept the mews part as her own home.'

'So that's why there's a lock on that connecting door, I suppose.'

'That's right. It was just for a bit of privacy. Not that she shut herself away – she wanted to be a friend to all the residents and help them, so she was always in and out of the main house, and they knew they could knock on her door any time and see her.'

'Was the door locked when you called in this morning?'

'Yes, it was.'

'But you have a key?'

'That's correct.'

'Of course. Do any of the residents have a key?'

'No.'

'But if any of them had knocked and she was in, she'd have opened the door?'

'Yes – she always wanted to be available if they needed anything.'

'And the back entrance – you have a key for that too?'

'I do, yes.'

'But not the residents, I assume.'

'That's right – they've no need for one.'

'Thank you, that's very helpful. Now, could you tell me who the other residents of the house are? We'll need to speak to all of them.'

'By all means. There's four of them. There's a lady called Ida Griggs – she was bombed out, over in the East End. Then there's Valerie Palmer – she's a volunteer ambulance driver with the London Auxiliary Ambulance Service at their station in Russell Court. That's in Woburn Place, not far from here. She was bombed out too, in Wapping. We've got a refugee – he's called Albert Nadelmann, and he's some sort of German professor. And then there's one more man, Charles Buckleby – he's a businessman, but I think he had a spot of bother and lost his money. He was already a lodger here when the council took the house over, so they've let him stay on. The two women are on the next floor up, and the men are on the top floor. Shall I tell them you're wanting to speak to them?'

Jago glanced at his watch. 'Yes, please, but it'll probably have to be tomorrow – we need to see Mrs Webster's next of kin first. We found a slip of paper in her identity card that gave his name as Flying Officer J. H. Webster. He's a relative, I assume?'

'Yes, that'll be Jack – he's her son. She only had the one child, as far as I know.'

'The note said "RAF Northolt" after his name. Do you know whether he's still stationed there?'

'Yes. That's where he was the last I heard – he was shot down, you see, and injured, and he's been recuperating there. It was very worrying for Mrs Webster, of course, but at least Northolt's not far away, so she's been able to visit him.' She paused, looking down at the floor as if distracted by the memory. 'And now she'll never see him again.' She pulled her shoulders back and returned her gaze to Jago. 'Anyway, you'll be breaking the news to him, will you?'

'Yes, we will.'

'Thank you – I'm glad it won't be me. I think he'll be OK, though – he's a strong young man, and Mrs Webster told me he was making a good recovery. She said it's very frustrating for him not to be flying, though – he can't wait to be back up in the air. Apparently the RAF's got him working on "special duties" now, whatever that means.

She didn't know either, but it sounds rather important, doesn't it? He said he wasn't allowed to tell her anything about it, so I suppose it must be.'

Jago noted the fact but said nothing. 'Did Mrs Webster have any other relatives?'

'She did, yes – she's got a brother. He's called Bowman – Gordon Bowman, and he's Canadian. Did you know Rosemary was Canadian?'

'Yes, I was told this morning. Do you happen to know how long she'd been over here?'

'In England, you mean? That would be since 1931, because it was later that year that I started working for her. Her husband had died, you see – in 1930, I think – so she decided to move to London. Jack came with her, of course – he was just a boy then – and she bought this place to live in.'

'Rather a large house for two people?'

'Her husband was some kind of successful businessman, and I think he'd told her property was the best investment, so I guess when she moved over here she was probably looking for financial security. But she always seemed to like having people round her and wanted to help anyone in need, so perhaps even then she was thinking about opening up her home to other people.'

'And why did she choose London?'

'She wanted to explore her roots. You know she was born here, don't you?'

Jago was beginning to wish Detective Superintendent Hardacre had briefed them in more detail. 'No, I didn't,' he said. 'When you say "here", do you mean in Britain, or in Bloomsbury?'

'Bloomsbury, I think.'

'So how did she end up in Canada?'

'Well, I don't know much myself. All I know really is that she was sent out to Canada as a child and adopted by a family there.'

'Sent out by whom?'

'By the local Board of Guardians.'

'Do you know why?'

'No, she never said, and I thought it wasn't my place to ask – I would've felt too much of a nosey parker. But there was a lady who came to see her once, and I think she'd been a member of the Board of Guardians back then. She'd probably know more about it, and I suppose if you're the police then it's your job to ask.'

'Do you recall her name?'

'I do. She was Mrs Cordingley – Mrs Pamela Cordingley, I think. I remember the name because there was a Mr Cordingley who owned a woollen mill in the town I grew up in. No relation, though, as far as I know. I think she lived somewhere round here – I don't know where, but she was quite a posh lady, so she's probably got a telephone. You might find her in the phone book.'

'Yes – thank you. Now, just to go back to what I was asking about relatives – you mentioned Mrs Webster had a Canadian brother, Mr Bowman. Was he a blood relation, or was he part of the family who adopted her?'

'He was the son of the Canadian family, so I suppose you'd call him her brother by adoption.'

'Did she have any other relatives?'

'Just her brother's family, I think.'

'Do you have an address for them?'

'Sorry, no, I don't, but I expect Rosemary's son will.'

'And can you tell me about the neighbours? I'm wondering whether any of them might've seen someone coming or going this morning.'

'That depends on where whoever it was came to – I mean, if they came to the front door someone might have seen them, but if they came to the back door, like you did, I don't think there'd have been anyone to see them.'

'So who are the neighbours at the front?'

'There's a man on that side,' she said, gesturing to her right, 'but he's out at work all day, and there's a lady on the other side who'd normally be at home most of the time, but she's away visiting her sister in Dover who's in hospital – she was caught in the shelling by those long-range guns the Germans have got on the French coast now. Dover's been a protected area since last April, so she had to get special permission to go, and it was terribly worrying for her, but Rosemary was a great support to her. So anyway, I think as far as neighbours are concerned your best bet is to speak to the lady in the house opposite, on the other side of the street – number 49. She's too snooty for my liking, but there's not much that gets past her round here. A regular curtain-twitcher she is – got her nose into everything. She's one of those busybodies the Ministry of Information gets to write reports on what people are thinking about the war, and what they say when they're in the shops or chatting in the pub. Not that she'd ever be seen inside a pub, mind you – she's far too respectable for that. "Cooper's Snoopers", that's what they call them, isn't it? She's one of them.'

Privately, it amused Jago to think that even the

supposedly sagacious prime minister, Mr Churchill, had apparently failed to anticipate when he appointed Duff Cooper to his post as Minister of Information that some unknown waggish member of the public or the press would inevitably come up with this obvious rhyming nickname. It did not do, however, for a police officer to betray even a smile of public amusement concerning members of His Majesty's Government, so his expression remained as impassive as stone.

'Can you tell me this lady's name?' he asked.

'Yes, it's Frobisher – Mildred Frobisher. A soppy sort of name, if you ask me, but she's apt to act like she's the queen of Guilford Street. And by the way, she's Miss Frobisher, not Mrs – she can get a bit prickly if you don't get that right.'

'Thank you. And just one last question, please. It was you who found the body, but it was the butcher's boy who ran to the telephone box and dialled 999. That's right, isn't it?'

'Yes, it is.'

'But when I was in Mrs Webster's flat just now I could see a telephone in the corner of the sitting room, just feet from where she was lying. Why didn't you use that yourself when you found her there?'

She looked confused. 'Well . . . I don't know – I think I just panicked. Seeing her there . . . it was shocking – I felt numb. Some instinct made me run for help, I suppose. I just remember screaming and running out into the street. It sounds foolish now, but I wasn't thinking straight, and when I ran into that butcher's boy and told him what had happened, he immediately dashed off, saying he'd call the police. That's all I can say, really.'

She dabbed at her eyes with her handkerchief. 'Will that be all, Inspector?'

'Yes, thank you, Mrs McCready. Is there anything else you'd like to add?'

She sniffed, wiped her eyes again and stuffed the handkerchief into her pocket. 'No. There's just one question that's been tormenting me since I found her, and I don't expect you to know the answer. It's just that Rosemary was so kind to everyone, always ready to listen and to help. I don't understand – why would anyone want to kill an angel of mercy?'

CHAPTER FIVE

Jago and Cradock took their leave of Annie McCready and headed back to the car via Rosemary Webster's flat. As Cradock closed the street door behind them, they saw a young woman hurrying towards them. Her coat had seen better days, and her gas mask case was the same battered cardboard as that of the humblest East End housewife, but when she opened her mouth she spoke with the same self-assurance as the country-squire officers Jago had rubbed shoulders with in the trenches, particularly when the High Command in its wisdom had seen fit to pluck him from the ranks and turn him into a 'temporary gentleman' with a pip on his shoulder and 'Second Lieutenant' in front of his name.

'Hello,' she said breezily. 'Are you friends of Rosemary's? I'm just on my way to see her.'

Jago raised his hand slightly, and she stopped, looking puzzled. 'I'm sorry, Miss, you can't go in at the moment.' He produced his warrant card and held it up for her to see. 'We're police officers – I'm Detective Inspector Jago, and this is Detective Constable Cradock. I'm afraid there's been an incident here.'

Her eyes widened. 'What do you mean? Is Rosemary all right?'

'Can I ask who you are, please?'

'Yes, of course. My name's Susan Ingram – and yes, you're right, it's Miss Ingram, as it happens – I'm a friend of Mrs Webster's, and we've arranged to go out for lunch together. What's happened?'

'I'm very sorry to have to tell you this, Miss Ingram, but Mrs Webster was found dead in her flat this morning.'

She recoiled, her mouth trembling, and for a moment looked unsteady on her feet.

'My car's right there,' said Jago, pointing. 'Let's get you out of the cold and sit down for a moment.'

She nodded mutely and followed them to the Riley. Cradock climbed into the back and motioned her to take the front passenger seat next to Jago.

'I'm sorry,' she said as she sat down. 'I'll be all right in a moment. It's just such a shock.'

Jago gave her time to compose herself, then continued. 'Could you tell me where you were and what you were doing between eight and ten o'clock this morning?'

She looked at him as though he was speaking a foreign language and then seemed to drag her thoughts back from some other unknown place. 'Of course, yes . . . I was in Kentish Town, North London, taking sandwiches to my father. He was working twelve hours a day as a volunteer bus driver because of the strike, and I was angry because he'd flatly refused to let me volunteer too, even though I could drive, just because I was a girl.'

Jago was puzzled. 'Which strike was that?'

'The general strike, of course.'

'But that was in 1926 – I'm talking about this morning.'

'Oh, forgive me,' she said with a start. 'You must think I'm mad. What I mean is I was at home, working on a story I'm writing – I was wrestling with one of my characters, trying to establish her essential motivation, and drawing on that past experience of mine during the strike for inspiration. I find first thing in the morning is the best time for that sort of creative thinking, because my mind's not cluttered with the events of the day – although I have to say these days it's often the events of the night that are the problem. All that crashing and banging of the bombs and the guns is not conducive to calm reflection, but still I must persist. It requires a hundred per cent concentration, and I have to immerse myself completely in the scene, so that in my imagination I'm actually there. Sometimes I even forget to eat. Not that that matters – I live alone, you see, so I can eat whenever I like. It's probably just as well I don't have a husband, let alone a child – their very lives might be at risk if I didn't remember to feed them.'

'Can anyone corroborate that?'

'My marital status, or my whereabouts?'

'Your whereabouts, if you don't mind.'

'Well, no, I'm afraid not – there was just me, at home, lost in my thoughts.'

'Can you tell me when you last saw Mrs Webster?'

'Yes – I spoke to her only yesterday, and everything seemed fine. We hadn't seen each other for a while, so we decided we'd meet up here and go to a little café we both like in Southampton Row. She was going to treat me. And now . . .' She sighed. 'Now I'll never see her again. How did she die, Inspector?'

'She had a fractured skull.'

'Was it a fall?'

'No – I'm afraid it was a homicide. We're treating it as a case of suspected murder.'

She gasped. 'Oh – that's not what I thought you were going to say. That makes it even worse. How could anyone deliberately kill her?' She took a deep breath. 'But I'm sorry, Inspector – I must pull myself together. There are people all over London who've lost loved ones closer than I was to Rosemary.'

'How close were you?'

'What can I say? She was like a second mother to me – perhaps the mother I never had.'

'I'm sorry. Were you orphaned?'

'No – except perhaps metaphorically. Are you local to this area?'

'Not to Bloomsbury, no.'

'Have you heard of the Bloomsbury Group?'

'The famous writers and artists?'

'That's one way of describing them, I suppose – yes.'

'Why do you mention them?'

'Because when I had some trouble in my life, Rosemary took me under her wing and tried to help me.'

'May I ask what kind of trouble that was?'

'You don't want to know my troubles.'

'If Mrs Webster was involved, I do.'

'All right, then. It was to do with the Bloomsbury Group

and my family – or to be more precise, since I have no siblings, my parents.'

'Do you mean your parents were members of the group?'

'Not actually members of it, no. I think they were more what you might call fans – in fact I'd say hangers-on. They moved to Bloomsbury before I was born, hoping some of the group's Bohemian intellectual glamour would rub off on them, I suppose, but I don't think they were ever admitted to the inner circle. They just wanted to be like them – free spirits. You know what people say about imitation.'

'The sincerest form of flattery?'

'Exactly. My parents didn't have the wit or the privileged background of the group itself, but I think they were infatuated with it and tried to ape its more outlandish attitudes, especially when it came to relationships.'

'Meaning?'

'All I'll say is that some of the members of that group had some rather avant-garde ideas about marriage, and my parents became rather taken with them too. If you ask me, things like experimental love triangles may be all very well if you're rich and famous, but for ordinary people like my parents . . . well, when I was a child I found it all very confusing and upsetting, and the worst of it was that I don't think they cared. To put it bluntly, by the time I grew up and met Mrs Webster, I was completely messed up – mentally, emotionally and socially. She helped to put me back together again – it was thanks to her that I got my life back on an even keel and started to live like a normal adult.'

'So how long have you known Mrs Webster?'

'Well, I'm sure you're too much of a gentleman to ask a girl her age, but as I said, I met her once I'd grown up, and I can tell you I came of age six years ago, in 1934.'

Jago did a quick mental calculation. 'So you're twenty-seven now.'

'You could say that, yes.'

'And apart from very caring, how would you describe her?'

'I'd say she was an unusual person – not just doing charitable works to be seen and admired, but really passionate about doing the right thing, even if it might be personally costly for her. She was involved in that project to bring Jewish children out of Germany before the war started – she was a volunteer at Bloomsbury House, and I believe that's been the headquarters for lots of groups involved in that work. I think she did a wonderful job, but I know some people were quite unpleasant to her about it.'

'Unpleasant enough to want to harm her?'

'That I couldn't say. People can be very well-mannered and yet still filled with spite on the inside.'

'Are you thinking of anyone in particular?'

'No, it's just a general observation. I like observing people – it feeds me with ideas for my writing.'

'Yes, you mentioned that you're a writer – is that in a professional sense?'

'Yes, and that's the only way in which the Bloomsbury Group has had a positive influence on me. When I was seventeen I read Virginia Woolf's novel *Mrs Dalloway* and fell in love with her writing. From that moment on I wanted to write novels, like her.'

'And you've done so?'

'Yes and no. You see, it's one thing to be driven to write, to know that it's what you were made for, but it's quite another thing to find a publisher willing to take you on. It's worse still if you're a woman, even in these supposedly enlightened days – a lot of female authors still find they have to write under a male name to get published.'

'Is that what you did?'

'I tried it with my first book, but I got nowhere – the publishers weren't interested. The problem is I'm a serious writer – I don't just churn out sentimental tosh like some I could mention, but it seems that's all most people want to read. The publishers' biggest customers are the lending libraries, like Boots and Smiths, but they want what's known as "popular fiction", the sort of books the man or woman on the Clapham omnibus wants to read – what you might call the lowest common denominator. But that's not art – it's not exactly breaking new ground in literary endeavour, is it? If I wanted just to earn a living, I'd write what people call "light romance", but I want to aim higher than that.'

'So are you still trying?'

'Yes, of course. If I don't believe in myself, who else will? The trouble is, all the successful serious writers of the past decade have been men, and most of them are privileged. Do you read George Orwell?'

'No.'

'Well, he said only last year that the problem is nearly all of them fit into what he called "the public school-university-Bloomsbury pattern", so for a young woman it's doubly hard to break in. I didn't go to Eton, nor to university, and although I may live here, I'd describe myself as "in Bloomsbury but not of it" – and yet I believe I have something important to say. And now we've got this blasted war, and that's really put the final nail in the coffin – it's virtually impossible for new authors to get their work published at all now. A writer friend of mine told me recently her agent said the best he'd been able to get for her was an offer from a publisher of forty pounds outright for the rights to her book, and he thought she should accept it. Forty pounds for two years' work! I could be an air raid warden and get a hundred a year. A girl needs a private income to become a successful writer these days.'

'And you don't have one, I suppose.'

She laughed scornfully. 'No, worse luck. There was a time when I thought my parents might support me in my literary career, but they died three years ago in a car smash on the Corniche, near Cannes.'

'I'm sorry to hear that – it must've been a terrible shock for you.'

'A shock, yes, but not a surprise. It was self-indulgence that killed them. They'd gone off pleasure-seeking in the South of France with their friends – I believe the French police thought it was their own fault, and I think snow was involved. And when I say snow, I don't mean they were on a skiing holiday – I mean snow as in cocaine.'

'Really?'

'Yes. I always knew they were self-centred and only interested in pleasing themselves, even when I was a child. I think they regarded me as an encumbrance. They packed me off to some ghastly cheap boarding school as soon as they could so they could be free to do what they liked. Then when they died I discovered they'd left me without a bean – they'd spent every penny on themselves. But that's not going to stop me.'

'With your writing, you mean?'

'Yes. My mother and father didn't believe in me, but now I've got a new idea for a novel, and I'm going to prove I can do it, even if they're not here to see it. Not that they'd be able to appreciate it, of course – deep down they were just a couple of philistines. They thought hob-nobbing with famous people made them special, but they weren't. I received a few letters of condolence after the crash – one woman said, "They were like a pair of shooting stars that brightened our lives all too briefly and were gone too soon", or some such nonsense. But that was probably just her arty sarcastic way of saying they were a flash in the pan – here today, gone and forgotten tomorrow. That's not how I want to be remembered – I want my new book to shine in the firmament as the defining portrait of British life in the 1930s, capturing and dissecting the zeitgeist of my generation.'

Jago could see Cradock reeling in the face of this verbal flurry and stepped in lest she should unleash a question at the defenceless constable. 'I see,' he said thoughtfully. 'An ambitious goal.'

'It is, but I'm ready for it.' She paused, as if expecting Jago to say something, but when he didn't, she stared accusingly at him. 'Aren't you going to ask me what it's about?'

'I wasn't sure you'd want to reveal that – isn't it all supposed to be a secret until you've finished it?'

She ignored his question. 'I'll tell you, then. It's about how my generation's inheritance was plundered and squandered by the previous one. When I was born, in 1913, my parents' generation had everything – peace, prosperity, an empire that stretched right round the world, political stability, sound money, even motor cars and aeroplanes. The future was bright. But they were selfish, and complacent too. They plunged us into the biggest war in history, that killed millions and left Europe in ruins, then they let millions more die of disease. They devastated the economy, destroyed businesses, and threw millions of people out of work, then let foreign dictators hurl us into a second world war. And now my generation is having to fight and die for them. I'll tell you the title of my novel too. It's called *Dispossessed*, because that's what they did to us – they stole our inheritance. They took everything and left us with nothing, and now my generation is paying the price. We are dispossessed, and it's their fault.'

Her words hung on the air while Jago waited, uncertain whether she was merely drawing breath for another round, but she seemed to have finished.

'So,' he said, 'a guilty generation, and your mother and father were part of it.'

'Yes, I believe they were.'

'And what about Rosemary Webster? The mother you never had, as you said. Was she tainted by that guilt too?'

'No, of course not. She was totally different. If it wasn't for Rosemary, I'd have given up writing, perhaps even given up life itself. It's only her kindness that's enabled me to keep pressing on. When I said Rosemary took me under her wing and tried to help me, I meant she gave me shelter when I had nowhere to go. She took me into her own home. She gave me a room in her house and never asked for rent. She gave me her time, listening to my troubles and encouraging me – she said she'd dabbled in writing fiction herself when she was younger and had high hopes, but unfortunately didn't have my talent. She even gave me money to live on so that I could fulfil my potential as an author, at least in the beginning. Virginia Woolf once said "A woman must have money and a room of her own if she is to write fiction," and that's what Rosemary gave me.'

'But you said just now that you'd arranged to meet Mrs Webster here, at her home. Does that mean you've moved out?'

'Yes, I have.'

'Why was that?'

'I just felt it was time I did, and Rosemary felt the same. It was time to stand on my own two feet, and in any case she couldn't necessarily keep supporting me for ever. I've got a little bed-sit over in Mecklenburgh Square now, and I'm still writing – if for nothing else, to show Rosemary I could do it and to thank her for her support.' She paused, head down, and wiped her eye. 'And now . . . Now she'll never know, will she?'

Jago waited for her to compose herself again. 'I think that'll be all for now, Miss Ingram, and I'm sorry we had to give you such distressing news out of the blue like that. We have to go and break it to Mrs Webster's son now.'

'Jack, you mean?'

'Yes – you know him?'

'Only slightly. He's in the air force, so he's not been around much. I've met him now and then when he's been visiting Rosemary.'

'How did they get on?'

'They got on well, as far as I know. She was rather protective of him, perhaps too much, but that's what mothers are like, isn't it? Most mothers, anyway – mine wasn't. I think Rosemary worried about him, but he's a grown man and old enough to make his own decisions, even if she didn't agree with them.'

'Right, thank you. And in case we need to speak to you again, can you tell me where exactly in Mecklenburgh Square you live?'

'Yes – it's number 51. It's only a couple of minutes' walk round the corner from here, and it's quite conspicuous – the house next door got bombed last September. That's probably why my room's the cheapest in the house – top floor back, so least protected of all if it gets hit. Beggars can't be choosers, though. Quite a few writers have lived in the square, so I'm hoping some of their success might rub off on me – even Virginia Woolf herself has a place there, I believe, although sadly I haven't bumped into her yet. Anyway, that's where you're most likely to find me. I'll probably be up there writing – and thinking of Rosemary. After what's happened to her it's going to be even more important to me to finish my book. And when I do, I shall dedicate it to her.'

CHAPTER SIX

'So, Peter,' said Jago when they'd left Susan Ingram to her literary endeavours and walked back to the car, 'what did you make of those two? Mrs McCready and Miss Ingram.'

'Well, they both seem like pretty reliable witnesses,' said Cradock. 'I mean they both knew the deceased lady quite well. But that author woman, Miss Ingram, she was a bit . . . er, I can't think of the right word . . . not quite real.'

'A tad theatrical?'

'Yes, that's right – very confident, but when she started talking about that book she's writing she got all dramatic, as if she'd got a script and was doing a performance. But maybe that's what authors are like – they spend so much time writing books, they end up talking like one.'

'You could be right – I got the same impression, and it made me wonder what might be going on underneath all that drama. She accused her parents of being self-centred, but it left me thinking maybe it runs in the family.'

Cradock nodded his head thoughtfully. 'I wasn't sure what to make of her, really. She sounded like what my mum used to say – like she'd swallowed a dictionary. I got lost after she said that zite-something – is that foreign? And what's a firmament?'

'The firmament is the heavens, Peter, and that zite-something, as you put it, is a German word, and it means the spirit of the age.'

'Oh, right,' said Cradock. It seemed to Jago that the boy was probably none the wiser for his explanation. 'Blimey, sir,' Cradock continued. 'You know a lot of words, don't you? How'd you manage that?'

'Well, I've never swallowed a dictionary, but when you were a babe in arms and I was a young lad working as a trainee reporter on the *Stratford Express* I did something a bit more achievable – I bought myself one, and every time I came across a word I didn't know, I looked it up. You could do worse than try the same thing yourself. Of course, when the government conscripted me and put me in khaki for a couple of years I didn't take it with me to the front, but when they let me out at the end of the war I dusted it off and started reading serious broadsheets like *The Times* or the *Telegraph* to try and make sense of what the whole war had been about, and I made good use of it again.'

'I've never read *The Times*, sir – never thought it was made for people like me. But, er . . .' He affected a knowing tone. 'Would that be our *Times*, sir, or the, er, New York one?'

'Don't be facetious, Peter – and if you don't know what facetious means, go and look it up.'

Jago knew he was being stern with Cradock, but it was his job to be stern. Nevertheless, it was an effort to stop himself smiling. The boy was clearly attempting what he no doubt considered a clever allusion to a certain American newspaper journalist of Jago's acquaintance, even though he must surely know that Dorothy worked for neither the *New York Times* nor the Printing House Square one – her paper was the *Boston Post* – but he found it surprisingly touching that his young assistant should presumably feel safe enough in his company to attempt a little gentle teasing. His thoughts wandered for a moment: he would soon be spending a pleasant evening with Dorothy. But he couldn't afford to let his mind drift too far from the case in hand.

'And what about Mrs McCready?' he said.

'Well,' said Cradock, 'she seemed to know a lot about Rosemary Webster, but I got a bit mixed up about whether she was really Canadian or British, what with Mrs McCready saying she was born here, like I was. Did Detective Superintendent Hardacre get it wrong?'

'Canadian by adoption – that's what she actually said. But in any case, all Canadians are British subjects. Didn't they teach you that when you were at school, on Empire Day? Or did you grow up in one of those places where the council wanted to abandon it and celebrate the League of Nations instead? International peace and goodwill, and all that.'

'I think we just had the standard Empire Day, sir – responsibility, duty, sympathy and self-sacrifice, that's what they used to say.'

'Well, if they ever mentioned Canada, they may've said it's a dominion. That means it's got its own government, but King George is the head of state, and all Canadians are British subjects.'

'Oh, yes, I, er, remember that now.'

Jago gave him a sceptical look. 'Very good. Oh, and by the way, as for Mr Hardacre getting it wrong, as you say, a word of advice that you might find helpful as your career in the Metropolitan Police marches confidently on. As I'm sure he'd remind you if he were here in person, a detective superintendent may on occasion be misinformed by less competent underlings, but a detective superintendent, especially if he's one you're working for, is never wrong.'

'Yes, sir.'

'Anything else before we go?'

'Well, yes, there is one thing. When she discovered that body lying there – don't you think it's a bit odd she didn't use the phone and dial 999? I mean, it was right there in the room with her, wasn't it? Basically she just ran off.'

'I agree, it is a bit surprising on the face of it. But as she said, when people are shocked by something like that happening they don't always necessarily think straight. And she did say the butcher's boy dashed off to report the incident as soon as she told him, so in her eyes that might've meant she didn't need to. You could say she fled the scene of the crime, but only as far as the street, so that's not really incriminating, is it?'

'I suppose not. I just thought it was a bit funny, that's all – you know, maybe trying to pull a fast one, take us for a ride.'

'Peter, you sound like someone out of a gangster movie. Have you been watching *The Saint* again at the pictures?'

'No, sir. Sorry, sir – I meant maybe she was trying to mislead us.'

'You mean she made a deliberate choice not to call the police and report the crime, and now she's trying to cover it up?'

'Yes, sir. Sorry, sir.'

'No need to apologise, Peter. It's a reasonable question to ask – but I don't think it puts her at the top of our list of possible suspects.'

Jago put the ignition key into the lock on the car's dashboard. 'So,' he said, 'do you think you'll be rushing out to buy Susan Ingram's book when it comes out?'

Cradock's eyes rolled. 'I should cocoa! Not my cup of tea at all.'

'I thought it might not be. And I'm no expert, but I can't help wondering whether when she said the publishers weren't interested in what she'd written, that was because they knew the readers wouldn't be interested either. But what do I know about it?'

'You mean it's a closed book, sir?'

'Very droll, Peter. But I can't help feeling sorry for her, slaving away in that cold little garret of hers on a book that might never see the light of day. They do say people like that have to suffer for their art, but it can't be easy.'

'Yes – and a pity she never got to have lunch with her pal Mrs Webster too. The poor thing'll be starving now, won't she?'

The humbly expectant glance he shot in Jago's direction was as lacking in subtlety as his attempt at a rhetorical question.

'Your compassion for that young lady does you credit,

Peter,' said Jago. 'I'm sure young Emily would be proud of you if she knew. You're still walking out with her, aren't you? Only I haven't heard much about it from her mother recently, and you know Rita likes to keep me up to date.'

Cradock's eyes widened in alarm. The thought of Jago discussing Emily and their love life with his old friend Rita was as disturbing as ever. 'Yes,' he said, 'everything's fine.'

'Good – you don't want to get on the wrong side of Rita. But I assume that compassion of yours has its origins in your stomach as well as your heart. Was it a hint that you'd like to treat me to lunch?'

Cradock's eyebrows rose another notch. 'No, sir, of course not . . . I mean—'

Jago laughed as he turned the ignition key and pressed the starter button. 'It's all right, Peter. I was already thinking perhaps it was time to haul you back from the brink of extinction. We'd better get over to the hospital now and see what Dr Gibson's managed to find out from his post-mortem, but I'll buy you a sandwich on the way – and perhaps a piece of cake.'

'Cor, thank you, sir,' said Cradock. His relief was heartfelt and doubled.

As they drove up Constitution Hill on their way to St George's Hospital, fortified by their sandwich lunch, the view ahead was impressive. To their left was Buckingham Palace, and to their right the ornate splendour of Canada Gate, a masterpiece in gilded wrought iron given to London by the Dominion of Canada in memory of Queen Victoria. He remembered his father taking him to see it when it was opened in 1911, when he was just a boy. Days that now seemed like distant history, two world wars ago. He also recalled a more recent moment, when he'd passed it in the May of 1939 and had his first sighting of BBC television cameras, a pair of which were mounted on the roof of a van parked beside the gate, ready to transmit images of the King and Queen setting off from the palace for their visit to Canada.

Like so many other things, that visit had been overshadowed by the threat of approaching war. The royal couple were supposed to have sailed on the battle-cruiser HMS *Repulse*, but at the last minute they switched to a passenger liner instead, the *Empress of Australia*, escorted by two Royal Navy cruisers, because, in the government's discreet words, it was thought preferable to keep the *Repulse* in European waters. Jago had taken this at the time as a sure sign that she might be needed closer to home to fight a war, and it was little comfort to be proved right less than four months later. He never saw the BBC's transmission, of course – like the vast majority of the population, he didn't own a television receiver. And probably just as well, he thought, because they cost anything up to thirty-five guineas and had become useless overnight when the onset of the new war meant the BBC's fledgling television service was shut down without notice for the duration.

He wondered whether Rosemary Webster had ever owned a television set, and whether she'd have been interested in seeing the King departing for a tour of her adoptive country. The size of her house in Guilford Street might suggest she'd once have been wealthy enough to buy one, but it was no guide to what her politics might have been. Whatever the case, though, he reflected wryly, her existence had now been cut off as abruptly as the BBC's television service, so he might never know.

Five minutes later they were in Grosvenor Crescent Mews, behind St George's, the big hospital by Hyde Park Corner. Jago parked the car, and they got out. Cradock seemed not to be bothered by the wintry weather, but Jago shivered as a gust of icy wind buffeted his overcoat. He rang the bell at the hospital's back door and waited, stamping his feet to keep warm, just as he had as a young constable on the beat twenty years before.

He was still stamping energetically when the door opened to reveal Spindle, Dr Gibson's lab technician and assistant, dressed in a clean white coat.

'Come in, gentlemen,' said Spindle gloomily, casting a wary eye at the snow-laden clouds above. 'You'll catch your death waiting around out there in the cold.' He paused as they squeezed past him into the building, then resumed in a morbid tone, 'Mind you, I suppose if you want to avoid catching your death, a mortuary may not be the best place to take refuge.'

Jago rewarded the technician's attempt at wit with a faint smile. 'Thanks for the tip, Mr Spindle,' he said. 'I trust Dr Gibson's finished his post-mortem examination?'

'Yes, he has, Inspector, and he's looking forward to discussing his findings with you,' Spindle replied as they set off down the corridor. 'Terrible weather, though, isn't it? We had a frozen pipe in here this morning.' Jago wasn't surprised to hear this: the post-mortem room had always felt too much like an icebox for his liking, even at the best of times. 'Seems they've got it worse in France, though,'

Spindle continued. 'Worst snow for fifty years, and two hundred thousand tons of it cleared from the streets of Paris, the paper said. Perhaps that'll stop those bombers coming over for a bit and give us all a little respite.'

'Actually, I don't think I heard any last night,' Jago replied. 'Do you think that could be why?'

'That and the RAF giving them a taste of their own medicine, perhaps. And not before time – as the good book says, "*As thou hast done, it shall be done unto thee – thy dealing shall return upon thine own head.*"'

'Does it really?'

'It does. I grant you it may not have been written with the Luftwaffe's bombs on London specifically in mind, but I think the general principle applies. It also says "*Though thou mount on high as the eagle, and though thy nest be set among the stars, I will bring thee down from thence, saith the Lord.*" Have you read the book of Obadiah?'

'I can't say I have, no.'

'Well, it won't take you long if you do. It's the shortest book in the Old Testament – about one page – and it's written by my namesake.'

Jago only just stifled a gasp of astonishment. 'You mean you're—'

'Yes, sir,' said Spindle. 'That was the name bestowed upon me in their wisdom by my dear departed parents – Obadiah Spindle.'

'Well I never. And what did he write about, this ancient namesake of yours?'

'Doom, sir, mainly.'

Jago was about to commend Spindle's parents for their foresight, but bit his tongue. Spindle, he thought, was a good and decent man, but never had he met one so characterised by doom and gloom. No man could have been so aptly named.

'But if we give them a taste of their own medicine,' he said, 'won't that same principle apply to us?'

'I fear, sir,' Spindle replied in a hushed tone, 'that it must, and I find that a most sobering thought.'

Jago's response was a silent, respectful nod of his head. This was not a popular sentiment, but Spindle clearly had the courage of his convictions.

They arrived at the post-mortem room, where Dr Gibson welcomed them. 'Hello again,' he said, his cheery voice a heartening contrast to Spindle's habitual lugubrious manner. 'I'm all ready for you. Now, first things first – I've heard the hospital refectory's offering mugs of hot chocolate today, so I think as the only doctor in the room I should prescribe one of those to warm you up before we start.' He glanced in Spindle's direction. 'And one for you and me too, I suggest.'

'Certainly, sir – I'll go straight away.'

'Thank you – and in the meantime we'll get down to work, shall we, Inspector?'

Spindle left, and Gibson took Jago and Cradock into his small office. 'Right,' he said. 'Where would you like me to start?'

'With the cause of death, please, if you don't mind. Would I be right in assuming the poor woman was bashed on the head with that poker?'

'Possibly. It wouldn't be the first time someone's life has ended in that way. Hospital doctors see a lot of injuries caused by pokers – I suppose it's because there's usually one to be found beside the fireplace, and while its normal use for keeping the fire going is innocent, if there's an argument or a fight in the room, it's all too easy for someone to grab the poker in anger and use it as a weapon. The consequences aren't usually lethal, though, and the assailant might get away with being brought before the magistrate on a charge of assault and fined a pound. Having said that, it's also true that whenever someone starts waving a poker round in anger, there's the chance that they'll inflict a fatal wound.'

'And what did your post-mortem tell you about the wound in this case?'

'It was actually a case of wounds rather than wound. There was the one above her left eyebrow that we noticed at the scene, but when I examined the body here in the hospital I also found a bruise behind the top of her left ear, and beneath it there was a depressed fracture of the temporal bone.'

'What's a depressed fracture?'

'It's what you get when a blow to the head fractures the skull and forces bone into the brain. A penetrating injury to the brain like that can put your life at risk.'

'And the temporal bone?'

'It's the bone that forms the lower part of the side of your skull, and the significant point is that it's where the skull is at its weakest, because it's so much thinner than the bones that make up the front and the back, and so it's also the most vulnerable to the impact of a blow.'

'And one of these wounds killed her?'

'I believe so, yes. As I said, blows from something like a poker aren't usually or necessarily lethal – you could be struck on the head two or three times and still survive, but equally one blow could kill you. It all depends on where the blow lands. A blow to the temporal bone won't necessarily be fatal, but in this case the injuries I found were severe.'

'So what's your formal judgement of the cause of death?'

'I don't think it was the blow to her forehead that killed her, although it may have stunned her. In my opinion her death was due to shock caused by a depressed fracture of the left temporal bone.'

'Thank you. Just a couple of questions – you said the first blow could've stunned her, but it was the second that killed her. So does that mean she would've collapsed after the first blow and the attacker would've had to strike her again while she was lying on the floor? I'm just wondering what that might tell us about the degree of intent involved.'

'Not much, I'm afraid. If the victim was stunned she might have fallen to the floor, but not necessarily, so I don't think I can infer anything about the degree of intent. But as you know, the law presumes that a person intends the natural consequences of his acts, so a homicide is regarded as murder unless the accused can prove it's not. In this case, the assailant might have struck her a second time in order to ensure she was dead, but equally might only have wanted to immobilise her in order to escape from the scene. Either explanation could be plausible, but whatever the reason, for your purposes I'd say the evidence of her wounds would be consistent with an act of murder.'

'And what will your formal report say about the weapon?'

'I shall say that the fracture that killed her was caused by a violent blow with a blunt object, and the injury produced was not inconsistent with what might be caused by an instrument such as the poker found at the scene.'

'And have you revised your estimate of the time of death?'

'No, I've found nothing to suggest we need to, so it remains between approximately two and four hours before I examined the body at the scene, in other words between about eight and ten o'clock this morning. But there's something else I can add – on the basis of my examination I'd say that death would probably have occurred within a few minutes of the injury being inflicted, and the victim would not have recovered consciousness. She probably died where she fell – it would have been like switching off the light.'

'Right . . . And just going back to that poker for a moment, it looked like there was what could've been blood on the end of it. Is that what it was?'

'Yes, I tested it, and it was human blood.'

'Were you able to establish whether it was the deceased's blood?'

'You mean so that we can say for certain this was the weapon that killed her?'

'Yes.'

'Ah, if only we could. I imagine that would make your job a lot easier in cases like this, wouldn't it? But unfortunately we can't be quite as certain as that. I think I recall from one of our earlier cases that you're familiar with the four blood groups?'

'That's right, although what I know about them could probably be written on the back of a postage stamp.'

Gibson laughed. 'It's not so long ago that doctors didn't

know about them either. They were only identified about forty years ago, and they solved the mystery of why some people died when they had blood transfusions. Even so, in the last war we only did transfusions on a very small scale. Since then, though, we've had the Spanish Civil War, and the evidence from that showed that blood transfusions saved thousands of lives, particularly among air-raid casualties. That's why we had that big drive in the summer before last to recruit blood donors and set up the big blood depots around London – now they're saving lives up and down the country every day, and it's all thanks to the discovery of blood groups.'

'But what can they tell us about this case?'

'Not a lot, I'm afraid. All I can say for certain is that the blood on the poker was of the same group as the deceased's. It's group O, which is the most common, and in emergency transfusions it's the most useful, because it can be given to a patient with any other blood group. For our purposes in this case, though, it's not so useful. If it had been of a different group, I could have confirmed that it's not the deceased's blood, but the fact that it's the same group as hers does not mean I can say this was the weapon that killed her – all I can confirm to you and in court is that the wounds to her body could have been caused by this poker.'

'Thank you – I think we can safely say we're treating it as a case of suspected murder, then.'

'Indeed you can. Now all you have to do is find out whose hand held the weapon.'

'As you say, Doctor – indeed.'

CHAPTER SEVEN

Jago and Cradock headed out of London on Western Avenue towards Middlesex, and half an hour or so later arrived at RAF Northolt, where they were instructed by a sentry that they must report to the station commander, Group Captain Dexter, in his office. Dexter was a middle-aged man with thinning hair and a strained look about his face, with a desk covered in papers. The medal ribbons on his tunic were the same as Jago's, from the 1914–18 war, and the pilot's wings badge with the letters RFC at its centre dated him back to the days when the RAF was still the Royal Flying Corps. He noted the detectives' names and ranks and got straight down to business.

'Scotland Yard, eh?' he said. 'So what brings you all the way out here? Not to admire the scenery, I'm sure.'

'No,' said Jago. 'We've come to have a word with Flying Officer Jack Webster, who we believe is stationed here. We need to let him know that his mother has died.'

'I see. And does the fact that you're a detective inspector signify that it wasn't of natural causes?'

'That's correct – we believe she was murdered.'

'I see – that's a bad show. There are enough people getting killed in the air raids without adding murder to the score. Webster's a good chap – one of our Canadians. You'll no doubt recall that Canada declared war just a week after we did, but the Royal Canadian Air Force didn't even have twenty modern warplanes to their name at that point, so they couldn't send any RCAF squadrons over at first. What they did send was men, to serve with the RAF, and Webster was one of them. He was posted to number 242 Squadron RAF, which was known as the Canadian Squadron because it had so many of them in it. Then eventually when the first RCAF squadron was deployed over here he transferred to that. The poor chap was shot down and now he's here recovering from his wounds. I'll get someone to take you to him.'

'Thank you.'

'You're welcome. But before you go, just a word of warning. A fighter pilot has to have tremendous resilience and determination, but the job is physically and mentally exhausting. He has to be supremely professional too, otherwise he makes a mistake and then he's had it. It's that professional pride that keeps these boys going – they know they're here to do a job, and they get on with it. When you're talking to Flying Officer Webster, though, there's one thing I'd like you to keep in mind – he's been fighting in conditions of intense stress, and I think by the time he was shot down he probably wasn't far off being grounded by battle fatigue. He's improved since then, and his morale is good, but all the same if you're here to tell him his mother's been murdered I'd ask you to handle him carefully. That's all.'

They found Webster in the officers' mess, a long, low red-brick building on the north side of the airfield with a columned entrance porch surmounted by a clock tower. He was dressed in uniform, with a 'Canada' flash on his shoulder and a single ring on his tunic cuff that signified the rank of flying officer. He rose awkwardly from his chair and steadied himself with a walking stick when they approached him and introduced themselves.

'Police, eh?' he said. He pulled a silver cigarette case from his pocket, opened it and held it out towards them. 'Cigarette?'

'No thank you,' said Jago.

'As you wish. Do you mind if I do?'

'Not at all.'

Webster lit his cigarette and blew a cloud of smoke up towards the ceiling. 'There's one thing I can say about the good old RAF – they never leave you short of cigarettes. And those girls who sell them in the NAAFI are peaches. Brave too, especially when the stations get bombed, which is not infrequently these days. I take it you don't smoke.'

'No, I don't.'

'Very sensible, I suppose. When you go for your medical board to join the RAF the doctors say airmen have to be fit, so you shouldn't smoke more than fifteen a day, although I suspect that advice may be more honoured in the breach than in the observance, as they say. But anyway, welcome to RAF Northolt. May I ask why you're here? Have I done something I shouldn't have?'

'No, Mr Webster, I'm afraid we're here with some bad news. Would you be more comfortable sitting down?'

'Yes, I would rather. It's this confounded body of mine – still doesn't work quite as it's supposed to. Let's go and sit over there.'

He led them to a quiet corner. 'So what's this bad news?'

'It concerns your mother. There's no easy way to say this, but I'm very sorry to have to tell you that she's been killed.'

Jago could see no trace of a reaction in Webster's expressionless face. It was a look he'd seen many times, and he wondered whether it was due to the battle fatigue the station commander had mentioned.

Webster took a long draw on his cigarette and exhaled slowly. 'What happened?'

'She was found dead at her home this morning.'

'Was it a bomb? Or did her heart give out or something?'

'I'm afraid it was neither of those things. According to the doctor, she was killed by a blow to the head, and we don't believe it was accidental. We're treating it as a case of suspected murder.'

Webster sank back into his chair and shook his head. 'But why would anyone want to do that? It doesn't make sense.'

'We don't know the answer to that question yet, but if there's anything you can think of that might help us, I'd be grateful to know.'

'I'll try, of course, but quite frankly I'm baffled.' He fell silent, as if wrestling with a puzzle. When he spoke again, his voice was flat. 'Look here, Inspector, I feel as though I should be crying my eyes out at this moment, and maybe that's what you're expecting, so please excuse me if you are – I just feel numb. You must think I'm heartless, but I fear that's what this war has done to me. I love my mother, and what you've just told me is terrible news, but the fact is I've seen too much death at close quarters and I've lost too many good friends, and there's never time to grieve. Tears don't come like they used to. I hope you understand.'

'I understand.'

'It is a shock, though. I've spent the past year and more worrying about what my mother would have to go through if I were killed, but I never really considered what it would be like for me if she died. And now she's gone – just like that. But I appreciate your coming out here to tell me – it can't be pleasant for you either. By the way, how did you manage to track me down so quickly?'

'We found a note inside your mother's identity card, naming you as her next of kin and giving RAF Northolt as your address.'

'I see – of course. I suppose I am her next of kin – I'm her only child, so that makes me her only blood relative.'

'Is there any more family we need to inform?'

'Just my Uncle Gordon, I think – his name's Gordon Bowman, and he's my mother's brother. He's Canadian, but he's based here in London, working for the Canadian government at the Ministry of Information in Bloomsbury. If you want his home address, he's got an apartment in Goodge Street, near where it meets Tottenham Court Road – it's in a building called Daventry Mansions, apartment 7. Would you like me to tell him, or would you rather do that yourself?'

'Thank you, but I'd prefer to do it in person.'

'That's fine with me. Is there anything else you need to know?'

'Yes. Could you just tell me where you were between eight and ten o'clock this morning?'

'Yes, I was here. Not right in this chair, of course, but on the station, or near it – mainly taking my daily exercise. Doctor's orders, you see.' He tapped his leg with his stick. 'If you go out of here and take your life in your hands and dodge the traffic racing up and down that new Western Avenue, which I can tell you isn't easy with a bad leg, there are some lovely fields and woods, and Yeading Brook, which is very calming for the soul, even at this time of year, and of course good for my recuperation. So I wrap up warm and hobble round there for a bit.'

'For how long?'

'Oh, about an hour – more if I can manage it, but that's usually enough.'

'So what time would that've been today?'

'Well, I had some breakfast first, so I probably went for my walk at about half past eight or a little later.'

'Could anyone else confirm that?'

'No, I was on my own – most of my colleagues here are rather too busy to go wandering around on a nature walk, if you know what I mean. But look, you're surely not suggesting that I—'

'No, Mr Webster, I'm not suggesting anything. It's just a question we have to ask to eliminate people from our inquiries.'

'Right. That's OK then. Anything else?'

'Yes. I understand your mother was born here in London

but was adopted in Canada and grew up there, but I wonder if you could tell us any more about the early part of her life.'

'No, I can't really – she didn't talk about her life here before she went to Canada. She was very young when she left, so I guess she didn't remember. She was adopted, as you say, by my grandparents. They were farming people in Ontario, so she grew up pretty healthy – probably healthier than she would've been if she'd stayed here. She said she liked it on the farm and she had a happy childhood. Then when she grew up she met my father – he was called Elliot Webster, and he was four years older than her. He worked in his family's lumber business. They got married in 1917, and I came along in 1918. That's about all I can say, but my Uncle Gordon may be able to tell you more.'

'Thank you. I'd be interested to know a bit more about yourself too. Group Captain Dexter told us you were one of the first Canadian airmen to come over here and serve with the RAF when the war started.'

'That's right. I was born in Canada, of course, but I came here with my mother in 1931, after my father died. I was just a boy then, but when I grew up I decided to move back to Canada, to figure out whether I wanted to live here or there. That was in 1938, and it soon became clear to me that there was going to be a war, so I volunteered for the Royal Canadian Air Force and got trained as a fighter pilot – and then as soon as Canada declared war they shipped me over here. I started out with 242 Squadron RAF – we got Hurricanes in January of last year and were sent to fight in France in May, but the tide had turned against us by then and we were pulled out in June. By the time we got home, the first RCAF squadron had been sent over here, and I was transferred to it in time for what people are calling the Battle of Britain, including the really big scrap on the fifteenth of September. I got shot down on the fifth of October, but that already seems a lifetime ago – and for some of my friends it is.'

He fell silent, and Jago waited before continuing. 'I understand you're recuperating from your wounds now,' he said.

'Yes, that's correct. I broke my leg in a crash landing and did something to my back too – the leg's healing up nicely, or so they tell me, but the back's still giving me grief.'

'What happened?'

'I was in a Hurricane, and we were attacking a formation of Me110 bombers over Maidstone. It had an escort of Me109s, and one of them suddenly dived down on me from nowhere and fired at me. Now, by the time those fighters get here from France, they've only got enough fuel to stay for ten minutes before they have to run for home. But unfortunately in those ten minutes he managed to hit my engine, and it started leaking glycol – that's the coolant it uses – and before I could get to the nearest airfield it seized up. I managed to make a crash landing, as I said, somewhere in Kent, but I was pretty badly beaten up in the process. I haven't been able to fly since, but they've got me here doing some dreary desk-bound duties while I recover. Meanwhile the rest of the squadron's been moved up to Scotland, so I'm here on my own. I'm still hoping I'll get up in the air again before it's all over, but things aren't looking too bright at the moment.'

'I'm sorry to hear that, Mr Webster – it must be frustrating for you.'

'It is. These wounds may be the end of my combat flying days. If I can't get back to full fitness it could mean the ATA for me.'

'The ATA?'

'The Air Transport Auxiliary – the chaps who ferry planes from the factories to the squadrons.'

'Ah, yes – I read about them in the paper. The article said it stood for something else too.'

'I know – "Ancient and Tattered Airmen", which is what I'll be if I don't mend enough to get back to my Hurricanes. It's quite appropriate in a way – they take all sorts of civilians who aren't fit enough for RAF service, and that means the front-line pilots don't have to do it. Don't get me wrong, though – I've met some of them, and they're made of strong stuff – flying fighters and bombers around unarmed and in all weathers, wherever they're needed. Some of them were even ferrying light bombers over to France when we were fighting there last year, and taking Hurricanes back. Some of them say ATA stands for "Anything to Anywhere".'

'I've read that they have women pilots too.'

'That's right – it was a bit controversial when it started, but they've proved they can do it. Terrible news about Amy Johnson, though. I expect you've heard – it's front-page news.'

'Yes – a very sad end. I understand her plane came down in the Thames Estuary.'

'That's right – just yesterday. I still remember when she first hit the headlines – first woman in the world to fly solo from here to Australia. She was the darling of the world. I was only twelve at the time and I thought it was amazing – people said she was the world's greatest woman flier. And after all those exploits and worldwide fame, last year she decided to join the ATA as an eight-pounds-a-week ferry pilot. She must have been the most glamorous and celebrated female pilot they've got, and now she's gone.'

'Do you know what happened?'

'It's not clear. From what I've heard, she was flying an Airspeed Oxford training plane from Blackpool down to RAF Kidlington, near Oxford, so why she was over the Thames Estuary I don't know. The weather was bad, though, and some people are saying she may have run out of fuel. Whatever happened, it's a tragic loss – she inspired no end of young people to take up flying, many of them serving in the RAF today. And in the Air Transport Auxiliary too – I believe it has twenty-five female pilots, and these days they're the only women in England allowed to fly. Which is more than I am, unfortunately.'

'Indeed. And I understand you're now on what was described to me as "special duties".'

Webster shot a suspicious glance at Jago. 'Who told you that?'

'Mrs McCready, your mother's housekeeper.'

'Well, she's no business to. We're all supposed to keep mum, aren't we, like those signs in the pubs say – not gossip.'

'I don't suppose she meant any harm – "special duties" could mean anything.'

'Yes, of course. In my case it's just sorting out some documents down the road at RAF Ruislip. It's only a mile or so from here, just across those fields you can see out of the window to the north – five minutes if you've got a car. It's not a flying station, just a maintenance unit and a depot for stores, but it's also where the RAF official records are kept, and that's where I'm currently flying a desk, worse luck. I'm supposed to be compiling information on RAF personnel who are listed as prisoners of war. Dull as ditchwater, but it's all I'm good for, it seems, at least until I'm mended. The only thing I want to do is get back to flying. I think it's what my mother would have wanted.'

'What makes you say that?'

'Just the fact that she brought me up to stand on my own two feet and fight my own battles. She also had a strong belief in duty – to your country, to your family, your neighbour, those less fortunate than yourself. I guess that's something I've inherited from her. She was a good woman.'

'And yet someone has killed her – do you know of anyone who might've wanted to harm her?'

'No. She had a habit of picking up waifs and strays and people down on their luck, and trying to help them, but I'm not aware of anyone like that who wanted to harm her.'

'And that included helping them financially?'

'Sure.'

'Mrs McCready told us she didn't think your mother was, as she put it, "too flush with money". Is that true?'

'That woman again – she's got a loose tongue. She should learn to keep her mouth shut. Look, I wasn't privy to all of my mother's financial affairs, and I don't suppose for a moment Mrs McCready was. But if she had one weakness, it was probably her desire to help anyone in need, and I guess that meant falling for the occasional hard luck story. I got the impression in the last year or so that she wasn't as well off as she used to be, but maybe that's just because I was over here by then and could see her in person, and also I was grown up now and more savvy about money myself. I used to warn her to beware of people who wanted her to bankroll them. I wasn't sponging on her and I didn't want anyone else to treat her like that – I was concerned she might end up with nothing left for herself.'

'Speaking of money, do you happen to know whether your mother had made a will?'

'Yes, I do. She made one some time ago, because she said it was the responsible thing to do – she didn't want to die intestate. I thought it wouldn't make any difference, because my father was already dead and I was her only child, so everything would come to me automatically, but she said if she didn't make a will it would involve more work for me. Apparently it's to do with probate and commissioners of oaths and other things I know nothing about, but she said I'd end up having to pay fees, and if she made a will I wouldn't. Then when I joined the air force and it looked like war was coming, she said I ought to make one too. I know some people are superstitious about things like that, but she wasn't – she was too sensible. So we both had wills – I left everything to her, and she left everything to me. Well, all except a few personal bequests, but basically everything.'

'Do you by any chance have a copy of her will?'

'I do, yes – she named me as the executor and made sure I got a copy once it was all signed and sealed.'

'Could you possibly let me see it?'

'Well, I suppose so – as long as you don't go round showing it to every Tom, Dick and Harry.'

'We won't do that. Do you have the copy here?'

'Yes, it's in my room. The whole country's been told we should all keep important things like that handy and take them with us into the shelter when there's an air raid, in case our home gets blown up, and I reckon the same applies if you're in the forces and stationed in England. I just don't take them with me in the plane, of course, because I figure even if the station's bombed they've got more chance of surviving than if they're up there in a dogfight with me. Would you like me to fetch it?'

'Yes, please, if you wouldn't mind.'

'By all means – it'll give me a little exercise. I'll be straight back.'

He got up out of his chair with some difficulty and left them, and returned a few minutes later.

'There you are,' he said, handing an envelope to Jago.

'Thank you.'

Jago took the will out of the envelope, unfolded it carefully and read it silently to himself. 'Hmm,' he said when he got to the end. 'That's interesting.' He folded the document and put it back in its envelope, then handed it to Webster. 'Thank you for letting me see that,' he said. 'What did you make of it when you saw it?'

'It seemed quite ordinary to me. I was just glad she hadn't sprayed money around to all those spongers.'

'Yes, I'm sure you were. Now, you mentioned that being over here in England meant you could see your mother in person – can you tell me when you last saw her?'

'Yes, it was last week – Thursday. I was with her for Christmas too – one of the few advantages of being temporarily laid up like this. It's still a bit uncomfortable driving, because of this.' He tapped his leg again. 'So I'm not as mobile as I used to be, which is a pity, as I managed to pick up a little MG two-seater for a song recently that goes like a rocket. But Ruislip Gardens Tube station is only round the corner from here, so on days when I'm not feeling quite tickety-boo I can get into town quite easily. I work office hours, from ten till six, and when I'm off duty I can come and go pretty much as I please – it's not like standing by waiting to jump in your plane and go straight into action whenever the enemy's sighted.'

'I expect she was pleased to have you with her at Christmas.'

'Yes, I think she was. I guess it was hard for her, being widowed, especially at Christmas time. She'd been on her own for several years.'

'Did she have any particularly close men friends?'

'You mean like a boyfriend? I don't think so.'

'No thoughts of remarrying, then?'

Webster laughed. 'If she did, she was keeping her cards very close to her chest. I don't think that was anywhere on the horizon.'

'And how did she seem when you saw her last week? Did she seem anxious about anything, for example?'

'No, she was just her usual self – I didn't get the impression that anything was particularly weighing on her mind.'

'What about money? You said just now that you thought your mother possibly wasn't as comfortably off as she used to be, but do you think she actually had real money worries?'

'I'm not sure. I don't think she could ever have been

called a wealthy woman. When my father died she was left with enough money to buy the house in Guilford Street, and I know there was a life insurance on his life that she invested and got a small income from, but apart from that, I don't think she had a lot of spare money.'

'Do you know if your mother had any debts?'

'You mean did she owe money to anyone who might have demanded repayment when she couldn't afford it, or might have wanted her to render some service to pay if off?'

'That sort of thing, yes – anything that might've given someone a motive to put pressure on her or threaten her.'

'Not to my knowledge, no.'

'I suppose handing her house over to the council must've helped her financially, bringing her outgoings down?'

'I guess it did a bit, but I'm sure that wouldn't have been her reason for doing it – she did that because she cared. And at least she didn't sell the place – she might've ended up with nothing then if she'd kept on giving money away.'

'You mentioned hard luck stories – do you know of anyone who'd been looking to her to back them in some venture or bail them out of their own financial difficulties of late?'

'I can think of one or two, yes. There's a woman called Susan Ingram who wants to be a great writer, and there's a man called Charles Buckleby who's some kind of businessman – she's talked about helping them, which to my mind means maybe they've been sponging on her. But I think she'd become a bit more secretive than she used to be. I don't know why, though.'

'Could it have been because she might think you'd disapprove of her generosity?'

'Possibly – if it was misplaced generosity, then yes, I would, and I'd let her know, for her own sake. But she was generous by nature, and I wouldn't try to change that – she was open-hearted and open-handed, and I always knew she'd be like that until the day she died.'

'Speaking of business, I've been told your father was a successful businessman.'

Webster gave an artificial smile, as if to signal that he knew who was probably the source of this information too, but this time made no accusation.

'Yes, he was a businessman, and I think he was successful – my mother certainly said he was, and we lived well. I was only twelve when he died, though, so I wasn't really old enough to judge for myself. He was my hero, and I thought everything about him was great. It broke my heart when he died.'

'I'm very sorry. How did it happen, if you don't mind me asking?'

'It was in the summer. I'd been away camping with the Boy Scouts for the first time, and when I came home my mother broke the news to me. She said there'd been an accident – he'd slipped on the stairs down into the basement and fallen down. I asked if he was all right now, and she said no, he'd broken his neck and died. I thought my whole world had come to an end. It was so unfair.' He fell into a short silence, then drew himself up in the chair. 'But I was just a boy. When you grow up you realise life isn't always fair, but you just have to get on with it.' He looked down at his tunic. 'And now I'm wearing this uniform, and that's never been more true in my life.'

CHAPTER EIGHT

Blackout time was just after half past five, and it was only a few minutes before that when Jago and Cradock set off on their return journey from Northolt. Jago checked his watch before starting the engine.

'I hope you haven't got any big plans for this evening, Peter,' he said, 'only we really need to see Gordon Bowman and his wife before the day's out. He may've found out already that his sister's been killed, but I don't want him to have to wait till tomorrow to hear it from us. We'll go straight to that flat of theirs in Goodge Street and hope he's got home from work by the time we get there.'

'That's all right, guv'nor, I wasn't planning anything special for this evening – just back to Ambrosden Avenue. Some of the lads at the section house are having a drink at the Windsor Castle, so I'll probably just pop round there and join them for a beer or two.'

'Good. But in any case, I'll make sure we've finished before eight – I don't want to ruin your evening.'

'That's very kind of you, sir.' Cradock was surprised at his boss's consideration. Jago, however, was thinking of his own plans. Dorothy had invited him to join her for a drink at eight in the somewhat more glamorous surroundings of the Savoy, temporary home for most of the American press corps, and he had no intention of ruining his own evening.

The onset of darkness meant it would take longer to drive back into central London than it had to drive out, particularly when the dual-carriageway sections of Western Avenue gave way to the built-up areas where the wartime blackout speed limit had been reduced from thirty to twenty miles an hour. The law, however, allowed Jago to exceed that limit when he was on police business, so he exercised his discretion and maintained a speed high enough to reach their destination as fast as possible without getting himself and Cradock, or anyone else, killed in the attempt.

'Good driving, guv'nor,' said Cradock when they arrived. He sounded excited by the experience.

Jago took a deep breath to relieve the tension of the drive. 'Thank you, Peter, but I have to say I'm looking forward to the day when we can drive at night with proper headlights on again.'

They parked in Goodge Street, near the corner with Tottenham Court Road as Jack Webster had directed, and managed to locate the nearby Daventry Mansions in the dark with the aid of Cradock's adequately screened torch. When they rang the bell of apartment 7, they were admitted by a smartly dressed woman who identified herself as Helen Bowman, wife of Gordon. She showed them into the drawing room.

'Gordon, dear,' she said, her voice quiet and uncertain, 'there are two police officers to see us. This is Detective Inspector Jago, and this is Detective Constable Cradock.'

'Well,' said Bowman, sounding the more confident of the two, 'that is a surprise. Do take a seat, please, gentlemen, and tell us why you're here.'

They sat down on a pair of strikingly comfortable armchairs.

'We've come with some bad news, I'm afraid,' Jago began. 'It's to do with your sister, Mr Bowman.'

'Rosemary? What's happened?'

'I regret to inform you that she's been found dead in her home today, and we're advised that it was not due to natural causes.'

'You mean—'

'Yes, sir – I'm very sorry to have to tell you this, but we're treating her death as a case of suspected murder.'

Bowman seemed shocked into silence. He stared at Jago for several seconds before speaking. 'Do you have any idea who did it?'

'Not yet, sir. Do you know if she had any enemies?'

'No – I don't think she was the kind of person who'd have enemies. She might've got a few backs up, but basically she seemed to get along pretty well with just about everyone, as far as I could tell. Not that I saw a lot of her – we both had very busy lives.'

'And you, Mrs Bowman, can you think of anyone who might've wanted to harm your sister-in-law?'

Helen Bowman twitched when he addressed her, as if not expecting to be drawn into the conversation. 'I don't think so,' she said. 'I agree with my husband – I can't imagine anyone wanting to kill poor Rosemary.' She shook her head slowly. 'It's just awful.'

'Mr Bowman,' Jago continued. 'You say she might've got a few backs up. Who would those people be, and why?'

'Well, I just mean the kind of work she did – Bloomsbury House and all that. It wasn't to everyone's liking. But that doesn't mean they'd get violent. By the way, is it OK for me to ask how Rosemary was killed?'

Jago glanced at Mrs Bowman, who gave an almost imperceptible nod of her head. 'Yes, it is,' he said. 'She suffered a blow to the side of her head, we think from a poker.'

'I see. Would she have died quickly?'

'Yes, she would. According to our pathologist, it would've been like switching off the light.'

'Ah – that's some comfort, I guess. But still, Rosemary was so full of life and energy – it's difficult to imagine her just going like that.' He turned to his wife, who was sobbing into her handkerchief. 'I'm sorry, Helen dear – I shouldn't have asked.'

'It's not your fault, Gordon – you were right to ask. But if you'll excuse me for a moment, gentlemen, I'll just go and fix my face.'

Bowman waited until she had left the room before speaking. 'I'm sorry, Inspector – news like this brings back sad memories for my wife. It's this damned war – we lost our son, you see.'

'I'm very sorry to hear that.' Jago glanced to his right and saw a framed photograph of a young man on the mantelpiece. 'Is that your son?'

'Yes, that's Harold. He was only twenty-two when he died.'

'What happened?'

'We're not exactly sure. It was last month. He was just a private, fighting the Italians somewhere in North Africa with the 7th Armoured Division – the ones they call the Desert Rats.'

'They won quite a victory, I believe.'

'Yes, they did, but there's always a price, isn't there, and Harold was part of it. He was riding in the back of a truck when it was hit by an enemy shell. And that was it – his life ended at that moment.' He paused, struggling to control his emotion. 'Such a waste – such a pointless waste. I know I shouldn't say that – they were fighting to save all of us and they won their battle, but why did it have to be him?'

'You have my sympathy, Mr Bowman.'

'Thank you. The worst of it is I feel like it's my fault.'

'Why's that?'

'If we hadn't brought him over here with us when I was posted to the High Commission, he wouldn't have been called up. Have you heard of the National Service (Armed Forces) Act 1939? It's the law that laid down the rules for enlistment of men in the armed forces.'

'I know of it, yes, but not in every detail. Why?'

'In my job I need to be aware of it too, in broad terms at least, but I didn't read it in detail either. But there's a sub-section that a colleague of mine brought to my attention – and by then it was too late. I thought because Harold was Canadian, like me and my wife, if he was going to be conscripted it would be in Canada, for the

Canadian forces. But when I read that little sub-section, I saw that although all male British subjects were liable to be called up, it said the act didn't apply to anyone who's a national or citizen of any of His Majesty's dominions outside Great Britain – which would include Canada, of course.'

'So he shouldn't have been called up?'

'That's what I thought. But it also said it was only if those nationals or citizens were "not ordinarily resident in Great Britain". Then when I read on I saw what that meant – it said "not ordinarily resident" meant you'd only been here for less than two years. Harold had been living here for four years, so he had to register, and by the end of 1939 he'd been called up. And then . . . well, you know what happened. If only we'd known, we could have sent him back to Canada.'

'But wouldn't he have been called up there?'

'Yes – Canada's in the war, and we've got conscription, but service overseas in the Canadian Army is only on a voluntary basis, so Harold would've been called up, but he wouldn't have gone off to fight somewhere like North Africa unless he wanted to. In the British Army he had no choice.'

Bowman closed his eyes, as if in physical pain. 'I can't stop thinking about what might have been, Inspector – do you think it ever ends?'

Before Jago could reply, Helen Bowman came back into the room. Her husband visibly pulled himself together and adopted a more controlled tone.

'Hello, Helen – I've just been telling the inspector about Harold, in the desert.'

'Oh,' she said, her voice flat. 'Could we maybe not talk about that?'

'Yes, of course, my dear.' He turned to Jago. 'Is that OK, Inspector?'

'By all means.'

'Thank you. So is there anything else you need to tell us?'

'I don't think so, but I'd be interested to know more about your sister's life. I understand she was adopted by your parents and grew up as part of your family in Canada.'

'Yes – who told you that?'

'It was her housekeeper, Mrs McCready, and also your nephew Jack. He gave us your address, too, which is how we found you here.'

'I see – that's OK then. He's a fine young man. As for my sister's life, well, she was six years old when she arrived in our family, and I was ten. She was very different from us then, and she spoke like a real old-fashioned Londoner, so I guess I didn't feel I had much in common with her. I knew she'd had to leave England because she was a poor orphan and needed a home, but I don't recall my parents telling me any more than that. I guess whatever her past was, they wanted her to have a fresh start and didn't want it hanging over her, but to be frank, I don't think I was all that interested anyway. Looking back, it seems to me we lived pretty separate lives, and that stayed the same when we'd grown up. Even when we both ended up living here we didn't see that much of each other – I guess we were both just very busy.'

'I understand your sister moved to England with her son in 1931. When did you come?'

'In 1936, with my wife and children.'

'I take it you and your wife are both Canadian?'

'That's right.'

'And your nephew also told us you work for the Canadian government at the Ministry of Information.'

'Yes, although strictly speaking I'm on the staff at the Canadian High Commission in Trafalgar Square, and—'

He was interrupted by the sound of a door slamming, followed by a shout from a female voice. 'Hi – I'm back!'

Seconds later a young woman entered the room, halfway through pulling off her coat.

'Oh,' she said, surprised. 'I didn't realise you had guests.' She smiled at the two visitors.

'These two gentlemen are from Scotland Yard, Claire,' said Bowman.

'Really?' she said with a breezy laugh. 'Come to arrest my dad, have you?'

Bowman saved Jago and Cradock from having to reply. 'This is my daughter, Claire,' he said. He turned back to her and continued, 'They're here on a very serious matter, Claire. It's about your Aunt Rosemary.'

Claire's expression turned to one of anxious concern. 'What's happened?'

Jago thought it was now his turn to spare Bowman having to break the news. 'I'm very sorry, Miss Bowman, but we're here to inform you that your aunt was found dead this morning, and we believe she was murdered.'

Claire slumped onto a sofa, wide-eyed, and said nothing.

Helen Bowman moved to her side and took her hand. 'There, there, my baby, it's all right.'

Claire pushed her hand away. 'No, it's not all right – someone's killed her. How can it be all right?'

Gordon Bowman took a step towards her. 'I understand, Claire. It's a terrible shock for all of us. I know my sister was precious to you, and she was precious to me too. We've all lost someone we love deeply, but life must go on.'

Claire gave no reply, and he moved away.

'This has been a challenging year for my daughter, Inspector,' he said. 'She was a student when the war started, at the London School of Economics – it's only about twenty minutes' walk from here, so she could keep living here. But then the buildings were taken over by the government to house the Ministry of Economic Warfare. The students and staff were evacuated to Cambridge, which turned out well because she was away from all the bombing here, but it was quite an upheaval for her. She's home for the winter vacation now, but she'll be going back soon for the new term.'

Claire rolled her eyes. 'You don't need to make excuses for me, Dad. I'm doing fine up there and I'm in no hurry to get back here. Two thirds of the LSE students are female, so we're giving the Cambridge women students a run for their money when it comes to competing for the men.'

Helen Bowman looked horrified.

'Don't worry, Mom,' said Claire, with theatrical exasperation. 'I actually spend all my time studying – I want to get a decent job when I finish.'

'Please excuse us, Inspector,' said Bowman. 'Perhaps I can get back to answering your question. As I was saying, I'm on the staff at the Canadian High Commission. I work in the information section as a liaison officer with the London-based Canadian press. That means I have an office at the Ministry of Information, where they get their briefings, and my job involves helping them with any difficulties they may be encountering, giving them a steer on any requirements the Canadian authorities may have, and also making sure they don't disclose sensitive information that hasn't been released by London. I also write reports and briefings for the Canadian government on how Britain is coping with the war, and for that I make use of the ministry's social survey reports. A humdrum kind of job, but I like to think I'm doing my bit, as everyone says these days.'

Jago smiled. 'Thank you – I'm sure it's valuable work.'

Bowman checked his watch. 'Is that all, do you think? Valuable or not, I have some work to do before I go to bed tonight.'

'Well, I won't keep you from that,' said Jago. 'That'll be all for now – we'll bid you good night.'

He and Cradock got to their feet.

'Did you come by car, Inspector?' said Claire.

'Yes, we did.'

'May I walk you down to it, then? I'd like a private word with you.'

'Claire?' said her mother.

'Yes, Mother dear, I'm grown up now and I'd like a word with the inspector in private. It's nothing for you to worry about.'

She guided Jago and Cradock to the door and put her coat on, then escorted them down to the ground-floor lobby of the apartment block.

'Take no notice of my mother, Inspector,' she said. 'She's just one of nature's worriers, and she still tends to treat me like a nine-year-old. She's one of two reasons why

I don't spend much time in that apartment – and the other one's up there with her.'

'Strong words, Miss Bowman.'

'Yes, well, I'm afraid I tend to have strong views – I think I take after my Aunt Rosemary in that respect. My father, however, is a diplomat by nature and by profession – that's probably how he got into the High Commission – and my mother doesn't like anything to upset her cosy little world, where everything's fine. But I'm not diplomatic, and if I see something that's not right I'll do my damnedest to get it fixed. So you can see why we don't get on too well. I probably used to spend more nights at Aunt Rosemary's place than I did here, because I found it more congenial.'

'Were you there last night?'

'No, I wasn't – I was visiting one of my friends from the LSE who lives in Islington and stayed the night.'

'What time did you get home?'

'About half past nine this morning, I think. Why? Was that when—?'

'We believe your aunt was murdered early this morning.'

'Oh . . . That makes it even worse – if I'd been there, perhaps I could have stopped it. If only I'd . . .'

'You can't blame yourself for not being there, Miss Bowman.'

'No – I guess you're right.'

'But what was it you wanted a private word about?'

'It's just all those things my parents said – my mother saying everything's all right when it obviously isn't, my father saying how precious my aunt was to him, how they loved her so deeply. That may be what they think, but it's not how I see it. I've never thought they got on well – I've always sensed this real friction between my dad and Aunt Rosemary. Maybe he calls that being diplomatic, but I call it hypocrisy and I can't abide it.'

'Friction over what?'

'That I can't say – I could never put my finger on it. I just sensed it.'

'Well, thank you for mentioning it. Is that all?'

'Yes, that's all. I guess I'd better go back up there and try to be diplomatic myself.'

CHAPTER NINE

'That's enough for today, Peter,' said Jago when they returned to the car. 'You can get back to Ambrosden Avenue and enjoy your beer now.'

'Thanks, guv'nor,' said Cradock. 'You, er . . . got any plans for the evening yourself?' he added, affecting a tone of innocent enquiry.

Jago was amused by the boy's cheek but would not indulge it. 'I do have another engagement, as it happens. Now, do you want a lift back to the section house or don't you?'

Cradock's curiosity was adequately satisfied, and he didn't want to push his luck by probing further. A tactful retreat would be in order.

'Actually, there's a Tube station just round the corner. I think I'll just jump on the train and leave you to it.'

'Very good – I hope you manage to get past all the shelterers.'

'That's a point, yes – last time I went on the Tube at this

time of the evening they were bedding down all over the platform – there was only about a foot of space left at the edge for people who actually wanted to catch the train, and the poor old porters had to keep pushing the shelterers back behind the white lines, otherwise nobody would've got on it. Still, it all makes the journey more interesting, doesn't it? One day we'll probably look back and think what fun it was.'

'You're beginning to sound like an old man. Go on, then – be off with you.'

'Good night, sir – see you in the morning.'

Cradock gave him a cheery wave and strode off in the direction of Goodge Street Tube station.

Jago started up the engine and drove south. The roads were quiet, and by eight o'clock he was sitting in the American Bar at the Savoy Hotel with Dorothy. As on previous visits, he felt like a fish out of water in such a prestigious establishment. If it hadn't been for the fact that Dorothy was a resident guest – and one whose stay there was no doubt being handsomely paid for by the *Boston Post* – he doubted he'd even have got past the doorman in the disreputable coat he'd taken to wearing on duty in these days of bombs and brick dust. He took it off once he was inside, and was relieved to see that some of the men who nodded to Dorothy as they passed and were presumably her American press colleagues looked more casually dressed than he was in his sober everyday suit. He got her a drink and they settled in the quietest corner of the bar they could find.

'I'm glad you made it,' said Dorothy, raising her glass to him.

'So am I,' he said, raising his own in reply. 'It was touch and go – Peter and I have had a busy day, chasing round town. But how about you? What's the latest news on the American front?'

'Well, let me see – we're still at the beginning of the year, so the paper's been reviewing the state of the world and trying to predict what's likely to come our way in the next twelve months. Not very happy reading, I fear – most of it gloomy. There was one bright spot for you British people, though.'

'Oh, yes? What was that?'

'Do you know about *Time* magazine's Man of the Year award?'

'I've heard of it, yes – is that when they put the man's picture on the front cover?'

'That's right – the editors decide who they think's made the most dramatic change in the course of history during the past year. It's always a man, of course, although Wallis Simpson did break the mould in 1936 and got on the cover as Woman of the Year. They've just announced that their Man of the Year for 1940 is Winston Churchill.'

'Not President Roosevelt, then?'

'No, but he's already won it twice. Anyway, it seems they think your prime minister's had a bigger impact on history than our president, which can't do your cause any harm.'

'Yes – but wasn't it Hitler a couple of years ago?'

'That's true, but it's not an award for the nicest man of the year. They chose him because of the terrible things he'd done in 1938, because they reckoned he was the greatest threat in the world to democratic, freedom-loving people, and that's why he'd had the biggest impact on history in that year. And do you know what they said at the end of the article they wrote about him? They said the Man of the Year for 1938 might make 1939 a year to be remembered. Boy, were they right – that should've got the prize for Understatement of the Year.'

'Quite.'

'But tell me, who is it you've been chasing round town today?'

'Oh, that's just the case we're working on – a woman was found murdered in Bloomsbury this morning. A Canadian woman actually, and her brother works at one of your old haunts – I wondered whether you might know him.'

'Which old haunt would that be?'

'The Senate House.'

'Ah yes, that skyscraper – London's little taste of New York, home of your famous Ministry of Information. I've spent many happy hours there cabling stories back to my paper. You know what people call it, don't you?'

'Tell me.'

'The Bloomsbury White Elephant – I suppose because it's so big and covered all over in white stone. But I think maybe they reckon it's just not much use.'

'Really? Why's that?'

'Well, I'm not saying they're right, but I've heard it said that it's amateurish and inefficient, and it's been stuffed full of people who had nowhere else to go. And one of your politicians said that all the curators who were put out of a job when the British Museum had to close down were given overpaid jobs in the ministry that they're not competent to do. Interesting, isn't it? Dare I ask the name of this man you thought I might know there?'

'Yes, he's called Gordon Bowman, and he said he works there as a liaison officer with the Canadian press. He's on the staff of the Canadian High Commission.'

Dorothy shook her head. 'No, I don't know him. But if he's working with the Canadian press I wouldn't be likely to run into him. Not that I've got anything against Canadians, of course – I like them. They're different from us – from us Americans, I mean – but they're good neighbours, and we haven't had a war with them since 1812, which is a pretty good record compared with Europe, I'd say.'

'That's a fair point. Who won?'

Dorothy laughed. 'And that's a fair question. I wasn't around at the time, but my understanding is that in those days we had a lot of grievances against you British. At the same time we were expanding westwards, and there were some who thought Canada should stop being British and become part of the United States instead, so our President Madison decided that with your country so occupied with fighting Napoleon it would be a good time to declare war on you and invade Canada. So we did. As for who won, well, I guess the fact that Canada never did become part of the USA speaks for itself. But the good thing is that there's been peace between us now for a century and a quarter and we've become good friends – and to my mind the fact that we share a four-thousand-mile border that's undefended says it all.'

'And now they're over here, helping us fight another war.'

'Unlike my country.'

'Your country's helping us in other ways. But I saw the Canadians in action in the last war and I was very glad when they arrived here for this one.'

'I actually covered that story, you know – the seventeenth of December 1939, when the first Canadian troops sailed in to what we were required to call "somewhere on the west coast". And I can tell you that wasn't the Ministry of Information's finest hour – it was more like a comedy of errors.'

'Are you allowed to tell me the story?'

'I'll tell you, and I guess then I'll have to leave it to you whether to arrest me.'

Jago smiled. 'I don't think that'll be necessary.'

'OK then. The ministry told the papers to send reporters, but then they messed up the travel arrangements. I managed to get there, but when we'd all written up the story the censorship people at the ministry said we couldn't publish it. They kept saying all day it would be too dangerous to release the information, but then that evening Churchill mentioned it in his broadcast, so why all the secrecy? And by the time the ministry lifted its ban, the story had moved on. I dare say it all made sense to the ministry, but to the press it seemed like one blunder after another. But listen, that's enough of my beefing. Tell me more about your case – who was this poor woman who's been murdered?'

'Well, we don't know a lot about her yet, but it seems she spent her time helping people and didn't have any enemies, so there isn't a strong motive for murder. As her housekeeper said, why would anyone want to kill an angel of mercy?'

'A good question. It reminds me of a woman I heard about in the States five or six years ago. She was known as an angel of mercy – always helping convicts, men who'd been on chain gangs, and homeless down-and-outers. She wasn't murdered, thankfully, but the thing about her was that she was voluntarily putting herself at risk, mixing with potentially dangerous people. So I guess I'd be asking myself who was your Canadian angel mixing with. People can do the most unexpected things, can't they?'

'In my experience that's definitely true. We're looking into it now.'

'Well, don't go putting yourself at risk.'

Jago noticed a softening of her voice and looked up. Her eyes expressed a gentle concern, something he'd rarely seen in his life, and he was touched.

'I won't,' he replied, and heard his own voice echoing the soft tone of hers. He didn't know what else to say, and there was a brief awkward silence before he spoke. 'And I hope you won't either – I know you have to get your stories, but this country's not a very safe place to work at the moment, is it?'

'It has its challenges,' Dorothy replied. Her voice was brighter now, and he suspected she was trying to help him out. 'But I've learned to be careful. I may have to crawl around bomb sites sometimes, but I'm not going to be the one who brings an incendiary bomb home as a souvenir, especially one that hasn't gone off yet.'

'Do journalists do that sort of thing?'

'Some do – but they're the ones who have a short career. I'm not like that. I don't go looking for danger.'

'What about working in that white elephant, though – the Senate House. It sticks out like a sore thumb, and all the German bombers that come over must know what it is.'

'Maybe, but they tell us it's a safe place. It's already been bombed – nine times, I think, but it didn't fall down, and the man who designed it said the base of the tower is the best bomb-proof shelter in London, so we know where to head for when the siren starts up.'

'I hope he's right.'

'I don't think we're in that much danger. Besides, there's a rumour going round in Bloomsbury that Hitler doesn't want to destroy the Senate House, because he plans to use it as the headquarters for his Nazi Party when he invades.' She laughed. 'But that plan doesn't seem to be going too well at the moment, does it?'

'No,' said Jago, 'and I very much hope it'll stay that way.' He checked his watch. 'And now I think it's time for me to reluctantly get back to my headquarters and leave you in yours. I'll see you soon.'

Dorothy smiled up at him as he got out of his chair. 'Yes,' she said, 'let's do that. Sleep well.'

CHAPTER TEN

When Jago stirred next morning in his temporary billet at Rochester Row police station, both his body and mind conspired to persuade him he'd only just nodded off. False witnesses, perhaps, but the overnight combination of freezing temperatures, the thunderous crash of anti-aircraft guns and even the well-meaning drone of the all-clear siren so deafeningly located on the police station's roof were not conducive to peaceful slumber, and despite Dorothy's parting wish he had definitely not slept well.

He washed and dressed quickly, grabbed some breakfast in the station canteen and drove to the nearby Ambrosden Avenue section house to pick up Cradock.

'Morning, guv'nor,' said the young constable breezily, his cheery demeanour suggesting that he'd discovered the secret of sleeping through the night-time clamour. 'Where do we start today, then?'

'In Bloomsbury Square, I think. I'm trying to piece

together what kind of woman Rosemary Webster was, and I still don't feel we've got a clear picture. What do we know about her so far?'

'Well, people've said she was open-handed and generous, although they don't seem too clear about whether she was as wealthy as they might've thought. She had strong convictions too, and believed in doing your duty, and she was passionate about doing the right thing, always helping people.'

'That's right – an angel of mercy, as Mrs McCready said. Do you think that sounds too good to be true?'

'Difficult to say, sir. Susan Ingram certainly seemed to think she'd been a big help to her.'

'But she said "at least in the beginning", didn't she? So perhaps it didn't last. There was also that thing her son said about falling for the occasional hard luck story. I wonder how that left her feeling, if it happened. And talking of beginnings, what no one claims to know much about is her past, except that she was possibly born in Bloomsbury and ended up in Canada when she was six, although no one seems to know why.'

'Her son said maybe she was too young to remember.'

'Yes, that sounds plausible. Annie McCready said Rosemary Webster moved back here because she wanted to explore her roots. I think we need to find out what those roots were, and I'm hoping that woman she mentioned, Mrs Cordingley, might be the person who can tell us. I looked her up in the phone book at Rochester Row this morning, and it gives her address as . . .' He checked his pocketbook. '10 Bloomsbury Square, telephone number Holborn 2463. According to my *A to Z* we'll be going past Bloomsbury Square on our way to Guilford Street, so I think we'll stop off there on the way and see if she's in.'

Number 10 Bloomsbury Square bore a discreet sign identifying it as a residential hotel, which to Jago signified the kind of place where people could live in comfort when they retired or for some other reason were no longer willing or able to live independently. A resident might have to pay four or five pounds a week for the privilege – or guineas for those establishments that considered themselves of superior quality – so they weren't a place for the hard up. When Mrs Pamela Cordingley had examined their credentials and admitted them to her small but tastefully furnished sitting room, her surroundings, clothes and demeanour, not to mention the electric fire burning extravagantly beside her, suggested that she could afford it.

She looked them up and down as if inspecting them on parade. 'Yes?'

Jago was struck by the incongruity of such an authoritative voice issuing from her frail and diminutive body. She was elderly, with steel-grey hair, and leaned on a stick, but her back was straight and her head and shoulders raised in a way that betokened youthful hours spent in deportment lessons. If so, he thought, that enforced practice of walking with a book balanced on her head had marked her for life.

'I'm sorry to disturb you, Mrs Cordingley,' he said, 'but we think you may be able to assist us with a matter we're looking into.'

'I shall certainly endeavour to do so,' she replied. 'In

days gone by I was a justice of the peace, so I'm clearly on the side of law and order. Besides, life is a little quiet here – sometimes too quiet for my liking.'

'It looks like a beautiful place to live, though,' said Jago, peering out of the window.

'The square, you mean? Oh, yes, it's one of the reasons why I decided to move here when I retired, as it were. Considering we're in the middle of London, it's particularly beautiful, especially in the summer, when the plane trees are in leaf and everything's green. I can't walk as far as I once could, but it's one of my pleasures to take a stroll round the square early in the day, before there's too much traffic filling the air with its noxious fumes.'

'No bombs on the square, though, I hope?'

'No, we've been spared so far, although when Great Ormond Street Hospital and the British Museum were bombed last September I heard the explosions and was concerned they might be heading this way. The only damage we've seen to our square was in 1939, when it became clear that war was coming and the council started digging trenches as quickly as they could for people to shelter in if we had air raids. It was the same story in several other squares in the area – they were ruined. I don't suppose the councillors had time to consider the aesthetic implications – I'm sure their minds would have been on their civic duty to keep the local residents alive, and that is of course commendable. But I'm glad to say that last year they found some money to put the damage right, and this and three other squares in Bloomsbury were restored to their former beauty. Now I can enjoy my little morning stroll just as I used to.'

'As a matter of interest, did you do that yesterday morning?'

'Yes, I did – I got up at eight o'clock, as usual, walked round the square for about half an hour to get my limbs moving, then came back for breakfast.'

'Do you ever venture further afield?'

'Not often. I have a daughter who lives in Chingford, out in Essex, so I occasionally catch the 38 bus here in the square and it takes me all the way there to visit her, but most of the time I'm here. Why do you ask?'

'I believe you may be acquainted with a Mrs Rosemary Webster. Is that correct?'

'Yes.'

'I was just wondering whether your walk might've taken you anywhere near her house in Guilford Street.'

'No, it didn't – but what's your interest in that?'

'I'm sorry to have to tell you, but I'm afraid Mrs Webster was found dead yesterday morning, and we're treating her death as suspicious.'

Mrs Cordingley gave a sharp intake of breath and swayed slightly on her stick. 'Oh, no – not Rosemary. Excuse me, Inspector – I'll have to sit down.'

Jago stepped forward to support her, but she waved him aside and sat on the nearest chair, then motioned him and Cradock to sit down too.

'What happened?' she said.

'We don't know yet. All I can say is that we believe she was killed by a blow to the head.'

'Could it have been an accident?'

'We believe not. We suspect it was murder.'

'Oh, dear – poor little Rosemary. To be cut off in her

prime like that. It's terribly sad – but how is it you think I can assist you?'

'We're talking to people who knew her, to find out more about her. We've been told you were involved in the board of guardians when she was sent out to Canada, and we thought you might be able to tell us about her early childhood before that.'

'Well, you're right, I was involved. I was elected to the board of guardians for the Holborn Poor Law Union in 1895 and served for several years. As I'm sure you'll recall . . .' She peered inquisitorially at Cradock over her half-moon glasses, as if estimating his tender years, and gave a polite cough. 'As you may be aware, those boards and Poor Law unions were abolished under the Local Government Act of 1929 and dissolved in 1930, but in my day each local board of guardians had its own workhouse, and in our case that was the one in Gray's Inn Road. I mention it because that's how I came to know Rosemary – she was born in the Gray's Inn Road workhouse.'

'Really? So presumably she came from a very poor background.'

'Oh, yes, definitely.'

'Did you know she came back to live in this country in 1931?'

'I did. Not at first, but she must have tracked me down somehow, because I had a letter from her out of the blue saying she'd like to meet me. She gave me her address in Guilford Street and invited me to join her for afternoon tea.'

Her reply conjured up in Jago's mind a prim and

proper occasion, but experience suggested it might just as easily have been a confrontation, especially if Rosemary Webster had harboured resentment at having been expelled by this woman from everything and everyone she knew to a strange country across the ocean.

'So how did that go?' he said.

'It was a very pleasant occasion. The shy little girl I'd last seen all those years ago had grown up to be a mature and intelligent woman, and confident too. She said she'd married a Canadian, although he had sadly died, and she had a young son who she seemed proud of.'

'Yes, we've met him. He's grown up now – a pilot in the air force.'

'Really? Well, I hope she was proud of him now too.'

'Indeed. Can you tell me more about what led to her being sent to Canada?'

'By all means. You'll have to excuse me if I don't recall all the details, but if you'll bear with me I'll check for you. I kept my copies of the minutes of our board of guardians meetings, for sentimental reasons I suppose, and I remember re-reading them before I went to tea with Rosemary. She was one of our 1902 cases.'

Mrs Cordingley crossed to the bookshelves on the opposite side of the room and took down a lever arch file. 'Here it is,' she said, holding it up for him to see. She thumbed through its pages until she found what she wanted. 'Here we are. Her mother had grown up in Compton Place, a sort of yard in Bloomsbury with a very unsavoury reputation. I don't know how well you know this area, but Compton Place was just a stone's throw from Tavistock Square, yet so rough that it had a mission hall at one end and its own police station at the other. She was destitute and ended up in the workhouse, and that's how Rosemary came to be born there. The father was unknown, and the mother had no support, so Rosemary lived there until her mother died – the poor child was barely six years old, and it fell to us, as the guardians, to decide her future.'

'So that's when she went to Canada?'

'Yes. We sent a lot of orphans and pauper children to Canada in those days, mainly to farming families in Ontario – it was the best way we knew to get them out of the slums and workhouses and give them the chance of a better life, growing up healthy and strong in families that cared for them instead of ending up homeless on the streets of London. There were two schools of thought in this country – some believed in sending these children to orphanages in Canada, but others thought they'd be more likely to prosper if they were placed in families. I and the other guardians for Holborn were strongly in favour of the latter. The people who took them in were not paid, but they were expected to feed and clothe the children and make sure they attended school and church.'

'And the family she went to did that?'

'Yes. I asked her that when we met for tea – she said they were good people, which was a relief to me, because it didn't always work out well for the children. They were farming folk, Mennonites, and she said they were kind to her and made sure she got a good education.'

'Mennonites? What's that?'

'It's an old Dutch religious sect founded by a man called Menno Simons about four hundred years ago.

Rosemary said there are lots of them in Canada – they sought refuge there when they were persecuted in places like Russia – and many of them are farmers. They believe in non-violence, and when I asked her whether they'd practised that in the home too she said yes, they never lifted a hand against her.'

'Pacifists, then?'

'Definitely. Apparently they have other strong convictions too – they object to taking oaths and won't go to the law, for example.'

'Interesting. Now, you mentioned "the people who took them in", but does that mean they adopted her?'

'Well, yes, but you need to understand that adoption then wasn't like it is now. In Rosemary's case it was what was called a Poor Law adoption, which meant we as the Poor Law guardians could decide it was in the child's best interests to be "emigrated", as we termed it, to Canada and adopted by a family, but there wasn't the same legal process that we have today. We've only had a law about adoption in this country since 1926, and I think in Ontario it was 1921. Before that it was all done on an informal basis.'

'I see. Now, there's just one more thing I'd like to ask you before we go. We were told that Mrs Webster came back to this part of London because she was born here and wanted to explore her roots. I assume everything you've just told us you told her too – is that right?'

'Yes, I think I did my best to answer her questions.'

'Did she say anything else about why she'd wanted to come here?'

'Yes. She said she was drawn back to Bloomsbury

partly because she was born here, but also because it represented where she wanted to get to in life. She loved Russell Square in particular, because it was a beautiful space with grass and trees where she felt free. I think it symbolised everything she thought was good about Bloomsbury. She even laughed and said it was where something called the Association of Special Libraries and Information Bureaux has its office, where professors and students and businesses can ring up and get answers to the most obscure of questions, and she wanted to find her own answers to life.'

'So she chose Guilford Street because it's close to Russell Square?'

'Not exactly. She said she chose that house because it was halfway between Russell Square and the workhouse. She'd come back to Bloomsbury because she'd heard it was a gathering place for free-thinking people who wanted to change the world, and that's what she wanted to do. Living in that house reminded her of her own journey. At one end Russell Square represented everything she wanted in life – knowledge, intellectual freedom and radical change – and at the other end Gray's Inn Road was everything she had left behind and wanted others to be free from too – poverty, abandonment and powerlessness. She said living there reminded her to keep pushing forward, and to help others do the same.'

CHAPTER ELEVEN

The change from Mrs Cordingley's stuffily-heated living room to the icy breeze sweeping across Bloomsbury Square was a shock to the system, and Jago noticed that Cradock was rubbing his hands together furiously to keep the chill at bay.

'Glad you weren't born in a workhouse and shipped out to Canada then, Peter?' he said.

'I certainly don't fancy the idea of the workhouse, guv'nor, but I wouldn't have minded growing up in Canada. All that space and fresh air, and I reckon they must get used to the cold. I'd have been a Mountie by now, probably, riding round on a horse all day nicking villains on the prairies instead of driving round smoky old London.'

'I suspect you may find they drive around in cars now, just like we do, but perhaps when this war's over you'll be able to go and find out for yourself. In the meantime, though, we'll hop into the old jalopy and nip round to

Guilford Street and start talking to the people Rosemary Webster had living in her house. But before we get involved with them I want to see that neighbour over the road from her, Miss Frobisher. If she's the curtain-twitcher that housekeeper said she is, maybe she saw something useful.'

'Ah, yes, the snooper.'

'Correct – but I don't want to hear that word pass your lips while we're there.'

'Yes, sir.'

Mildred Frobisher proved to be a middle-aged woman with hair permed in the style of the twenties, a well-modulated accent and an austere manner.

'I was expecting you to call,' she said, once they'd introduced themselves and gone into the house. 'It's about Mrs Webster over the road, isn't it? I imagine you'll want to know whether I saw anything.'

Jago wondered whether she was perhaps aware of her reputation, assuming, of course, that there was any truth in what Annie McCready had told them about her. 'Yes, that's correct – and anything else you may know that could be helpful to our inquiries.'

'Of course. It's a terrible business – struck down in her own home and left to die on the floor.'

'You seem to know quite a lot about it, Miss Frobisher – how's that?'

'News travels fast, Inspector – that's what they say, isn't it, although news is not always accurate. In this case, however, I happened to look out of the window yesterday morning and noticed a policeman standing outside Mrs Webster's front door, so I knew something was amiss. I went over and spoke to that Scottish woman, the housekeeper.' Her tone of voice put Jago in mind of a duchess speaking of the lower orders. 'She told me what had happened. Was it murder?'

'We have reason to think so, yes. Can you tell me where you were between about eight and ten yesterday morning?'

'So that's when it happened, is it?'

Jago ignored her question and waited for an answer.

'I was here, of course,' she said. 'And I live alone, so if you're about to ask whether there's anyone who can corroborate that, the answer is no, there isn't – just as it would be if you asked a million other people who choose to live alone. The fact of the matter is that I don't need to take in lodgers because I have sufficient means of my own, and I prefer to come and go as I please. So I'm afraid you'll just have to take my word for it.'

'Thank you, Miss Frobisher. Did you see anyone entering or leaving the house between those hours yesterday?'

'No, I didn't. But Mrs Webster lived at the back of the house and had her own entrance there, so if they used that I wouldn't know. And in any case, the fact that I don't have to work for a living doesn't mean I stand around all day staring out of the window. I have things to do, you know.'

'I'm sure you do. Now, do you know of anyone who might've quarrelled with Mrs Webster or had anything against her?'

'No, I can't say I do. But that doesn't mean she would

have been the front-runner in a Guilford Street popularity contest. I think there was a feeling generally in the street that she and her acquaintances had rather lowered the tone, as it were, although I have to say it's been generally deteriorating for some time.'

'I'm not sure I know what you mean.'

'Well, let me explain. This house has been in my family for three generations – my grandparents bought it in 1865. In those days Bloomsbury was a respectable area, but it's a matter of great regret to me and some others in this street that since then it's gone decidedly downhill. Half the properties have degenerated into boarding houses and what people call bed-sits, and it's just not what it was. If you tell anyone in London that you live here now they'll sneer at you. "Ah," they'll say, "Bloomsberries, are you?" It's as if they think we're some kind of delicate soft fruit that's of no serious use to man or beast. And perhaps they're right – when I was a young woman I was proud to be a daughter of the empire on which the sun never set, but now Bloomsbury's full of people who sneer at such ideas. It's widely regarded as the haunt of idle artists, philosophers and so-called intellectuals who wear corduroy trousers. You've heard of the Bloomsbury Group, I imagine?'

'Yes.'

'Need I say more, then? I think the rot set in with them, but now the whole area's gone to the dogs. Everywhere you look you see communists, crackpots and other undesirables. And I don't like to say this, but I think Mrs Webster rather went with the tide on that matter.'

'In what sense?'

'Undesirables, Inspector. I'm thinking of some of the people she had living in her house. She took in all manner of waifs and strays, and apparently she did some work involving refugees. I believe she even had a German living there – I mean, really. Quite frankly, that place seems to have become a magnet for shabby foreigners and other uncouth types that bring the neighbourhood down.'

'Do you know of anyone in particular who might've wished to harm her?'

'Oh, no, of course not – I mean, I sometimes happened to see some questionable-looking characters coming and going, but I didn't actually know them or anything about them.'

'How did you get on with Mrs Webster?'

'We were on speaking terms, but I didn't know her well in the personal sense – I've never been inside her house.'

Jago glanced at the window and couldn't help studying the position of the curtain. 'I understand you do some work for the Ministry of Information,' he said.

She looked surprised. 'As a matter of fact I do. Who told you that?'

'Mrs McCready – Mrs Webster's housekeeper.'

'Ah, yes. I believe she's known locally as a bit of a gossip.'

The words 'pots and kettles' came to Jago's mind, but he decided to let her comment lie where it fell. 'Am I right in thinking that you write reports for the ministry on public opinion?'

'Yes, I work for the Wartime Social Survey. They have people like me sending in reports from all over the country on what ordinary people are saying about the war. In Germany, people aren't allowed to say what they think, but in this country they are, and these reports are an excellent way of ensuring that the government keeps aware of public morale and of what issues are troubling the man and woman in the street.'

It seemed to Jago that Miss Frobisher would certainly not categorise her work as snooping, so he phrased his next question carefully. 'So how do you find out what they're thinking?'

'We do door-to-door surveys and we keep our ears open,' she replied. 'Take the problem of rumours, for example. We should all be aware of the harm they can do by now, but there are still those chatter-bugs, as that man from the ministry called them on the wireless, people who can't resist passing on rumours, or even starting them. If I overhear anyone doing that, it's my duty to make a note of it and report it. The government needs to know what rumours are going round so that it can refute them before they do irreparable damage.'

'Well, if you hear of anything that might have a bearing on what's happened to Mrs Webster, please let us know.'

She nodded. 'I'll keep my ear to the ground, Inspector – it's part of my job. Just ring Whitehall 1212? That's the number for Scotland Yard, isn't it?'

'Yes, that's right – call any time, day or night. Now, unless you have anything else to tell us, that'll be all for now.'

'I don't think I've anything to add, Inspector. I wish you success with your inquiries and I hope you find out who did it, so we can all sleep soundly in our beds – or at least as soundly as Mr Goering's aeroplanes allow. Whoever it was surely can't be of sound mind, but finding a crackpot in Bloomsbury, well, that might be like trying to find a tree in a forest. Judging by the flotsam and jetsam I've seen going in and out of that house over the past few years, if you're looking for suspects you'll probably find a whole gang of them as soon as you cross the threshold.'

'Well, thank you very much for your help, Miss Frobisher, and don't hesitate to get in touch if you think of anything else that might help us.'

'I shall, Inspector. Goodbye.'

'Do you know what a collective noun is, Peter?' said Jago as the door shut behind them.

'No, sir,' said Cradock with endearing transparency.

'Never mind – it's not essential knowledge. But a gang of suspects – that's an interesting one. I wonder how many of these people are in it. Let's pop over the road and put her theory to the test.'

CHAPTER TWELVE

From the outside, Rosemary Webster's four-storey Georgian terraced house looked like a solid, comfortable residence, and Jago guessed it would have cost her a pretty penny to buy it. As he and Cradock stood waiting for someone to answer the doorbell, however, the peeling paint on the front door and window frames made him wonder whether this sign of neglect was evidence of a more recent lack of cash on Rosemary's part or simply lack of interest. His train of thought was interrupted when the door creaked open to reveal the housekeeper.

'Good morning, Mrs McCready,' he said, doffing his hat. 'We've come to talk to your residents. Do you happen to know who's in?'

'Yes,' she said, 'but come in first – I don't want to let all the cold in.'

They stepped into the gloomy hallway, where an old bicycle was propped against the wall.

'You'll have to excuse that,' said Mrs McCready. 'It

belongs to Miss Palmer, but she's out at work, at the ambulance station. Mrs Griggs is in, but the others are out too – Mr Nadelmann's round in Russell Square, I think.'

'Do you know where in Russell Square?'

'Probably that publishing company – Faber and Faber I think it's called. I believe he does a bit of work for them from time to time, but I'm not sure exactly what.'

'And Mr Buckleby?'

'Oh, he's gone off somewhere but said he'd be back in time for lunch. So it looks like it'll have to be Mrs Griggs, doesn't it?'

'That's fine. Could you show us to her room please?'

'Of course. Follow me.'

She took them up two flights of stairs and banged on a door. It was opened by a young woman with tousled hair and nervous eyes, with a grubby apron tied round her waist.

'Police want to talk to you, Mrs Griggs,' said the housekeeper.

Ida Griggs glanced from Jago to Annie McCready and back again.

'That'll be all, thank you, Mrs McCready,' said Jago.

'Oh, all right. Shout if you need me.' She retreated down the stairs.

'Good morning, Mrs Griggs,' said Jago when they were in her room. 'We'd just like to talk to you about what happened here yesterday morning.'

'Mrs Webster, you mean?' She shook her head sorrowfully. 'Shocking business – I couldn't believe it. What would you like to know?'

'Could you tell us how long you've known Mrs Webster?'

'Since last October, after the council took over this house. We'd been bombed out, you see – I was living in Shadwell, and the little place we were renting copped it in one of those big air raids on the docks. I was all right, because I was in the shelter round the corner, under St Paul's – not the cathedral, of course, just our local church. But anyway, it was chaotic, and people were panicking. Then when the all-clear sounded and we came out, I discovered that what'd been our home when we went in was gone – it was just a pile of bricks and wreckage.'

'You said the little place "we" were renting – was that you and your husband?'

'Yes, but he'd gone by then, so at least he didn't have to see it. He used to work at the Godfrey Phillips tobacco factory in Commercial Street, but now he's in the army somewhere in the desert, driving a tank. We've got a daughter too, Poppy – she's ten, and she was evacuated to Cornwall last year, so she's well away from all this terrible bombing. I've only been down there once to see her, and that was only because Mrs Webster gave me the money for the train fare. She was very thoughtful like that, and I'm sorry to see her go. She was Canadian, wasn't she?'

'Yes, I believe she was.'

'I'd never met a Canadian before – I don't think we had 'em in Shadwell. But I see a lot of them now over by the Senate House – I do a bit of cleaning there in the mornings, and just up the street there's a big place that Mrs Webster said used to be where the women students at the university lived. It's been taken over now by something called the Victoria League so the Canadian soldiers can stay there when they're in London for a weekend's leave or training courses or what-have-you. The shops and pubs like it, because those soldiers get paid more than our boys and don't mind spending a bit.'

'Good for business, then.'

'You bet. Mrs Webster even said a new shoeshine bloke set up his pitch outside Russell Square Tube station last year just because there was so much demand from the Canadians. It's all good for the area, I suppose, although there was that one a few weeks ago, wasn't there? At the Kingsley Hotel, near Bloomsbury Square.' She clearly assumed Jago knew what she was talking about, so he adopted a non-committal expression of interested ignorance, and she continued. 'That Canadian corporal – the staff reckoned he'd nicked something, but he pulled a gun out and threatened to shoot them, then legged it. One of your boys found him hiding under the bed in a maid's room. Still, I suppose every country has its bad 'uns, doesn't it? You can't trust 'em all, even if most of them are nice. Even Canadians.'

'Quite.'

'It didn't put Mrs Webster off, though. There was some local campaign to get people to offer hospitality to the Canadian troops, and she used to have them round for tea. She was very kind like that. So sad to see it all end like this.'

'So tell me, Mrs Griggs, have you seen or heard anything since you've known Mrs Webster that might shed any light on why she was killed? Anything out of the ordinary?'

'No, except— No, it's nothing.'

'What were you going to say?'

'Well, it was you saying anything out of the ordinary, it just reminded me . . . You know how sometimes you discover another side to someone that you never knew was there? It was a bit like that with her.'

'Tell me more, please.'

'Well, since I moved here I've managed to get a little job – a bit of cleaning at the Senate House, like I said. That big, tall government place over in Malet Street.'

'Yes, I know it.'

'Good. So anyway, there's another cleaner there, and we were having a chat one day, and it turned out she used to do some cleaning here, for Mrs Webster. She told me something a bit surprising – it really made me wonder whether there was more to Mrs Webster than met the eye. Still, it's a free country, isn't it? Not for me to judge.'

'What did this other cleaner tell you?'

'Oh, it was just about something she'd found in the house.' She hesitated.

'Yes?' said Jago.

'Actually, I don't think I should say any more than that. It's only something some woman said. I don't even know whether it was true.'

'What's she called, this other cleaner?'

'She's Mrs Lock – Vera to her friends.'

'And do you know where she lives?'

'Yes, she invited me round for a cup of tea once. She's got a little council flat in the Coram Buildings in Herbrand Street, where the slums used to be – number 52, on the top floor. Would you mind speaking to her yourselves?

Then I won't feel as though I've gone behind Mrs Webster's back. It's silly, I know, but you do understand, don't you?'

'Yes, we understand – we'll have a word with her. And before we go, can you tell me where you were between about eight and ten o'clock yesterday morning?'

'Yes, I was sitting in here on my tod. To tell you the truth, I was feeling sorry for myself. I miss my little Poppy and my hubby – she's growing up without me, and he's out there in the desert up to I-don't-know-what, and I don't even know whether he's alive or dead. I know I should be brave and all that, but it's hard when you're on your own. Sometimes your thoughts run away with you, if you know what I mean, and it's like you're not yourself any more. But you don't want to know about all that – you get out there and find out who did that terrible thing to Mrs Webster.'

CHAPTER THIRTEEN

Having been assured that Russell Court, where Valerie Palmer worked, was only a short walk from Rosemary Webster's house, Jago and Cradock set off on foot. Turning right at Russell Square, they passed the breathtakingly ornate Victorian façade of the Hotel Russell, complete with statues in wall niches that wouldn't have looked out of place on a medieval cathedral. Crossing a side-street and continuing northwards, however, they found a striking contrast: Russell Court turned out to be an austere apartment block in the modern style, ten storeys of red brick and steel-framed windows towering over Woburn Place. It seemed an unlikely location for an ambulance station, but when they got as far as the junction with Coram Street they found that the north-west corner of the block appeared to have been purpose-built to house a garage, fronted by a row of petrol pumps on a small forecourt.

It wasn't like the greasy back-street petrol stations Jago had grown up with in West Ham. The art deco sign that swept across its front proclaimed that it was a Moon's garage, part of a London-wide chain, and the premises looked smart and clean. He recalled that just a few months before war broke out, two Moon's garages in different parts of the city had been robbed on consecutive nights by masked men with revolvers. Was that the price of success? Perhaps. Maybe twenty years as a policeman had skewed his thinking, but he couldn't help feeling that if people knew how often success bred jealousy, violence and crime, they might not so readily pursue it.

He shrugged off the thought and approached the only person in sight, a man he assumed was the petrol pump attendant. 'Excuse me,' he said. 'Have we got the right place for the ambulance station?'

The man nodded and jerked his thumb towards the side of the garage. 'Down there,' he said. 'Underground garage. You can't miss it – but I hope the Germans can.'

Jago thought perhaps this last remark was supposed to be witty, but the man's voice was so flat and expressionless that he couldn't tell. He confined himself to a simple 'Thank you,' and he and Cradock followed the direction of the attendant's thumb.

They found a ramp going down, at the bottom of which a large subterranean space opened up before them. 'Wow,' said Cradock. 'That's what I call an underground garage. Great place to keep ambulances safe from the bombs.'

'Yes,' said Jago. 'Mind you, they don't look so safe for driving around in an air raid, do they? Not exactly armoured cars.'

The space surrounding them was filled with grey-painted vehicles of all shapes and sizes, most of which seemed to be either former commercial vans and trucks or saloon cars newly fitted with box-van backs, and all of which bore the sign 'Ambulance'. Some were neatly parked in a row, looking ready for action, while on the side opposite them men and women in grease-stained overalls were busy checking oil levels, pumping tyres and in some cases washing the vehicles with bucket and sponge.

Jago interrupted the nearest of them, a young woman, to ask where they might find Valerie Palmer.

'I think she's just popped into the office over there,' she said, motioning with her head towards the back of the garage. Jago could see that a small area was partitioned off with flimsy board walls and glass.

He thanked her and crossed the garage with Cradock in tow. 'Miss Palmer?' he enquired when they reached it.

'That's me – but do call me Valerie. We're always called by surnames only here, and it can get a bit tedious. And you are?'

'I'm Detective Inspector Jago, and this is Detective Constable Cradock. We're from Scotland Yard.'

'Scotland Yard? What brings you here?'

'It's in connection with Mrs Rosemary Webster. Mrs McCready told us you live in the house.'

The sunny expression on her face turned abruptly serious. 'Oh, yes,' she said, her voice now sombre. 'Of course – poor Rosemary. It's a terrible business, isn't it? What happened?'

'We're treating it as a case of suspected murder.'

'How dreadful. But look – if there's anything I can do to help you, please just ask.'

'Thank you, Miss Palmer,' Jago replied. Despite her invitation to informality, it wasn't his practice to address adult members of the public by their first name when on duty, especially young women, and more particularly it wasn't a habit he wished Cradock to get into. 'I'll try to be brief,' he said. 'I can see you're all very busy here. I must say I didn't expect to find an ambulance station underneath a block of flats – I'm surprised that ramp's got enough headroom.'

'As well you might, Inspector. There's actually about ten feet, so plenty for our ambulances. The thing is, this was a commercial garage until it was taken over by the ambulance service, so I suppose it catered for larger vehicles as well as cars, and it's turned out to be very suitable for what we do. It's not the actual Bloomsbury ambulance station – that's round the corner in Herbrand Street, but it's not big enough for all the extra vehicles we've got now because of the war.' She paused as if a question had just occurred to her. 'So was it Mrs McCready who told you where to find me?'

'Yes, she told us you worked for the London Auxiliary Ambulance Service.'

'Ah yes – the fount of all knowledge, that's our Mrs McCready. No one has any secrets from her. But she's a sweet thing, really, I suppose. Anyway, this place is now Auxiliary Ambulance Station 56A, and everyone here's in the LAAS – ambulance drivers and attendants, and mostly women.'

'And I think she said it's voluntary work?'

'Yes. I got involved when the call went out before the war started for women volunteers to drive ambulances –

my dad's a motor mechanic in Streatham, and he taught me to drive when I was a kid. I never imagined that'd come in handy in a war, but it has done, because I can drive more or less anything, and we've got all sorts here – mostly either requisitioned or donated. The one I mainly drive was a laundry van until war broke out, and now instead of sheets and pillowcases it carries stretchers and patients.'

'And how long have you known Mrs Webster?'

'Not long – since last October. I was originally based at the auxiliary station down in Wapping, at the old soap works in Brewhouse Lane, and I had a room in a house a few streets away, but that got bombed while I was on duty one night. I came home to find the whole place was gone, and the few possessions I had were all gone with it. I had nowhere else to go, so I was stuck in the local rest centre for a few nights, and then the council moved me over here, to the one in Taviton Street. A couple of nights later they said they'd found me a billet – a room in Rosemary's house. So I moved in and got a transfer to the Bloomsbury station, and here I am.'

'So what can you tell me about Mrs Webster?'

'Well, I'd say she was a very kind person, always willing to lend a hand, especially when someone's down on their luck, like I was. Strong principles, mind – very black and white in her views. If she thought something was right, she'd give it everything, and if she thought it was wrong, she'd fight it tooth and nail. Not someone you'd want to get on the wrong side of, but fortunately I never did. We got on like a house on fire from the moment I moved in, and I think it was because I wasn't one of those society debs who help at the soup kitchen then get driven home in their Rolls-Royce. I grew up with no advantages in life, no rich parents, and I've always had to pay my own way. I think Rosemary understood that – she hadn't had an easy start in life herself. I worked in a ladies' hat shop – or a milliner's, as they like to call it if they want to sound posh – and I got paid next to nothing, but I've always known there are plenty of people worse off than me and wanted to help them in any way I could. I suppose that's why I joined the ambulance service.'

'You said you're a volunteer, so is that unpaid?'

'It is if you're a part-timer, but I'm a full-time volunteer, so I started out on the princely sum of one pound eighteen shillings and ninepence a week, and now that's gone up to two pounds three. The men are paid more, of course – they get three pounds three and three a week, but that's another war we need to fight, and I'm not sure which one we'll win first.' Jago knew better than to comment on political matters, so he said nothing, and she continued. 'But it's more than I got when I was a volunteer in Spain – which was about two pounds three shillings less than I get now.'

'You were in Spain?'

'Yes – didn't Mrs McCready tell you?'

'No, she didn't mention it.'

'Well, that's a surprise. I think she regards me as a bit exotic for doing that – if not eccentric. I went out there to drive an ambulance with the British Medical Unit. That was only four years ago, but things were very different then – the International Brigades that were fighting Franco's rebels only took men, but now our government's so short of ambulance drivers it's the women they're asking to step up.'

'You must've felt very strongly about what was happening in Spain to go out there like that.'

'Oh, yes – I had no doubt at all that I had to do it. The way I saw it, the issue was clear – it was black and white. There was a right side and a wrong side, and I couldn't stand by and see the wrong side win.'

'You used those words to describe Mrs Webster too, just now – black and white in her views, strong principles. Do you think you were similar to each other in that respect?'

'I suppose we were, yes. I like to think I've got principles, like she did. Not necessarily the same principles, but strong, like hers. I know my own mind, and when I've made a decision I stick to it, whatever the consequences.'

'What did Mrs Webster think of your work in Spain?'

'She was very interested – she wanted to know all about the things I'd seen and done there. I remember she asked me to talk to her nephew Harold about it too. He was a lovely boy – very thoughtful about other people, about life. I was very fond of him. He was interested in doing some ambulance work at the time, and I think he found it very helpful. I didn't spare the detail, and I thought that might put him off, but to be fair to him it didn't. I think he'd already heard some stories from one of Rosemary's friends in the FAU.'

'The FAU? You mean the Friends' Ambulance Unit?'

'Yes, that's it – the Quaker thing, although I don't think you have to be a Quaker to be in it. I believe they're open to anyone whose religious convictions mean they don't want to fight but do want to help people in need or in danger – and so many are these days, aren't they? They're all volunteers, and the headquarters are here in Bloomsbury – at number 4 Gordon Square. Rosemary used to call in there from time to time – she knew quite a few of the young men working there, and I think she did her best to support them and encourage them.'

'Do you know of anyone she might've been particularly close to?'

'Yes, Arthur Murray. He's a Quaker, and he's the friend of hers in the FAU that I was referring to – he works round at Gordon Square. You might want to talk to him – he probably knew her better than most. I think she was fond of him, because he cared about the kind of things she was passionate about – doing your best to help other people, not kill them.'

'Values close to your own heart too?'

'Yes, I suppose they are, and I think she understood there's a price to pay if you believe things like that. I don't just mean financially, although that's true enough – I didn't have any money in Spain, but people at home used to collect money for us and send it out so we had something to live on. Then there were the terrible wounds and dead bodies to deal with – you don't sleep very well after days like that. But you – are you an old soldier?'

'Yes, I am.'

'At the front?'

'Yes.'

'You'll understand what it's like, then. But I have to say I'm glad I went through it four years ago, because that meant when it all started here I knew I could cope with it. Not that that makes it any easier – even that Herbert Morrison in the government said last week that driving ambulances is dangerous work. And it doesn't just mean taking injured people to hospital. We have to drive around picking up the bits that are left after someone's been blown up by a bomb too. I've lost count of how many times I've driven odd limbs down to Billingsgate fish market – they go into the big fridges there so that people can try to identify them and work out who the victim was. I'll tell you something – I'd never realised how heavy a human leg can be.'

Her words brought a flood of pictures into Jago's mind, his own memories of what artillery shells, shrapnel and machine-gun bullets could do to a human body – images that he thought would haunt him for the rest of his days.

He was brought up with a start as Valerie Palmer continued. 'There are things you see that you can never get out of your mind,' she said. It was as if she'd been reading his thoughts. 'I know I did the right thing in Spain, and I feel the same here, now, but sometimes I worry about what it'll be like when this is all over, if I'm still here, and what kind of person I'll be. It can harden you, can't it?'

Jago nodded silently.

'I wonder if I'll ever have a normal life.' She sighed. 'I felt young when I went to Spain, but I'm twenty-eight now and thinking maybe I've left it too late to find someone I can settle down with and be a housewife. But then I don't think I could do that anyway, so I'm still hoping I'll find a man who's not looking for that kind of woman, someone who's still got a thirst for adventure in him.' She flashed him a brief smile of resignation. 'But time waits for no man – and for no woman either, so I may just have to settle for being an old maid who used to drive ambulances in the Blitz and lives on her fading memories. How's that for an inspiring prospect?'

Her question hung on the air. Jago was not going to pursue the subject.

'Before we go,' he said, 'can you tell me the last time you saw Mrs Webster?'

'Yes, it was about the middle of last week – Wednesday, I think.'

'And how did she seem to you?'

'Just her normal self, really – very chatty, full of questions about how I was getting on, how the work was going. She always took an interest.'

'And did she say anything about how she was getting on herself?'

'No, but then she tended not to talk much about herself. She wasn't one to wear her heart on her sleeve – too busy thinking of others, I think.'

'Thank you. And can you tell me where you were between eight and ten o'clock yesterday morning?'

'Yes, we'd had a gift from the American Red Cross – a consignment of warm clothes and boots and shoes for children as well as grown-ups. There was more than we needed here, so I was driving some in one of our car ambulances over to the station in Wapping where I used to be based. They're crying out for things like that for the people round that way that've been bombed out. It's a bit of a job getting there, with so much damage to the roads in the East End, so I set off from here at about half past seven or so. The LAAS people at Brewhouse Lane were thrilled to receive the clothes and things and insisted I stay for some breakfast and a general catch-up, then I drove back and was here by about ten-thirty.'

'Thank you. And just one last question – can you think of anyone who might've had reason to harm Mrs Webster?'

'Harm Rosemary? No – I can't imagine anyone would want to do that.'

'And what about those strong principles of hers that you mentioned? Could they've brought her into conflict with anyone?'

Valerie Palmer paused for thought. 'Well,' she said, 'I suppose there might well be some officious bureaucrats out there that she came to blows with – but only metaphorically. She was only interested in helping people who were suffering or in danger. Surely no one would want to kill her for that?'

CHAPTER FOURTEEN

Their walk back to Guilford Street would take them past Russell Square, so Jago decided to call in at Faber and Faber on the off-chance of catching Nadelmann there doing whatever the work was that Annie McCready had mentioned. A news vendor directed them to the publisher's office at number 24, a large building on the north-west corner of the square that looked as though it might once have been the home of a wealthy Victorian family. The fact that most of the windows on the side of the building were bricked up was presumably a result of the window tax imposed generations ago to raise money for the government, but now in the age of air raids it seemed more like a sensible precaution against bomb damage.

Once inside the building, they were taken to a tiny office with a single wooden chair and the smallest of desks strewn with books and papers, where they were introduced to Mr Nadelmann. He was a short man with thinning hair and a serious expression. His manner was formal, and he spoke in slow, measured tones. His English was fluent, but his accent, though slight, was unmistakably German.

'I apologise for the fact that there's no room in here for you to sit,' he said. 'Would you like me to try to find somewhere more comfortable?'

'No, this will be fine, Mr Nadelmann,' Jago replied. 'We won't be long – we're just speaking to the residents in Mrs Webster's house, and we believe you're one of them.'

'That is correct. It is a matter of great sadness to me that she has been taken from us so cruelly – Mrs McCready told me she'd been struck on the head with a poker. It was to get away from such violence that I left my country, and she gave me a place of refuge, took me into her own home.'

'Yes, so I gathered. How did that happen?'

'It was through her work at Bloomsbury House. Until 1938 I was a lecturer at Heidelberg University on Renaissance prints and drawings, but then . . . well, I'm sure you know what happened to people like me in Germany. The Nazis dismissed me from my job, and even worse they confiscated my personal collection of drawings, which were not only beautiful but also very valuable. I had to flee to England – I could see which way the wind was blowing, as I believe you say in English, and I could see no future for the likes of me in Germany. I arrived as a refugee with just one suitcase and nowhere to live, but I was told that Bloomsbury House was where I'd find help, so I went there and registered. Mrs Webster said I could have a room in her house, which to me at that time was better than a palace. She was a wonderful person.'

'And how did you end up working here at Faber and Faber?'

'Well, to start with, dear Rosemary put me in touch with a friend of hers – a close friend, I believe – who was working with something called the Society for the Protection of Science and Learning, in Gordon Square, just up the road from here. It was set up some years before the war started by a group of British academics to help refugee lecturers who'd been driven out of their jobs by the Nazis. He arranged for the society to give me a little money to cover my immediate needs and he said he would try to find me some work.'

'And the name of this close friend of Mrs Webster's?'

'It's Masterson – Godfrey Masterson. He's an academic, like me, but he's a professor of law at University College London, here in Bloomsbury, so more distinguished than me.'

'I think I'd like to speak to him if he was a close friend of hers. Where would I find him?'

'I would try University College first, in Gower Street – that seems to be his main base when he's in London.'

'Thank you. And did he help to find you work here, with Faber and Faber?'

'No, it was with the British Museum. When Professor Masterson heard of my field of study, he spoke to the Keeper of Prints and Drawings, a man who I thought must have been very important because he had an official residence at the museum. I was delighted, because he gave me a little work, helping to update the catalogues of their enormous collection. At first I was just what they called an unpaid voluntary assistant, but later the museum's trustees agreed that I could be paid for "occasional assistance" at a rate of one pound a day. Not what I would earn if I were still a lecturer, of course, but as we say in Germany, in times of need, the devil eats flies.'

'Ah, yes – I think we'd say beggars can't be choosers.'

Nadelmann paused to digest this unfamiliar expression. 'Thank you, yes. But I must say it was a pleasure to do this work. The British Museum has a unique collection of beautiful prints and drawings by Albrecht Dürer, worth a great deal of money – one that I particularly like, of a peasant woman, was bought by the museum in 1930 for five thousand pounds. My own collection was not as illustrious as that, of course, but even so it was precious to me.'

'So things were working out well for you?'

'At first, yes, but ten days before the war started the museum was closed down and about three-quarters of its collection of prints and drawings were evacuated – they were moved to a bomb-proof emergency storage shelter tunnelled into the rock below the National Library of Wales, in Aberystwyth. It was a huge operation, but a wise decision, considering the number of bombs that have hit the museum in the last three months.'

'So was that the end of your job?'

'Not at all. The collection was evacuated to Aberystwyth, as I said, and the staff were evacuated with it, including me. I was put up in a nice little hotel on the seafront, but then I had a whole story I won't bore you with, having to go before an enemy aliens tribunal in October but being exempted from internment because I was categorised as a refugee, then interned last June when all the Germans were rounded up, then being released again thanks to the intervention of Professor Masterson.

I am indebted to him. Eventually after all that I came back to Bloomsbury, because Faber and Faber offered me some part-time work as an advisor on a book they plan to publish. I think Professor Masterson had contacted them and put in a good word for me. It's a book about prints and drawings created by the Old Masters – which is exactly my expertise. So here I am, and I'm happy to be working again.'

'You said it's a part-time job – what are your working hours?'

'They pay me for twenty hours a week, but unless they want me to attend a meeting I can be quite flexible about what time I come in and how many hours I stay on any particular day, as long as it adds up to not less than twenty over the week. Sometimes I work more, because it's something I really enjoy, but I don't get paid for that. Today, for example, I started at nine-thirty and I'll probably finish quite soon, but tomorrow I'm planning to come in later as I need to do some shopping.'

'What time did you start yesterday?'

'At nine-thirty, the same as today.'

'And can you tell me what you did before that?'

'Certainly, but it's not very interesting. I have a routine, you see – I rise at seven o'clock, I wash and dress, and at about seven-thirty I go down to the front door to find *The Times*, which the paperboy has put through the letterbox some time before that. I bring it upstairs and read it for one hour, from eight till nine, while taking my breakfast – usually a cup of coffee with whatever I can find to eat. Yesterday I left there at nine-fifteen and walked round here – it doesn't take more than ten minutes to get here.'

'Could anyone confirm what time you left the house yesterday?'

'I hope you're not thinking that I perhaps had something to do with what happened to poor Mrs Webster.'

'It's just to help us eliminate you from our inquiries, Mr Nadelmann.'

'I'm glad to hear that. The only person who saw me before I left was Mr Buckleby, but he didn't actually see me leaving the house. I called on him briefly on my way out, to pass the newspaper on to him – we share it, you see. Even so it may seem to you a luxury for someone in my circumstances, but the thing is, I don't just read it, I study it – in the evenings too, if he's finished with it. When I was living and working in Heidelberg I thought I'd be there for ever, but then life brought me to Britain, and I want to be British – and that means I must learn to speak English properly. If I want to have an academic career here and lecture to students I must have an excellent command of your language. So I read *The Times* carefully, with a dictionary beside me, and every time I find a word or an expression that's new to me, I look it up and write it in my notebook and do my best to learn it. Even for the work I'm doing here for Faber and Faber it's very important, because I'm writing some of the chapters for the book they're planning to publish. It's just a pity that the shortage of paper means it won't come out until the war is over – it's not so easy to get things published in the present situation.'

'Yes. That reminds me of someone else we've been speaking to who writes books. She's finding it difficult to get published too, albeit for different reasons. She used to live in Mrs Webster's house, so I imagine you probably know her – Susan Ingram.'

'Yes, I know her. But her work is totally different to mine – it's fiction, I believe, so not serious, and I must confess I'm not interested. Rosemary seemed to think my working for Faber meant I might be able to get Miss Ingram an introduction or something, and I would have done anything to help Rosemary, but the only person I know in the company is the editor of the book I'm working on, and I don't think whoever handles fiction here would be interested in a recommendation by a foreign expert on Renaissance drawings. I had to tell Rosemary no, I couldn't do it, and her friend would have to find a publisher by her own efforts. And in any case, I understand the young lady's doing a different kind of work now – something to do with pigs, I believe. If you know anything about the Jewish faith, you'll understand that working with pigs is of even less interest to me than writing fiction.'

'I'm glad to hear things seem to have worked out well for you, though. It sounds as though this Professor Masterson's been a great help to you.'

'Yes, although I think it was Rosemary who persuaded him – she wanted to help me get back to the work I love, and that's what happened, which is very good. But there's something else going on which is very bad.'

'Really?'

'Yes. You see, I mentioned earlier that the Nazis had confiscated my collection of prints and drawings, but what that means, of course, is that they stole it from me. That was bad enough, but later when I was checking the catalogues I discovered that some of my items are now in the British Museum's collection.'

'You mean the museum's acquired them from the people who stole them?'

'Not necessarily directly – there may have been any number of middlemen involved – but the fact remains that the museum has bought them, and the money has gone into the pockets of those Nazi criminals. Those works are my property, and I want them back.'

'Have you taken this up with the museum?'

'I have, but I'm getting nowhere – I believe you call it red tape. I'm a peaceable man, Inspector, but we all have our limits, and I will not stand idly by while someone cheats me of what is rightfully mine.'

CHAPTER FIFTEEN

Jago and Cradock left the Faber and Faber offices and continued their walk across Russell Square to Guilford Street, where they climbed the stairs to Charles Buckleby's room on the top floor. They knocked on the door, and it opened to reveal a lean-looking middle-aged man in a business suit that hung a little too loosely on him, as if he'd lost weight since buying it. What appeared to be a small food stain was visible towards the bottom of his lapel.

'Ah,' he said when Jago and Cradock produced their warrant cards and introduced themselves, 'Mrs McCready told us all we might be getting a visit from the police. This'll be about Mrs Webster, will it?'

'That's correct, sir,' said Jago.

'You'd better come in, then.' He bustled about the room, clearing a cardigan and a newspaper from a sofa that was threadbare on the arms.

'No need to tidy up for us, sir,' said Jago, sitting down.

'No, of course . . . Actually, I was just about to have a

quick bite of lunch. Would you like to join me? It'll only be toast and peanut butter, I'm afraid, but you'd be very welcome.'

Cradock's eyes lit up, but Jago, mindful of Annie McCready's comment about the businessman losing his money, nipped any potentially enthusiastic response by his young colleague in the bud. 'That's very kind, Mr Buckleby, but we're fine, thank you. We'd just like to see what you can tell us about Mrs Webster.'

'By all means,' said Buckleby, fidgeting with the grubby shirt cuff that protruded from his jacket sleeve. 'I still can't believe it's true – she was so full of life.'

'Can you tell us when you last saw Mrs Webster?'

'Yes, it was the day before yesterday, but just in passing – she seemed fine, just her usual self.'

'Was there any hint that she was apprehensive or afraid?'

'What, you mean as if she knew someone was going to attack her? No, I should say there wasn't.'

'Was there anyone she'd had trouble with recently?'

'No, not that I'm aware of.'

'Can you tell us what you were doing yesterday morning?'

'Not a lot, really. I'd been down in the basement for most of the night, after the sirens went off, trying to sleep but failing, as I usually do, then when the all-clear sounded at about six o'clock I came back up here and tried to get a bit of sleep. I managed to doze for a couple of hours, then woke up and had a bit of bread and jam for breakfast, and I spent the rest of the morning here in this room.'

'Can anyone confirm that?'

'No, I was on my own. The only caller I had was Mr Nadelmann – he dropped in at about a quarter past nine to give me the paper. We neither of us have the same money we used to, so we go halves, and then it only costs us a penny each instead of tuppence. He gets first go of it, because he's got a job to go to, then he passes it on to me. He was on his way to work, so he didn't stay for more than a quick chat, then when he'd gone I read the paper in bed. And my bed's strictly single occupancy, I regret to say, so no witnesses.'

'And you didn't see or hear anything of Mrs Webster?'

'No – like I said, the last time I saw her was the previous day.'

'How long had you known her?'

Buckleby perched on an armchair. 'I first met her ten years ago, when she moved here with her boy, Jack, after her husband died. Considering she was quite recently widowed, I was impressed by how well she was coping. A woman of some strength, I'd say, and she was a great help to me.'

'How did you come to meet her?'

'I knew her husband, Elliot. He was Canadian, but during the last war he came to Britain with the Canadian Forestry Corps – we were getting very short of timber for the war effort, so the Canadian government sent thousands of lumbermen over here to maximise our production of timber. Elliot was in the lumber business, you see. When the war ended he went back to Canada, but I started doing business with him.'

'What kind of business was that?'

'I was in concrete.' He paused, as if expecting a reaction,

but got none. 'I used to say that as a joke, but it's not funny, is it? What I mean is I had a company – Buckleby Concrete Construction. You need a lot of timber for formwork when you're building with concrete, and I managed to do a good deal with Elliot, importing timber from him. That all ended when he died, of course. I'd never met Rosemary, what with them being on the other side of the Atlantic, but we knew of each other's existence because of the business connection, and when she moved to Britain she looked me up.'

'How well did you get to know her?'

'Very well, I'd say – she was a warm and friendly person, and she took an interest in me. I got to know the whole family – her son, Jack, and her brother and his family too.'

'How did she get on with her brother?'

'I couldn't say, really – just like an ordinary brother and sister, I suppose. Why do you ask?'

'Only because someone's suggested there was some friction between them.'

'I see – well, maybe they're right, but if there was I never noticed it.'

'You say you had a company – what became of it?'

'Ah, well that's the sad story of my life, unfortunately. At first it all went splendidly. Seven or eight years ago I started getting big contracts from the Air Ministry to build sound detectors. Are you familiar with them?'

'I've heard of them – something to do with spotting enemy aircraft approaching?'

'That's right – some people call them acoustic mirrors, or even concrete ears. You may have seen some of them, especially down by the coast.'

'No, I can't say I have.'

'Well, they're quite striking to look at – they're big concrete walls and dishes designed to pick up the sound of approaching bombers before they get here, so we can send up our own fighter planes to intercept them. I don't know how they work, but the fact that they were big and concrete meant my company got a lot of work and we made some good money. But unfortunately, a few years later the ministry said they'd got a better idea – they wouldn't tell me what it was, but I think it was something to do with using radio waves instead. Anyway, the main thing as far as I'm concerned is that they cancelled my contracts overnight, and that meant no more concrete ears – and it was the end of my business. All over, just like that.'

'I'm sorry to hear that. So was that when Mrs Webster was such a help to you?'

'It was, yes – when the company went bust I lost my home as well as my money, and she let me have this room.'

'I see. So what else can you tell me about her?'

'That's simple. When the world turned its back on me she was the one who helped me. When I was down and out, she lifted me up and put me back on my feet. When everyone said I was a failure, a has-been, she believed in me – and made me believe in myself again.'

'So she was a real friend to you?'

'More than a friend, Inspector. She was the finest woman who ever walked this earth.'

'Praise indeed. How close were you?'

'That's a difficult question to answer. She understood me in a way that I don't think anyone else did. She was someone I loved being with, even if it was just talking or going for a walk. I trusted her, and I think she trusted me, and she was the one person I knew I could rely on. Most of all, I think, I admired her – for the kind of person she was and the way she lived, what she'd done with her life. I've never married, but I suppose you could say she was the woman of my dreams.'

'Were you romantically involved with her?'

Buckleby replied with a brief laugh, but there was a bittersweet ring to it. 'If I'd met her when I was younger I'd have asked her to marry me. But look around you – what could I have offered her now? To tell the truth, I think I was never really convinced that I'd be good enough for her, so maybe I'd have to just let myself worship her from afar and leave it at that. Sometimes perhaps it's better to be content with the little you have than to risk all and lose everything. And besides, it's not a crime to dream, is it?'

CHAPTER SIXTEEN

'Well,' said Jago as they left the house in Guilford Street, '"the woman of my dreams," indeed. It looks like someone loved her.'

'Yes, and it sounds like they didn't have to use one of those matrimonial agency things,' said Cradock.

'Speaking of which, now that we've seen the residents, I think maybe it's time we paid a visit to ABC Introductions.'

'To fix ourselves up with wives, sir?'

'I don't think I'd rate your chances of survival very highly if Emily found out you were doing that, Peter. But I do think we should see what we can learn about what Rosemary Webster was getting up to with those letters. Before we do that, though, I want to visit that young man Miss Palmer mentioned – the one with the Friends' Ambulance Unit. Murray was his name, wasn't it?'

'Yes, sir. Er . . . any chance of a bite to eat, sir?'

Cradock's face took on an expression that Jago took to be a naive attempt to feign the incipient pangs of starvation. He stopped and stared at the detective constable sceptically. 'I know it must've been difficult for you to forgo Buckleby's offer of peanut butter on toast, Peter, but that poor fellow probably didn't have two brass farthings to his name.'

'Yes, sir.'

'If this Murray's a Quaker, like Valerie Palmer said, he'll probably feel sorry for you and give you his own lunch if you look at him like you looked at me just now, and I don't want to have to arrest you for demanding food under false pretences. But neither do I want you collapsing from hunger, so we'll find a little bite to eat on the way. But no loitering.'

'Thanks, guv'nor,' Cradock replied with a sigh of relief. 'That's very kind of you.'

After a rapidly consumed sandwich, they arrived in Gordon Square. Number 4, the address Valerie Palmer had given them, was an anonymous-looking house with a green door in the south-west corner of the square. Jago rang the bell, and after a brief wait the door was opened by an earnest-looking young man in a shapeless brown knitted jumper and worn corduroy trousers. 'Yes?' he said with a smile. 'Can I help you?'

'I'm looking for Mr Arthur Murray – I understand he works here. Is he here today?'

'He is, yes – I'll fetch him. Can I say who's calling?'

'Yes – the Metropolitan Police. I'm Detective Inspector Jago, and this is Detective Constable Cradock.'

'The police? Is he in any trouble?'

'Not as far as I'm aware. We just want a word with him.'

'Well, you'd better come in out of the cold while I look for him.'

He stepped back and let them into the entrance hall, shutting the door after them. 'Shan't be long,' he said, and disappeared down a corridor.

Jago looked around. The hall was spacious but filled with mounds of winter overcoats and bundles of other clothing, and a table in the corner was loaded with a stack of plain cardboard boxes. He was still wondering what was in them when the man returned.

'Please excuse the mess,' he said, following the direction of Jago's gaze. 'Coats for distribution and medical supplies. We get a lot of stuff passing through here and we run out of space for it, but it all makes a big difference to people who need it. Anyway, here's Mr Murray – I'll leave you to talk.'

He ducked away again down the same corridor and disappeared. Murray stepped forward and greeted them. He was a tall young man of athletic build with an untidy shock of fair hair, in clothes that looked even more battered than those of his colleague.

'Welcome to the Friends' Ambulance Unit,' he said, in a voice that suggested to Jago's ears a private education. 'How can I help you gentlemen?'

'We'd just like a brief word, sir. We're making inquiries in connection with the death of Mrs Rosemary Webster, and I gather you knew her.'

'Ah, yes. Poor Rosemary – it was a terrible shock. I had a phone call from a young lady who works for the London Auxiliary Ambulance Service – she told me what had happened.'

'That would be Miss Palmer?'

'Yes – she knew I was very fond of Rosemary, and she said she'd mentioned me when you spoke to her. But look, let's not stand around here. I'll take you upstairs to the common room – it seemed to be empty when I passed it just now.'

He led them up the stairs to a room furnished with sagging sofas and easy chairs that looked as though they'd come straight from the local junk shop. There was no fire in the grate, and the room was cold. Murray must have assumed they'd want to keep their coats on, because he made no offer to take them.

'I'm sorry it's a bit chilly in here,' he said. 'But funds don't stretch to much coal, even if you can get it, and besides, we rarely have time to take breaks.'

'Yes,' said Jago. 'It looked rather busy downstairs when we came in. I understand this is your headquarters – is that right?'

'It is, yes. We moved in here last September. There's a lot to do, and there's never enough of us to do it.'

'And you're all volunteers?'

'That's right. None of us gets paid, which can make life a bit tricky at times, but we get free board and lodging, and some of us who don't have any other support get a little pocket money – a pound a month – from a fund that the unit maintains. I probably don't need to say that we all work for love rather than money.'

'Yes, I dare say. Now, I don't want to keep you from your work, Mr Murray, but I'd just like to ask you one or two questions.'

'By all means. But before you do, Miss Palmer told me

you're treating Rosemary's death as suspected murder. Is that correct?'

'I'm afraid it is.'

'But she was such a kind-hearted woman – she was a saint. Who'd want to kill her?'

'That's what we're trying to establish. Can you think of anyone who might've wanted to harm her?'

'An enemy, you mean? No, I can't. I mean she was always trying to help people, and I can't imagine anyone wanting to do her harm. But I suppose anyone can have enemies, can't they, even if they're trying to do good. I just feel guilty that I wasn't there to prevent it – maybe it was something I could have helped her with.'

'Are you thinking of anything in particular?'

'No – it's just that the idea of somebody hurting her, even killing her, has been haunting me. I can't get it out of my mind. Do you think you'll find out who did it?'

'We'll be doing everything we can, yes.'

'I'm sure you will, of course – but please, if and when you do, could you let me know? I'm desperate to know who took her life – and even more why they did it.'

'I shall. But tell me please, how did you come to know Mrs Webster?'

'Well, she was involved in lots of humanitarian work around Bloomsbury and used to drop in here to see how we were doing. I got chatting with her one day, and we became friends – I think she felt we were like kindred spirits. She was quite a bit older than me, but she was very interested in the work we do, especially my overseas experiences with the unit.'

'Where was that?'

'Mainly in Finland, after the Russians invaded it in December 1939. We took twenty ambulances and fifty men out there and worked at the front, transporting the wounded to hospitals, but then the Finns had to sign a peace treaty, and the area we were in became part of Russia. All the Finns left, and we got out just before the Russians arrived. The conditions were terrible, of course, with blizzards and freezing temperatures, but we moved further west and carried on helping in any way we could, transporting civilian evacuees and wounded soldiers. Then when April came we got news that Germany had invaded Norway and we were sent to help there, but it wasn't long before Norway fell and we had to be evacuated. Half of us escaped at the last moment on a French ship – thankfully we got back in a convoy to Scapa Flow, but two destroyers were sunk on the way.'

'And the other half?'

'They had to make their way overland to Sweden. It meant they reached a neutral country, but it proved very difficult for them to get home from there – some of them could only get out via Russia and Turkey, and they ended up working as voluntary drivers for the Red Cross in Cairo.'

'And you're driving ambulances in London?'

'Well, no, actually – that's the frustrating thing about it. Most of the ambulances we took to Finland and Norway were destroyed there, and the rest we had to abandon, but in any case it seems there's already enough volunteer ambulance drivers here – people like Valerie Palmer – so they don't need us to do that.'

'So if you're not required for ambulance work, what are you doing?'

'Since the Blitz started, most of us have been working as orderlies on hospital wards, and others are providing help in air-raid shelters and in rest centres for people whose homes have been destroyed. I work at the rest centre in Taviton Street, just over on the other side of the square here, and there's always something to keep us busy. I've been working on the night shift there for the last two nights, and then coming over here to do a bit of work in the afternoons.'

'I know what night shifts are like – it's very tiring, isn't it? What hours are yours?'

'Eight in the evening till eight in the morning.'

'Longer than I used to do when I was a police constable. And then you've got to try to sleep. I used to go to bed as soon as I got off duty and sleep for a few hours if I could, but everyone else is making noise by that time of day, so it can be difficult. Is that what you do?'

'Yes. I live at the FAU hostel in Nassau Street. It's actually some evacuated wards in the Middlesex Hospital, above the outpatients department. We started using them last month, and it's a good arrangement, because for the hospital it means there are always some fit young men available at night for fire-watching or stretcher-bearing, and for us it means we get accommodation for free. All the men who live there are rest centre workers, like me. If I've been on a night shift at Taviton Street I go back there – it's only about twenty minutes' walk – and go straight to bed and sleep till about lunchtime.'

'Is that what you did last night?'

'Yes.'

'And you're back here again working already?'

'Yes – I had a quick bite of lunch and then came straight down here.'

'And what about yesterday – was it the same routine?'

'Yes – I finished my shift at eight, walked back to the hostel, slept till lunchtime, then came here.'

'That's very dedicated of you.'

'Not at all – it's simply doing my duty. There's work to be done, and I'm here to do it – and as I said, we do it for love, not for money. People who end up in rest centres are suffering much more than I am, and from where we're standing here, the ones in Taviton Street are almost literally our neighbours, so to me it's just a case of loving your neighbour. Those places are a lifeline, and we none of us know when we might end up in one ourselves.'

Jago nodded. 'Miss Palmer told us she spent a few nights in a rest centre over in Wapping, when the house where she lodged got bombed, and then some more at Taviton Street.'

'Yes, that's where I first met her – at the Taviton Street one. You know, those places were only supposed to be somewhere for bombed-out people to find shelter for a day or two, but the air raids have gone on for so long now, for a lot of people they've become home – there's just nowhere else for them to go. That's why I thought it was so good of Rosemary to turn her house over to the council – it may be only a drop in the ocean, but it means a few people get a proper home.'

'Quite. When we met Miss Palmer, she spoke highly of Mrs Webster – she said she was very kind and always willing to help people in need. It sounds as though you share that view – is that correct?'

'Yes, it is, but don't get me wrong – I don't think there was anything sentimental about Rosemary. She could be tough with people when she felt it was necessary. She was fond of Valerie, but even so I remember once she spoke quite harshly about her to me. I must have made some complimentary remark about Valerie, but Rosemary said something like I should be careful, she's clever but cynical. She said sometimes even the most attractive woman can have a heart of stone, and a man can be blind to it until it's too late. Now, I knew her nephew Harold had a bit of a crush on Valerie at the time, so I thought she was talking about him, but then I got the feeling maybe she was trying to warn me off. I was rather taken aback by that, but I think that's just the way Rosemary was – she wasn't one to mince her words.'

'I see. Miss Palmer mentioned that you knew Mrs Webster's nephew – she said he was interested in doing ambulance work.'

'That's right. As you may know, Harold wanted to be registered as a conscientious objector.'

'No, I wasn't aware of that.'

'Right – well, I put him in touch with the Central Board for Conscientious Objectors. They've got their office just five minutes' walk from here, round in Endsleigh Street. They coached him for his tribunal so he could make a good case for being registered, and in due course he appeared at Bloomsbury County Court. But unfortunately it didn't work – the tribunal turned down his request.'

'And I understand he was called up into the army and killed.'

'Yes – a tragedy. He was so young and talented – wise

for his age, people used to say. He had a passionate belief in what the Bible says about war – you know, the idea that one day God will judge between the nations, and they'll stop having wars and turn their swords into ploughshares. That's what he dreamed of, and his conscience wouldn't let him take up a weapon to kill. When he died, it was . . . well, it was like losing a brother I loved. He had so much to offer, and I can only imagine what a positive contribution he would have made to the world if he'd lived. When Valerie told me he'd been killed I felt awful about it – I couldn't help thinking I was to blame. I'd tried to prepare him for that tribunal, you see, but I'd failed him. If they hadn't turned down his appeal, Harold would still be with us today, possibility working right here with me. It was a terrible blow to learn of his death, but for his parents . . . I just can't imagine. It must've been like the end of the world, especially if there was still pain between them and him.'

'Pain?'

'Oh, I'm sorry – it was just something Valerie said in passing once. I think she'd got that impression from Rosemary. Some trouble, but whether Rosemary herself was mixed up in it I don't know.'

'Well, if you think of anything else that might be helpful to us, please get in touch.'

'Yes, of course. And if you need me again, you'll probably find me here or at the rest centre in Taviton Street. Nothing can bring dear Rosemary back now, but I'll do anything I can to help you find whoever did that dreadful thing to her. Some people just don't deserve to die.'

CHAPTER SEVENTEEN

'Working for love rather than money – that's what he said, wasn't it?' said Cradock as Arthur Murray waved them off in the direction of Museum Street, the home of ABC Introductions. 'I was just thinking – that's what we do, isn't it?'

Jago laughed. 'If that's your subtle way of complaining about police pay, you should be thankful you weren't a policeman before the strikes – back then you might well have found yourself earning less than the man digging up the road that you'd just walked past on your beat. It was only after virtually the whole Met came out on strike that they got a half-decent pay rise.'

'Did you go on strike, sir?'

'No – it was before my time, 1918. I was still in the army then – I didn't join the Met until 1919, and it was pretty much all over by then.'

'I reckon that Murray bloke ought to think about going on strike – he looked as poor as a church mouse in those scruffy old clothes of his.'

'I suspect you'll find he regards his work as a vocation, Peter, as I'm sure you do yours.'

'Oh, of course, sir – no doubt about it.'

'But having said that, I think he may be in for a little surprise.'

'Really? What kind of surprise?'

'A pleasant one. In that will of Rosemary Webster's.'

'Ah – you didn't mention that when you had a look at it.'

'Only because I didn't want to discuss the contents with Jack Webster.'

'So what did it say?'

'Basically she left everything to her son, as he said – the house and all her chattels. But it was those specific bequests he mentioned that were interesting. One was to Annie McCready – a hundred pounds, with thanks for her loyalty and faithfulness, which I suppose is quite normal for someone who'd had long service from her housekeeper. The other one was to Arthur Murray. That was for five hundred pounds, with a simple message – "Follow your dream."'

'I see what you mean – that will be a nice surprise for him. Will you be telling him?'

'No – he'll find out in due course. Strictly speaking, that will's private until probate's been granted, and that can take a while, so it's not for us to go round blabbing the contents. Which reminds me, have you made a will?'

'No – my mum says it's unlucky.'

'Why?'

'I don't know – she reckons if you make a will you'll die sooner.'

'With all due respect to your dear mother, Peter, that's nonsense. Has she ever made one?'

'No, but she says she's got nothing to leave except her wedding ring and a few old sheets that she reckons she's pawned more times than she's had hot dinners, so she's playing it safe – not tempting fate, she says.'

'Well, all I can say is if you're thinking you might marry that poor helpless girl Emily someday, I'd advise you to make one – being in the police is a dangerous job, even without having to be out at all hours, not to mention air raids. Like Webster said, you don't want to make her life any more complicated by not leaving a will.'

'Have you made one, sir?'

'No, I haven't, actually – but I haven't got anyone to leave anything to, have I? Anyway, my advice is do as I say, not as I do. Is that clear?'

'Totally, sir. And that reminds me – that other thing Murray said was interesting, wasn't it?'

'Which particular thing are you thinking of?'

'About dying. He said "Some people just don't deserve to die." That's a bit funny, isn't it? I mean, is he saying some other people do deserve to die?'

'My goodness, Peter – have you taken to reading books of philosophy?'

'No, sir – that's not what you might call my cup of tea. It's just that I'd have thought a pacifist kind of bloke like him would say nobody deserves to die, if you know what I mean.'

'I do, Peter. So you think maybe he's the kind of person who'd believe that rule in principle but be prepared to make an exception if necessary?'

'I think that's what I mean, sir, yes.'

'Well, good for you – I realise it may be just because that sandwich we had has given your overworked brain a bit of a boost, but I'm pleased to see you thinking carefully about what people say. Whether you're right or not I couldn't say at this stage, of course, but well done all the same.'

Cradock felt a flush of embarrassed delight creeping across his face. 'Oh, thank you, sir. Very nice of you to say so.'

'All right – don't let it go to your head. Now, let's see what ABC Introductions have to say for themselves.'

Hadleigh Mansions was a four-storey building, and the ABC Introductions office was on the top floor. Jago and Cradock climbed the stairs, knocked on the door and were admitted by a young woman in a smart fawn-coloured jersey jacket suit with a pleated skirt. She beamed a wide smile at them, which Jago judged a little over-enthusiastic, and made quite a performance of seating them on a pair of comfortable chairs facing the desk behind which she proceeded to sit.

She looked each of them in the eye, Jago first and then Cradock, with an air of intense interest.

'Good afternoon, gentlemen,' she cooed, 'and welcome to ABC Introductions. It's always a delight to meet people looking for that special someone in their life. Would one of you be desiring our assistance in seeking a matrimonial alliance? Or is it both of you? I can assure you of our utmost attention, and I'm confident we'll find just the right woman for you – there'll always be someone out there, but the challenge is to find them. Happy is the man who finds her for himself, of course, but sometimes we all need a helping hand. The quality of our female clientele is probably the finest in the world, and . . .' Her eyes strayed to Jago's somewhat disreputable overcoat. 'And we, er . . . cater for all tastes and classes.'

Jago ignored the implication of her comment. 'I apologise for the state of my coat, Miss, er?'

'Stevens – Miss Beryl Stevens. There are three of us who run the company – my colleagues Miss Alison Archer, Miss Christine Dawson and myself. We wanted to use our initials for the name, but our surnames would have spelt SAD, which we thought inappropriate for a matrimonial agency, so we used our Christian names, and that gave us ABC. We like to tell our clients who've struggled to meet the right person that with us it's as easy as ABC.'

'Quite,' said Jago, suspecting this might not be quite the original promotional masterstroke she seemed to think it was. 'I don't suppose I'd come up to scratch if someone was looking for a well-tailored gentleman, but I blame this coat on the Blitz.'

'Of course – and I'm sure we can find you plenty of ladies who are more interested in a man's character than his coat.'

'That's very reassuring, but I should explain that we're not here looking for wives – we're police officers.'

'Oh, I see – in that case please forgive my misapprehension. But even so, if you happen to be bachelors you might still want to consider the potential benefits of registering with us and partaking of our services. We are the experts.'

'That won't be necessary, Miss Stevens. I'm Detective Inspector Jago, and this is Detective Constable Cradock, and we're making inquiries in connection with the death of a woman who we suspect may have had some contact with you.'

'As a client?'

'Possibly.'

'Can you tell me her name?'

'Yes. It's Mrs Rosemary Webster – a widow.'

'Ah, yes, that name rings a bell, but only a faint one.'

'So what can you tell me about her?'

'Well, we hold our clients' personal information in the strictest confidentiality, of course, as I'm sure you'll understand, but since you're the police I'll give you every cooperation I can. What is your particular interest in Mrs Webster?'

'I'd like to know whether Mrs Webster was actively seeking a husband, and if so, who are the men you've put her into contact with.'

'Isn't that rather intrusive into her private affairs?'

'It may seem that way, but we're treating her death as a case of suspected murder, so the answer is no.'

'I see. In that case I'll check. Bear with me for a moment.' She swivelled her chair round and began to search through a card index. 'Here we are,' she said, pulling out a card. 'Mrs Rosemary Webster. It says here that she came to see us towards the end of last year and spoke to one of my colleagues about possibly going on our books, and they came to a mutually advantageous arrangement.'

'What does that mean?'

'I'm not sure – it could have been a small discount, perhaps. Some of our clients are not wealthy and – how shall I put this – they have very specific requirements in terms of the man's income, although on the other hand we sometimes find the women have money of their own and are equally specific about how much of it they'd be willing to let their husband have. And of course, as you can imagine, many of the ladies have a very particular view of what kind of man they're looking for with regard to looks, character and disposition, although we did have one poor soul recently who told us she just wanted a husband and didn't mind how ugly he was. But that's rather the exception in our experience.'

'Do you have a record of what Mrs Webster was looking for?'

'Yes. It says here "Strong moral principles, compassion for those less fortunate, faithful, reliable, steady temperament."'

'But you haven't found anyone so far to match that?'

'It seems not, but it looks as though she hadn't formally registered with us yet. As I said, she only came to see us towards the end of last year, and judging by the date here it was actually three weeks ago, since when we've had Christmas and air raids to keep us busy. But I'm sure we would have succeeded in finding her a match before long.' She stared out of the window for a moment. 'Such a pity that it's too late now.'

Jago found himself wondering whether Miss Stevens's response reflected a genuine compassion for the departed or disappointment at a lost business opportunity, but he didn't ask.

'I'm curious about how your business works,' he said. 'Could you explain it, please?'

'Yes, of course. Our clients pay a modest registration fee of two guineas, and we then create what we call a psychographic profile of the client. That includes their age, their appearance – colour of hair, height, build, that sort of thing – plus their religion, their professional status if they're working, their social class, their hobbies, pastimes and interests, and of course what they're looking for in a wife or husband, as the case may be. Then we make sure we've noted anything else they may mention, for example they hate cats but love dogs. It's all about identifying the qualities you're looking for in a life partner, you see, and then finding someone who has them. Once we have all that information, we use our skills and experience to match them with potential prospective partners from amongst our huge bank of clients of the opposite sex, and write to them with the details of the client by way of introduction. If none of our introductions proves suitable, that's the end of it – although of course we rarely fail – but if our service results in an engagement both parties pay us a further fee, and then another if it yields the happy result of a marriage.'

'So when you write to the potential partners, do you write yourselves or do you get the client to write a letter of self-introduction and send that?'

'We find the latter is the more productive approach, but we insist that the correspondence goes through us rather than directly between the two parties. That's so we can check the client's letter before we send it on, to make sure it's consistent with the profile we've built up for them on our records, on the basis of which we've selected the potential partners. Also, of course, we control the correspondence to protect the client against the very small risk that the person we send their letter to proves to be unreliable or objectionable in their behaviour.'

'Quite a rigorous procedure, then.'

'We like to think so. We also require that their letter of self-introduction be handwritten, because I happen to know a lot about handwriting – I have considerable experience in the skill of handwriting analysis. You could present me with any two specimens, and I'd be able to tell you whether they were written by the same person. But that's just the simple matter of comparing how they form their letters – the real skill is in the interpretation. In the right hands, a piece of handwriting is like a window on the soul of the writer. I can look at what someone's written in their own hand and identify their personality traits, their emotional make-up and other characteristics. We call it the science of graphology, and I'm an expert graphologist.'

'Really – where did you learn that?'

'I'm self-taught, Inspector. It's not something you can learn at a university. It's intuitive, a gift, and some of us simply have it. When we combine it with our psychographic profiling, it's what gives ABC Introductions its commercial edge – it's been a key factor in our success.'

'I see. Just one more question – did anything emerge in your dealings with Mrs Webster that might've suggested someone could be a threat to her?'

Miss Stevens looked shocked. 'Certainly not – we would never have anyone like *that* on our books. The very thought of it sends shivers down my spine. No, Inspector, we are a very respectable company, and we only take on respectable clients.'

'Thank you – that was very helpful. But before we go, I wonder if you could help me with this.' Jago took Rosemary Webster's envelope from his pocket and handed it to her. 'Addressed to ABC Introductions, as you can see. Could you take a look at the contents, please?'

She took the two letters out, read them quickly and swallowed nervously. 'Yes?'

'Rather odd, don't you think?'

'Er, yes, it does look rather unusual on the face of it.'

'And to your expert eye, written by the same person?'

'Yes.'

'Right. Now, we found those letters in Mrs Webster's flat. They look to me like the kind of thing you might pass on as your female client's introduction to the men on your books. But tell me, why would Mrs Webster want to send you two contradictory letters like that?'

'I've no idea.' She paused to think. 'But clearly she didn't actually send them to us, and since she hadn't formally registered with us as a client or paid the fee, we wouldn't have supplied her with the names of any of our male clients. I can only guess that perhaps she wasn't sure how to present herself to the possible contacts, and that these were perhaps her experimental drafts – a work in progress, as you might say. Obviously we tell our clients to be honest in the way they describe themselves, but at the same time human nature dictates that they'll want to present their best side, and sometimes they exaggerate their qualities. But in the end it's up to them what they say. If we assume she was intending to register with us, she may have drafted these with a view to deciding when the time came which one to send and discarding the other one.'

'She'd got as far as addressing the envelope to you with both letters in it, though, hadn't she?'

'Yes, but the envelope's not stamped or sealed, is it? So we can't tell whether she intended to send both letters to us or not. And I suppose that since she clearly hadn't got to the point of posting that envelope, we'll never know.'

'You may be right,' said Jago. 'Thank you.'

CHAPTER EIGHTEEN

'I noticed you didn't ask that Beryl Stevens to give you a quick profile of Mrs Webster's character from the handwriting in those letters, sir,' said Cradock.

'No, I didn't,' Jago replied. 'I remember seven or eight years ago some graphologist came over to Scotland Yard from America when Lord Trenchard was the commissioner and tried to persuade them graphology would revolutionise crime detection. I think they did some tests, but I never heard anything more about it. I have to say I'm happy to go to court with Dr Gibson giving evidence on the basis of opening up someone's chest and looking at a stab wound, but I don't think calling a witness to a deceased woman's character because they can open up a window on her soul would cut much ice with a judge.'

Cradock laughed. 'I see what you mean, sir. She was a bit scary, though, wasn't she? I'm not sure I'd like to fall into her clutches. All that business about registration fees and matrimonial alliances and psycho-whatsit profiles –

not very romantic, is it? She made it sound like some sort of factory where they feed you in at one end and you come out the other end married. A bit too impersonal for my liking – and probably a bit too pricey.'

'Yes,' said Jago, 'I suppose there's still a lot to be said for falling in love with the girl next door. Wouldn't you say so?'

Cradock eyed him cautiously: he'd never actually lived next door to Emily, but Jago's meaning was clear. 'I suppose so, yes,' he replied, anxious to extricate himself in the least impertinent way possible. 'Although it's a bit different nowadays, isn't it, what with all the trains and ships and aeroplanes. You can meet people from much further away.'

He knew he'd failed as soon as the words left his lips, but if Jago's thoughts had flitted to Dorothy, his face betrayed nothing.

'You can indeed, Peter,' he said. 'But what I'm thinking about right now is something else to do with Rosemary Webster – from what Miss Stevens said, it seems she never actually signed up with the agency or paid her registration fee, so I'm wondering how serious she was about looking for a man, if at all. It's not that she didn't have male admirers – that Buckleby said she was the finest woman who ever walked this earth, and Nadelmann said she was wonderful, didn't he?'

'But her son didn't even think she had a boyfriend, never mind any plans to remarry.'

'Yes, so no sign of a spurned lover lurking in the wings, more's the pity.'

'Revenge, you mean?'

'Yes – it's a common enough motive, and we seem to be lacking one so far. But I don't think we're going to find one standing around here getting cold. Let's pop over to that cleaning woman Ida Griggs mentioned – I'd like to know what it was she found in the house that made Ida think there was more to Mrs Webster than met the eye.'

Coram Buildings was a long, red-brick block standing at right angles to Herbrand Road and facing an identical building across a small yard. It was modest in style, but tidy. Jago and Cradock went in at the ground-floor door and were greeted by a cold lobby with painted brick walls, a concrete staircase and a smell of disinfectant. They climbed the stairs to the top floor and knocked at the door of flat 52, where Vera Lock, a shy-looking, plainly dressed woman with tired eyes, admitted them once they had identified themselves and showed them into her small living room. A wireless was playing light music and the space in the middle of the room was dominated by an ironing board.

'Please excuse the mess,' she said, taking the iron off its asbestos stand and folding the board's wooden legs away before removing the two items to an unknown destination outside the room. She tutted when she spotted her ironing pile on the table, as if someone else had carelessly left it there, and removed that too before returning, turning off the wireless and taking a seat.

'There,' she said with a meek smile, 'that's better. I'm sorry my hubby's out – I expect it's him you want to speak to really.'

'No, Mrs Lock,' said Jago, 'it's you, actually. I understand you work as a cleaner at the Senate House – the Ministry of Information. Is that correct?'

'Yes, it is. But what's it to you? I haven't done something wrong, have I?'

'No, not at all. It's just that we were talking to Mrs Griggs. She works there too?'

'Yes, she does. So?'

'She told us you used to clean for Mrs Rosemary Webster in Guilford Street. Now, I'm sorry to have to tell you this, but unfortunately Mrs Webster has been killed.'

Vera's hands flew to her face. 'Oh, no – poor woman. What happened?'

'We're treating her case as suspected murder, I'm afraid.'

'Murdered? That's even worse – but who'd want to do that?'

'That's what we're trying to find out. I'm hoping you might be able to help us.'

'Me? I shouldn't think so – I only worked with her for a bit, and then when the council took the place over in October they made their own arrangements for the main house, and I just used to do an occasional bit of cleaning for her in the little flat. I couldn't really say I knew her.'

'I understand, but there's one small matter you might be able to shed some light on.'

'Well, of course, if that'll help – what is it?'

'Mrs Griggs has told us that you once mentioned you'd found something rather surprising in Mrs Webster's home. Do you have any recollection of that?'

'Yes, I do, actually, because I thought it was a bit odd.' She hesitated. 'But look, I don't know as I should say what it was – I don't want to get anyone in trouble.'

'We're investigating a murder, Mrs Lock, and I'd appreciate your cooperation. It would be as well for you not to withhold information that might be relevant to our inquiries.'

'Right, I see what you mean. Well, it's just that I was doing some dusting in the bedroom – Mrs Webster's bedroom, that is – and I found some cigarettes. That was strange, because I didn't think she smoked, but then I noticed they were a bit funny-looking, and when I sniffed one I could tell by the smell what it was. It was Mary Jane.'

'Mary Jane?'

'Oh, I'm sorry – that's slang. It means that drug – marijuana.'

'I see – and you could tell immediately that's what it was? Do you come across a lot of that in the course of your cleaning?'

'No, but I did when I worked in one of those dodgy clubs in Soho. Reefers, that's what those cigarettes are called. You used to be able to buy them there, four for five shillings – not that I ever did, of course.'

'And these were just lying around in the bedroom?'

'Well, no, not exactly. I know I'm not supposed to, but I was having a bit of a nose around in the drawers on her dressing table. Just curious, you know, and I saw them there. There was something else too – just a plain little box with no writing on it, next to those reefers. I had a look inside and saw a bit of white powder, and I was suspicious, so next time I went round there to clean I took an envelope with me and put a tiny bit in it, then showed it to someone I knew in that club. He put some on his tongue and said it was cocaine – said he could tell by the taste. He said I wouldn't like it, because it had a nasty bitter sort of taste. I said I wouldn't like it for a lot more reasons than that – I'm not such a mug as to take drugs.'

'And did you ever find out why they were there in Mrs Webster's house?'

'No, but it made me wonder what sort of game she was involved in. I mean, either she must've been using it herself or she was selling it to make some money, or she was just looking after it for someone else. Whatever it was, I don't suppose she should've been doing it.'

'Did you ever ask her?'

'No. I know my place – and besides, she might've taken offence if she knew I'd been poking around in the drawer. I don't suppose it matters who knows now, though.'

'Indeed. And did you tell anyone else apart from Mrs Griggs?'

'Not as I recall, no – I think she's the only person I've met since I left there who knew her, and I only told her because it sort of slipped out when we were comparing notes on what she was like to work for. I hope I haven't spoken out of turn.'

'There's no need to worry about that. Now, is there anything else you can tell me about this whole business?'

'No – I think that's all I know.'

'Well, thank you for your time, Mrs Lock. That'll be all for now.'

'So what do you make of that, Peter?' said Jago as they went back down the stairs from Vera Lock's flat.

'It's quite an eye-opener, isn't it?' Cradock replied. 'I mean Rosemary Webster being mixed up with drugs – just being in possession would've got her a fine if she'd been caught, or even a spell in jail, let alone dealing in them.'

'Yes, but it doesn't seem to fit with what we know about her, does it? People can always do things that are out of character, but even so, it just seems a bit unlikely she was using dangerous drugs or buying and selling them.'

'But Annie McCready did reckon she wasn't too flush with money, and her son said she wasn't as well off as she used to be. Supposing she needed the cash?'

'Well, yes, maybe.'

'Vera Lock thought she might've been looking after it for someone else, didn't she? Maybe that's it. But who? Did she know anyone who might've been handling that kind of stuff?'

'Good question – that's something we'll have to think about, isn't it?'

CHAPTER NINETEEN

'I trust you slept well,' said Jago the next morning when he collected Cradock from the police section house in Ambrosden Avenue.

Cradock slipped into the passenger seat of the Riley and rubbed his eyes in a way that reminded Jago of babies in prams. 'Mustn't grumble, sir,' he said. 'There's plenty worse off than me, with their roof blown off or whatever. It's just when those perishing anti-aircraft guns start blasting away – it's such a row. I just hope they manage to hit something up there – they must keep the whole city awake. I managed to get a bit of sleep when they packed it in, though.'

'So it wasn't the memories of that young woman at ABC Introductions giving you nightmares that kept you awake, then?'

'No – I think I've recovered from that. But I still reckon I'd rather go to the dentist than sign up with her and her crew – it sounded like a right old rigmarole.'

'Well, you know what they say – there's no gain without pain.'

'Yes, sir, I'm sure you're right. I suppose I'm just not keen on that kind of pain. Which reminds me, I was thinking about pain when I was awake. It was that thing Arthur Murray said about Harold Bowman and his parents – he said there was pain between them. What do you reckon that was?'

'Hmm . . . I've been wondering that myself. He made it sound as though there'd been some kind of trouble between them in the past. Of course, we don't know whether there really was any – he only said Valerie Palmer had mentioned it in passing, and he thought it was an impression she'd got from Rosemary Webster. So it's not exactly first-hand evidence, is it? But still, it might be worth having a word with Miss Palmer to see if she can tell us anything more about it.'

They returned to the auxiliary ambulance station and found her in dirty overalls, bent over the engine of an ambulance. 'I'm sorry to interrupt you, Miss Palmer,' said Jago, 'but I wonder whether we could have a quick word.'

She straightened up, with a dipstick in one hand and a rag in the other. 'That's fine. I was just checking the oil in case it needs topping up – we can't afford to have an engine seizing up on us. Will here do?'

'Yes, of course.'

'Before we start, I must apologise for going on about my search for the right kind of man and all that when you were here before. I'm afraid I have a reputation for speaking my mind, and sometimes I speak first and think later. It's just that people are always telling me there's someone out there who's the perfect man for me, but I've never found him. I thought I had in Spain, but he was killed, and if I found someone now he'd probably be even more likely to be killed. In any case, by the time this war's over I'll definitely be past my prime – I'll probably end up one of that army of superfluous women, like we had after the last war. So there – my apologies. Now, what did you want to know?'

'It's to do with Mr Murray at the Friends' Ambulance Unit in Gordon Square. We've been talking to him, and he said you'd mentioned to him in passing that there'd been some pain between Mr and Mrs Bowman and their son, and he wondered whether Mrs Webster was mixed up in it in some way. Can you shed any light on that for us, please?'

'Well, I'm not sure. I don't know a lot about it, but I'm pretty sure Harold and his parents weren't particularly close at the best of times, especially him and his father. His dad's some sort of bigwig in the Canadian High Commission, but I don't think that impressed Harold very much – he told me once that he thought his dad was up to something at work, something suspicious that Harold didn't approve of, but he didn't say what it was. But as for the pain you're talking about, that was to do with the conscientious objector business – you're familiar with that, are you?'

'Yes – Mr Murray said he'd wanted to register.'

'Right, well, he'd talked with his parents about it back before the war, and they weren't keen. I think they wanted him to be a success, not a rebel. In the circles they moved in, the thing for young men like him to do was to get a decent military record behind them and then land a good job when it was all over. I think he said his father hadn't been called up in the Great War and had always felt the lack of a good service background in his career.'

'And Mrs Webster? Was she involved in this?'

'I don't think she was closely involved, but with Rosemary's interests you can probably imagine that she'd have been sympathetic to young men whose convictions meant they wanted to help their fellow man, not kill him, even in war. I think when she discovered he wanted to register as a conscientious objector she supported him.'

'And what did his parents think of that?'

'I've no idea. I don't know whether she ever discussed it with them, but clearly if she had they'd have been on different sides of the argument, and I suspect she wouldn't have been shy about making her views known if they'd asked. One of the things I liked about Rosemary was that you always knew where you stood with her – she was a forthright kind of person. If you asked her for advice she wouldn't pull her punches – she'd tell you exactly what she thought. But only if you asked – I don't think she'd go round poking her nose in where it wasn't wanted just for the sake of it. I got the impression she'd learnt to be discreet, and I think she'd have been more likely just to encourage him quietly from the sidelines. But in any case, I believe it all changed when the war started.'

'How was that?'

'From what Harold said, I think when war broke out his parents changed their minds. He was their only son, after all, and I imagine when there's actually a war on that puts a different complexion on things. As far as I know, they were suddenly more concerned about his survival than his career prospects. Not that it made any difference in the end.'

'You mean they lost him?'

'Yes – I can't imagine what their pain and grief must have been. But what I do remember very clearly is the effect his death had on Rosemary. She only had one son too, and he was her only child, and he'd joined up as a volunteer. It really brought home to Rosemary that he might die too – and I think that had an unfortunate effect on her relationship with him.'

'In what way?'

'Well, as I said, I don't know much about it, but I do recall her telling me she'd said things she regretted. She didn't go into detail, but she said she'd lost her temper. I think that's what happens sometimes, isn't it? We're frightened we're going to lose someone we love, but it comes out wrong and we get angry with them and blame them for being irresponsible. Afterwards she felt really bad about it – she said she'd pushed Jack away when he might have needed her.' She shook her head in silent thought. 'Nothing good comes of war, does it? I think a lot of people are finding out now what I found out in Spain.'

'And what's that?'

'It's simple – that war turns your life upside down and inside out, and you're never the same again. The things I saw in Spain changed my outlook on life. Before I went there, I had hopes and dreams about all the good things life might bring my way in the future, about being happy. But dealing with people who'd been maimed or bereaved or blown to pieces put paid to all that. Now I don't expect anything from life, and I don't care whether I live or die. You may think that's shocking, but it's the truth.'

'I don't find it shocking,' said Jago, 'even though I think perhaps I should.'

'In that case you're probably an exception. Most people seem to think I'm callous and heartless. But I think I'm just brutally realistic, because that's what the world's made me. I'm not subtle and I'm not polite – like I said, I see things in black and white, not shades of grey. I hate the rich and love the poor. I hate privilege. I hate lots of things, but I love justice, and I love seeing bad people get what's coming to them. I expect that'd make me a good policeman, wouldn't it?'

'If you're content to serve justice, then yes, perhaps it would. But not if you want to take it into your own hands – that can land you in a lot of trouble.'

She gave a bitter laugh. 'I reckon I've had enough trouble for more than one lifetime already, and I'm not looking for more. But all the same, if that's your official advice, I'll be sure to watch my step.'

CHAPTER TWENTY

Valerie Palmer escorted the two detectives back to Jago's Riley Lynx and insisted on checking the oil before casting a few admiring glances over it. 'Nice car,' she said. 'Sporty but practical.'

'It does the job,' Jago replied. Fond though he was of the Riley, he didn't have much time for men who slavered over their vehicles as if they were Hollywood starlets. It was a reliable machine that got him from A to B, and that was enough for him.

Valerie stood back while he and Cradock got into the car, and waved them off as they departed.

'That was very considerate of her, wasn't it?' said Cradock.

'Yes,' Jago replied. 'She said her dad was a motor mechanic, so maybe it's something she learnt from him – looking after engines, and good manners to please your customers. I can't help thinking of what Susan Ingram said, though. Do you remember? It was something like

"People can be very well-mannered and yet still filled with spite on the inside." It seems to me we're meeting quite a lot of well-mannered people here – Jack Webster, officer and gentleman, Gordon and Helen Bowman, cultured diplomat and wife, Albert Nadelmann, university lecturer, even Susan Ingram herself – but it makes me wonder what spite there may be on the inside.'

'You're right, guv'nor – and what about that Mrs Cordingley? She was the well-manneredest of the lot.'

Jago winced. 'Peter, please – don't murder your own language. That fellow Nadelmann speaks better English than you do.'

'Sorry, guv'nor – she was the most well-mannered of the lot. But what I'm getting at is that if we're looking for spite, who knows what might've been going on if we've only got her side of it? I mean, she's the woman who sent that little orphan girl Rosemary off to Canada. She says Rosemary invited her to tea and all that, like it was all lovey-dovey, but for all we know Rosemary might've hated her.'

'You make a fair point, Peter, although I can't quite see Mrs Cordingley managing to beat someone to death with a poker at her age. I think I'd like to go back and talk to Susan Ingram again – she's an ambitious young woman with more than one chip on her shoulder, as far as I can tell, and I'd also like to find out what that business of working with pigs that Nadelmann mentioned is all about.'

Susan Ingram's flat wasn't difficult to locate: the bombed remains of the house next door in Mecklenburgh Square were conspicuous, as she had said. They found her at home.

'Sorry to disturb you, Miss Ingram,' said Jago, 'but we'd just like a quick word. Are we interrupting your writing?'

'No, not at all. I've run up against something of a brick wall in my plot, so I'm taking a little break to clear my head and hoping I'll be able to find a way round it later today. Do come in.'

She took them up to her bed-sitting-room on the top floor. It was a cramped and untidy space, in stark contrast to Rosemary Webster's flat. 'Welcome to the reality of life in Bloomsbury,' she said. 'It used to be such a grand place, and there are still the leafy squares and some nice houses, like Rosemary's, but it ended up one of the poorest parts of London and now it's full of cheap, dingy boarding houses and rooms like this, with landladies still protesting because the war's damaged their business so badly they can't afford to pay their rent and rates.'

She moved to the window and pulled the curtain back as far as it would go, as if to relieve the gloom. 'Did you see that film that came out last year – *Tilly of Bloomsbury*?' Jago and Cradock both shook their heads. 'No, I don't suppose it's the sort of thing policemen go for – "Country gentleman falls for daughter of working-class Bloomsbury boarding-housekeeper, with hilarious consequences." Amusing to some, I suppose, and people might think Bloomsbury's just the kind of place that could happen. But the reality's more like what you see here.' She gave a dismissive laugh. 'Anyway, this place it too pokey to stand on ceremony – all I can offer you to sit on is the divan.'

They accepted her invitation and perched on the divan,

which Jago assumed doubled as her bed, while she sat on a stool in front of what looked like a combination dressing table and desk, on which a fountain pen rested beside a pad of foolscap paper covered with scribbled handwriting. 'So,' she said, 'how are you getting on with your inquiries?'

'We've met the residents in the house,' said Jago, 'and Mrs Webster's family – her brother and his wife and daughter, and Mrs Webster's son – you know him, don't you, if I recall correctly.'

'Yes, I do. He's a nice young man, rather dashing I suppose, but then all those RAF boys are, aren't they – so young and so brave. Rosemary told me he was a pacifist when he was younger – got it from his grandparents, apparently – but then changed his mind and volunteered for the Canadian air force. I must say I rather admire him for that – it shows moral courage, don't you think?'

'Every man has to make his own decision when war comes – we all have a job to do.'

'Indeed we do, and even authors have to pay the rent. I've got a job now, and I like to think it's helping the war effort.'

'I got the impression from our previous conversation that you were a full-time author.'

'Well, I suppose I didn't mention the job because writing novels is so much more interesting than the boring drudgery of the kind of work ordinary people do.'

From the look on her face, Jago suspected she regarded him as one of those ordinary people.

'It's only a part-time job, thank heaven,' she continued.

'And something to do with pigs, I believe,' said Jago.

'Who told you that?'

'Mr Nadelmann. I assume you know him from the house.'

'Yes, I do, but not well. A horrid little man, by all accounts.'

'What makes you say that?'

'He took advantage of Rosemary, after all she'd done to help him – I think he's involved in something dishonest and put her in a very nasty position.'

'Really? Can you tell me more?'

'I don't know any more. It's just something I was told.'

'By whom?'

'Her housekeeper – Annie McCready. I'm sure she'll be able to tell you all about it – she's quite the village gossip, you know.'

'Thank you. Are you aware of any tensions between Mrs Webster and any of the other residents in the house?'

'Not particularly – Valerie Palmer's always seemed a sweet thing, and Ida Griggs, well, she's what people call the salt of the earth, isn't she? I don't think Rosemary would have had any problems with them. I'm not so sure about that fellow Buckleby, though – he seems to dote on her, but I don't trust him. He disappeared very suddenly for a few months last year and then turned up again without a word of explanation, as if he'd never been away. I wondered whether he'd been hiding from someone. He was behaving oddly too. I bumped into him on the landing one evening, and he just stared straight through me as if I wasn't there, like the zombies in that Bela Lugosi horror film, *White Zombie*. I don't know whether you've seen that one, but a friend of mine persuaded me to go the summer before last – she said it was a great spine-chiller, but to me it was so corny it was more like a pantomime. Suddenly seeing Buckleby like that was much more scary.'

'I see. But to get back to those pigs Mr Nadelmann mentioned – is it true?'

She sighed, as if pigs and anything to do with them were beneath her dignity. 'Yes, it is. I've left it now, but I had a part-time clerical job at the Small Pig-Keepers' Council. Have you heard of it?'

'Can't say I have, no.'

'Neither had I. I was never entirely sure whether it was to do with people who keep small pigs or small people who keep pigs, or even a small council for people who keep pigs, but it was set up a couple of months after the war started and it's based at Victoria House, on Bloomsbury Square. It's that big classical building on the east side of the square. Do you know it?'

'We called on someone on the west side of the square yesterday, and I could see a long building on the other side through the trees, but I didn't have time to study it.'

'Well, it's very grand and it looks as though it must be very old, but it was actually only built about ten years ago, for Liverpool Victoria, the insurance company. The council occupies only a very small corner of it, of course, and it's quite an odd contrast when you consider the work they do – they encourage people to set up pig clubs and feed them on kitchen waste. Apparently there are more than three hundred of them now – clubs, that is – which means the country's producing an extra ten thousand hundredweight of pig meat a year.' She rolled her eyes. 'Fascinating, isn't it? Did you know there's even one run by the Metropolitan Police?'

Jago's face must have betrayed his ignorance of this fact.

'Yes, it's surprising,' she continued. 'What with the bombs and the blackout and all the crimes, you wouldn't have thought they had the time, would you? But a couple of them came to visit us at the office for advice – they said they were from Hyde Park police station, and that's where they'd set up their club. Do you have any interest in pigs, Inspector?'

'No – I'm too much of a townie for that.'

'Nor I, sadly – I wouldn't know one end of a pig from the other, and the thought of devoting my spare time to their company leaves me cold. I'm glad I've managed to escape.'

'So you've left the job?'

'Yes, I've found some much more congenial employment – still part-time, of course, so I can concentrate on my real job.' She waved her hand in the direction of the paper and pen on her desk.

'So where do you work now?'

'At the Ministry of Information. I'm in the Press and Censorship Division, but in a very minor clerical role again, filing press cuttings. The pay's only a pound a week, but they only want me for two or three hours at different times of the day, so I still have time to write. I have to say it's pretty dull, but it's more interesting than pigs.'

'I dare say. Mrs Webster's brother, Mr Bowman, told us he works for the Canadian High Commission as some kind of liaison officer, working with the Canadian press at the Ministry of Information. Do you know him?'

'I know of him – Rosemary mentioned that he worked

there when I told her about the new job – but I can't say I know him. I don't come into contact with him through my work, but that's hardly surprising – I haven't been there long, and I'm only part-time, and I understand he's something much higher up than me. Besides, it's a big place. Apparently there was a big fuss made when the ministry started up at the beginning of the war because there were nine hundred and ninety-nine people working there, but now I believe there's about twice as many as that, and people are saying it's hugely overstaffed. They're supposed to be reducing the numbers, so I'm hoping I'm not one of the people they're planning to cut, although I suppose that would give me more time to write.'

'Yes. By the way, I've been thinking about what you said, about the subject matter of your novel. You said your parents' generation had stolen everything from yours, but I was wondering, wouldn't Virginia Woolf have been part of that generation, perhaps even the whole Bloomsbury Group? And yet you said she'd inspired you.'

'It was her writing that inspired me – her style, not her friends. I don't have much time for them. They thought they were pioneering some new and liberated way of living, but if you were to ask me now I'd say it was all just the self-indulgent antics of the privileged rich. And I am neither privileged nor rich – I want to be as successful as Mrs Woolf, but I have to accept that I've never had her social advantages, not to mention her background, her connections or her money. If I'm to achieve anything, it'll have to be on my own terms.'

'And that'll be part of the story in your book, I suppose.'

'Yes. The central character – the heroine, if you like – is a young woman grappling with misfortune, but her story stands, of course, as a metaphor for the experience of my generation, and it captures the broad sweep of a changing world as it lurches from one degree of chaos to another. She's a woman of our time, living in a world where the women haven't married because all the best men are dead, and the men haven't married because their hearts have been shrivelled by war. She wants to be free, but she's shackled by the mundane mediocrity of society, by the dull, malignant economic forces that govern our lives, by powers beyond her control. She can see little prospect of joy in the future – just the daily grind of existence, the grim reality of 1930s Britain. And as I mentioned before, she's been dispossessed of her inheritance, of everything noble and beautiful she had hoped for.'

She sounded to Jago as if she were reciting something from a book herself, and he wondered how many people would want to spend their leisure time reading about grim reality when their everyday lives were already so full of it. 'Yes,' he said. 'And do you think this new book will stand a better chance of finding a publisher?'

'Well,' she replied hesitantly, 'I'm, er . . . in discussions with potential publishers at the moment and hoping to have a deal very soon. But one has to be patient in these matters.'

'I see,' said Jago. 'I'm sure one does. Is that something Mrs Webster was trying to help you with?'

'No, and I hadn't asked her to – I wanted to do this by myself, for myself.'

'Someone we've spoken to who knew Mrs Webster said

you always knew where you stood with her. Would you say that's true?'

'Yes. Rosemary was a no-nonsense kind of person – she didn't mince her words. She always called a spade a spade.'

'Forthright, then?'

'Yes, it pains me to say it, but she was the sort of woman who said what she thought was true and right, regardless of what effect it might have on others. Some people are like that, aren't they? Being cruel to be kind, that's what they say. It's like the woman friend who tells you your waistline isn't attractive and you ought to lose some weight. Unfortunately Rosemary was like that about my writing – she said I was trying too hard to be taken seriously and it wasn't working. She thought I should write something more marketable, just so I could earn enough money to pay the bills, like romantic fiction, for example – there's a big market for it, you know.'

'The sort of thing you referred to as "light romance"?'

'Exactly. As a matter of fact, three or four years ago Rosemary persuaded me to enter a romantic novel competition, in the *Daily Mirror* of all things. Not a newspaper I'm in the habit of reading, but the prize was two hundred and fifty pounds, which is not to be sniffed at if you're a person of straitened means, and there was a chance of being published. I entered under a pen name, of course, because I thought if I win it I don't want to risk becoming identified as a romantic novel writer – it could be the kiss of death to my future career as a literary novelist, but there's a lot I could do with two hundred and fifty pounds.'

'And did you win?'

She looked at Jago with an expression somewhere between pitying and patronising. 'No, I did not. And the woman who did . . . Well, no one could ever accuse me of being a snob, but I ask you – she was a short-hand typist from Torquay, and she wrote about a typist who falls in love with the man she types letters for. Not only that, she said she wrote the novel for fun. For fun? When did I ever write anything for fun? Writing serious literature has nothing to do with fun. And to add insult to injury, the wretched novel was published, and I believe she's had a couple more published since.'

'But as you say, there's a market for it – there must be plenty of people who want to read it.'

'Yes, there are – women who long to meet a man who's a romantic hero, not the dull sort we seem to meet in reality. I think there was something of that even in Rosemary, you know.'

'You mean she was looking for a man like that?'

'I don't know, but I wouldn't be surprised – she'd been alone for ten years, since her husband died, and I do recall her saying quite recently that she wished she had a man about the house.'

'Do you know whether she ever contacted a matrimonial agency?'

Susan laughed. 'Rosemary? Now there's a thought – but then again, why not? People do, don't they? But as for having a man about the house, it's the sort of thing any woman might say if she wanted a shelf putting up, although if she did I'd say "Put it up yourself, girl." But I suppose if that's what she was really thinking she might well have gone to one of those places. I've never been to one myself, though, so I couldn't really say.'

'And you didn't take her advice about writing romantic fiction?'

She laughed again. 'Of course not. I think it was what the government calls defeatist talk, and that's against the law now, isn't it? Rosemary was mistaken, and that's sad – I really think that's all she thought I was capable of.'

CHAPTER TWENTY-ONE

Cradock shivered as they left Susan Ingram's flat. 'That was a bit weird, wasn't it? Buckleby acting like a zombie and all that? I mean, maybe they've got them in Haiti, but not in Bloomsbury, surely.'

'Haiti?' said Jago. 'Miss Ingram didn't mention that. Do I deduce that you've seen the film?'

'Well, yes, actually,' Cradock replied bashfully. 'Just for a laugh, of course. I don't suppose you have, sir, have you?'

'No, I haven't, Peter,' said Jago, suppressing a smile. 'But it takes place in Haiti, does it?'

'Yes, sir. There's this creepy mad bloke, played by Bela Lugosi—'

'Of Dracula fame?'

'Yes, he's a voodoo man, and he puts a tiny bit of some drug into people that sends them into a sort of trance, like they're dead but they're not. They're zombies. It was on at the Coliseum in Upton Park just a week or two before the war broke out.'

'I'm sorry I missed it. But seriously, if that's what Mr Buckleby looked like, given what Vera Lock says she found in Rosemary Webster's bedroom, I think we should have a word with him.'

'There's just a small point we'd like to clear up with you, Mr Buckleby, if you don't mind,' said Jago when they returned to the house in Guilford Street.

'Sure – what is it?'

'We've been told that sometime last year you suddenly disappeared from Mrs Webster's house and weren't seen for a few months, and I wondered whether you could tell us why that was.'

'Well, it's a bit of a painful subject for me, but if you must know, it was due to the financial difficulties I was having a while back. I told you my business went bust, didn't I?'

'Yes, you did.'

'Well, the thing is, everything I had was in that business, and I was declared bankrupt. That really knocked me for six – in my head, you know? I didn't know where I was – I just went to pieces.'

'So you went away to recuperate?'

Buckleby gave a bitter laugh. 'No such luck. I ran into a spot of bother when I wrote a cheque one day and it bounced. I thought I might get away with a polite letter from my bank manager, but no – I ended up being taken before the magistrate for obtaining credit while being an undischarged bankrupt. It was only for twenty-two pounds ten, but the magistrate set bail at two hundred pounds. There was no way I could find that much money, and if it hadn't been for Mrs Webster I've have been put on remand. She stood as surety for me, and if she hadn't I'd have gone to prison.'

'But that surety would only have meant you didn't have to stay in prison while you were on remand. What was the final verdict in the case?'

'Ah, yes, well, it didn't end well. I pleaded guilty to obtaining credit without revealing that I was an undischarged bankrupt, and of obtaining money under false pretences, and the magistrate sentenced me to three months' imprisonment. He said it could've been six, but he'd only given me three because of the relatively small sum involved and because I'd pleaded guilty. I can't describe what it was like to go to prison, and I don't want to talk about it. It broke me, and when I came out I just couldn't face life. Before I wrote that confounded cheque I'd been hatching a plan to start making pre-cast reinforced concrete air-raid shelters, but that conviction put the tin lid on it. It's as much as I can do to get out of bed these days, let alone try to make a living. You probably think that's a disgrace and I ought to be out doing some vital war work, but I reckon I did my bit for the war effort building those concrete ears, not to mention trying to build shelters, and where did that get me? Precisely nowhere, so I've given up – I've had too much bad experience.'

'I see. And did that experience lead you to seek solace in drugs?'

Buckleby looked sideways at him. 'Why do you say that?'

'Because we have a witness who saw you displaying signs of behaviour that I would associate with that.'

'All right, then – I've got nothing to be ashamed about. Yes, I did. Not much, mind, just a bit. What with the business, the bankruptcy and prison, I had some kind of nervous breakdown. I was in such a bad way, I felt as though I'd gone down a deep hole and there was no way out. I started smoking things you shouldn't smoke, just to calm my nerves.'

'And what would that be?'

'What people call Mary Jane. You know, Mary Jane gaspers?'

'You mean marijuana cigarettes?'

'Yes, marijuana, hashish, reefers – call it what you like, it was stupid of me. I knew how to get hold of them, and I thought they were quite cheap. Fortunately for me, though, I suppose, the war did me a favour – the bloke I was buying them from said his supply chain had been disrupted.'

'When was that?'

'About June of last year. Anyway, it made me think, and it probably saved me. I'd been getting worried, you see – I'd been smoking more of them and I was scared that if I didn't stop I was going to get addicted and might end up taking cocaine or something like that. I was angry too – I felt as though I'd been taken for a mug, and people were taking money off me that I couldn't afford. So anyway, one way or another I stopped, and I haven't touched one since.'

'Who was selling you these cigarettes?'

Buckleby was silent. His face suggested he was torn. Finally he spoke. 'All right. I suppose nothing I say could hurt poor Rosemary now.'

'Are you saying it was Mrs Webster who supplied them to you?'

'No, but that's not far off – it was him, her son. Jack Webster, the golden boy hero.'

CHAPTER TWENTY-TWO

A lone double-decker bus rumbled conspicuously past as they walked back to the car. Conspicuously not in the sense that they hadn't seen any buses on this street before – the aftermath of air raids regularly necessitated improvised detours these days – but because instead of the standard red of London buses it was garishly painted green at the top and orange at the bottom, separated by a belt of cream on which were the words 'Glasgow Corporation'. Jago recalled his surprise at seeing such a sight earlier in the Blitz when buses had been drafted in from provincial services to make up for the losses to fire and bomb-blast on the streets of London. Nowadays it was not such a surprise, but still odd enough to warrant a second look. And it wasn't the first surprise of the day, he reflected.

'How the mighty are fallen,' he said, half to himself. 'If it's true, of course.'

'Sir?' said Cradock, loping along beside him.

'What that man Buckleby just said – that Jack Webster

was supplying him with marijuana cigarettes. It's not what we might think of as conduct becoming an officer and gentleman, is it? We need to see what Flying Officer Webster has to say on the subject.'

They drove to RAF Northolt, where Jack Webster invited them to join him for a light lunch of soup and bread in the officers' mess. It was the start of the lunchtime period, so they managed to find a quiet corner where Jago could be confident they would not be overheard.

'So,' he said once they were seated with their food, 'how's your leg?'

'Steadily improving – that's what I say when people ask,' Webster replied. 'I have to tell myself too, first thing every morning, to keep myself going. I don't want to hobble around on a stick for the rest of my life – I want to fly again. You can't imagine what it's like, flying one of those modern fighter planes – you soar up into the sky like an eagle looking for its next prey. You're free from everything, except the risk of dying, but I don't have any intention of doing that. And when we get through this war I want to be fit and well, so I can make a half-decent husband to some lucky gal. And the good news this week is that the Canadian government's said I can.'

'Get married?'

'That's right.'

'You need their permission?'

Webster laughed. 'Not now, but until a couple of days ago I did. There was a regulation, you see – no officer in the Royal Canadian Air Force below the rank of flight lieutenant was allowed to get married unless he could prove he had a private income on top of his salary, and that included me, because I'm just a humble flying officer. Don't ask me why – rules is rules, that's what they say. But anyway, now the government's abolished it, and any officer who's been in the service for at least six months can marry, as long as he gets permission from his commanding officer. So I guess we'll be seeing a big rush to the altar now.'

'Do you have any plans in that direction yourself?'

'No. I'm going to wait until we have peace again and then see how things shape up.'

'I see. Speaking of peace, someone told us you used to be a pacifist but changed your mind and volunteered for the air force.'

'Who said that?'

'It was Miss Ingram – she said your mother had told her.'

'Susan? I guess she thinks I'm a bit weird.'

'No, I don't think so – I think she rather admired you for having the courage to do it. It can't have been easy.'

'Well, it's not what I planned. My mother's adoptive parents were Mennonites, you see, and they had a big influence on me when I was growing up.'

Jago nodded. 'We've been told that the Mennonites believe in non-violence.'

'That's right. So my mother was raised in a pacifist family, and I guess it rubbed off on me.'

'So what made you change your mind?'

'Well, to be honest, I found the whole thing just too complicated. I mean the Bible says "thou shalt not kill", of course, and Christ said we should love our enemies, but it also says you should defend the weak, the widows and orphans. So what do you do when there's something evil like Nazism on the attack? Maybe you should turn the other cheek if someone's threatening you, but should you turn away when they're threatening your neighbour?'

'Not an easy matter, I'm sure.'

'Correct. And people come to different conclusions. My mother and I were still in touch with some of our Mennonite family and friends back in Canada, and my impression is that about half of them are against getting involved in war and half think it's right to take up arms in a situation like the one we're in today. I thought about it a lot, and in the end I became convinced that if people in London were going to be bombed, including my own mother, it was my duty to protect her and them, and therefore to fight.'

'What did your mother think of that?'

'She believed in peace and pacifism, but she also believed in duty. She knew it can sometimes be hard to reconcile the two, but I think she understood why I'd joined up and she respected my decision. It was just a question of principle.'

'Yes.' Jago paused. 'There's something else I'd like to ask you, and that's about a question of principle too.'

'OK – fire away.'

'It concerns Mr Buckleby. He's told us he's been smoking marijuana cigarettes – what some people call reefers.'

'Really? Well, I have to say I'm not surprised – a thoroughly disreputable fellow, if you ask me.'

'That's as may be, Mr Webster, but what concerns me is that he said he'd bought them from you. Is that true?'

Webster laughed. 'Of course not – I'm a fighter pilot, not a drug peddler.'

'But you know Mr Buckleby, don't you?'

'I know him, yes, but only because he was one of my mother's lodgers. An odd sort of character, from what I could make out. If what my mother told me is anything to go by, I got the impression he used to swoon every time he saw her. As for reefers, if he needed them, I say good luck to him. As far as I know he was a failed businessman and a bankrupt, so I'd imagine that doesn't make him a very credible witness.'

'What makes you say he was a bankrupt?'

'My mother told me – and she'd got it from Buckleby himself. I wouldn't be surprised if he was trying to make her feel sorry for him so he could chisel her out of more cash. Besides, smoking that kind of stuff addles the mind, so you can't rely on what he says.'

'You seem quite well informed about marijuana, Mr Webster. Do you partake of it yourself?'

Webster replied cautiously. 'If you must know, yes, I have done – but I was only using it for the pain, from my wounds. Someone told me it was good for that, so I got a few reefers to try them, and they helped.'

'Did you sell any of these cigarettes to Mr Buckleby?'

'No I did not. I gave him some, as a gift. I was just doing him a favour. A pal of mine told me marijuana was very good for relaxing the mind, and poor Buckleby had been through the mill, so I got hold of a few and gave them to him – I thought they might help him.'

'Did your mother know about this?'

'Yes, unfortunately Buckleby told her how grateful he'd been for my help, and when she asked him what kind of help, he mentioned the marijuana. The man's a fool, but he'd been under a lot of strain, and I know what that's like so I can't really blame him. To be perfectly honest, I think he's got a screw loose.'

'And what did she think of it?'

'She hated it. She said she loved me as her son but couldn't condone what I'd done, because it was a crime. But that's not how I see it. I'm over here fighting to defend her and everyone else from Hitler. He's the one who's a criminal – what's a few exotic cigarettes compared with what he's done? My mother was too soft-hearted – she even had a German living under her own roof.'

'Mr Nadelmann is a refugee from the Nazis.'

'Yes, well, that's his story, isn't it? As far as I'm concerned they're all the same.'

Webster's tone was pugnacious, but if this was bait, Jago wasn't going to rise to it. The man's sharp response might be just one symptom of the intense stress he'd been under.

'One last question, Mr Webster. We've spoken to someone who claims they found drugs in your mother's bedroom. Do you know anything about that?'

'Drugs in her bedroom? That's ridiculous – she wasn't interested in drugs. What evidence do you have?'

'It's a claim that we're trying to verify.'

'Well, I'd say it's false – she had no time for that kind of thing.'

'Did your mother know you were using marijuana yourself?'

Webster's voice dropped to a softer tone. 'As a matter of fact she did, but she knew why – it was for medicinal purposes, as I said. She didn't approve of things like that, but my mother loved me, and I loved her. Nothing ever came between us.'

CHAPTER TWENTY-THREE

Western Avenue, the main road leading out of London towards Oxford, had been under construction for twenty years, and on the rare occasions during that time when Jago had driven on it, he'd seen it gradually develop as a modern highway complete with stretches of dual carriageway and even innovative cycle tracks alongside it, the first in England. By the time the outbreak of war in 1939 put a halt to all construction of trunk roads, it had been completed as far as Uxbridge, which was a couple of miles beyond RAF Northolt, so he expected a fast drive back to London.

His expectation was short-lived. Not long after starting off, he had to brake sharply when he saw that two lorries in an army convoy ahead of them appeared to have skidded, blocking part of the road. He stopped the car, and they waited for the obstruction to be cleared.

'So, Peter,' he said, 'what did you make of Jack Webster's story?'

'I reckon there's something not quite right about it.'

'In what way?'

'Well, Webster said he gave those reefers to Buckleby as a gift, didn't he? But Buckleby said he was selling them – so they can't both be telling the truth, can they?'

This struck Jago as a statement of the blindingly obvious, but he didn't like to discourage the boy. 'Yes, Peter – you're right. If it's Jack Webster who was lying it'd make sense, because he wouldn't want to admit to us that he'd been selling dangerous drugs – he must know that's illegal. And he could easily just deny it – I don't suppose drug dealing's the kind of business where he'd be handing out receipts to his customers.'

'Yes, but if it's Buckleby who's lying, he must know that could get Webster into a lot of trouble, not least with us. So why would he want to do that? To get his own back on Webster for something? But for what? Or maybe it was to put pressure on Webster, like a sort of blackmail – Buckleby gets us breathing down Webster's neck to frighten him, and if Webster pays up or whatever, Buckleby just tells us he'd got a bit mixed up and withdraws his statement.' Cradock paused. 'But why would Buckleby want to put pressure on Webster? Just for money? Or maybe to make him keep his mouth shut about something?'

'I don't know, Peter, but it's an interesting question. I think we may have to ask Mr Buckleby to substantiate his claims. Anything else?'

'Yes. Webster said flat out that the idea of his mum having drugs in her bedroom was ridiculous, so that doesn't fit in with what Vera Lock told us, does it?'

'Indeed it doesn't. It suggests one of them's not telling the truth, although in Jack Webster's case it could be just that he *thinks* she wouldn't have anything to do with drugs and hasn't seen any evidence to suggest she would. Let's knock on Vera Lock's door when we get back and have another word with her.'

Looking ahead, Jago could see that the army appeared to have got its convoy back into order, and the lorries were starting to move off one by one, each leaving the regulation twenty-five-yard gap between them. It seemed to take for ever for the entire line of vehicles to get under way again, but eventually Jago was able to follow them, and finally to pass them when the road widened to two lanes. When they got to London, he drove straight to Vera Lock's flat in Herbrand Road.

She was at home when they arrived, and when they followed her into the flat, a woman sitting in a chair with her back to them turned round. It was Ida Griggs.

'Good afternoon, Mrs Griggs,' said Jago. 'I didn't expect to find you here.'

'I didn't expect to see you turning up while I'm having a quiet little cup of tea with my friend either,' she replied. 'Do you want me to go away?'

'No – since you're here, there's something I'd like to ask both of you.' He turned to Vera. 'Mrs Lock, you told us about finding some drugs in Mrs Webster's bedroom, and you said you hadn't told anyone else apart from Mrs Griggs.'

'That's right – it's not the sort of thing I'd go blabbing about to everyone.'

'And you, Mrs Griggs, once you'd heard Mrs Lock's

account of what she'd found, did you have any opportunity to verify it?'

'What, do you mean did I go and poke around in Mrs Webster's bedroom to find out? Of course not – suppose she'd found out? I'd never have heard the end of it – she'd probably have reported me.'

'So, Mrs Lock, am I correct in assuming that you didn't report what you'd found to the police?'

'Why would I do that?'

'Because it's an offence to be in possession of dangerous drugs.'

She snorted. 'Look – I've been round the block a few times – I know how things work. People like Mrs Webster who have big houses and don't have to scrape a living like I do, they all know each other, don't they? They stick together, cover each other's backs, and half of them are mates with the high-ups in the police. What's in it for me if I go running to the police about something like that? Nothing but trouble, that's what. I've learnt to keep my nose out of things that don't concern me.'

'So no one else can confirm your account of what you found?'

'What? Are you calling me a liar?'

'No, I'm not saying that. I'm just trying to establish whether anyone else knew those drugs were there.'

'Well, all I can say is what I know, and what I know is what I saw. What you do with that is your own business. Will that be all? My tea's getting cold.'

'Yes, that'll be all, Mrs Lock – and you too, Mrs Griggs.'

* * *

Jago and Cradock walked back down the stairs from the flat. 'So we've still only got Vera Lock's word for it,' said Cradock. 'Do you think she's telling the truth?'

'What do you think?' said Jago.

'I thought it was interesting that she said "What's in it for me?" I know she was talking about not reporting it to the police, but it made me think there could've been something in it for her if she kept her mouth shut. I mean what if she let Mrs Webster know what she'd found? There'd be a risk of her getting sacked, but if she threatened to go to the police, it might've been worth a few bob to Mrs Webster to pay her to keep her mouth shut. Maybe there was something in it for both her and Ida Griggs, being as they're such pals.'

'You mean a spot of blackmail? An interesting possibility, but if the two of them were doing that, why would Vera have told us all about what she found in such detail? Wouldn't it have been better for them if they'd both kept quiet about the whole thing? I'm not so sure.'

'Right – yes, I hadn't thought of that,' said Cradock thoughtfully. 'So, where are we going next?'

'I think it's time we had a word with Professor Masterson. If he was as close a friend of Rosemary Webster as Mr Nadelmann said, it could be interesting.'

CHAPTER TWENTY-FOUR

Jago had never visited University College London before, and when he and Cradock arrived in Gower Street and stopped at the lodge to identify themselves, he realised he was not seeing it at its finest. A columned portico presided imperiously over the quadrangle before them like a classical temple, but the burnt-out skeleton of what must once have been an elegant dome on its roof and the smoke-blackened stonework of the walls on either side of it betrayed the impact of bombing.

The elderly gentleman manning the lodge deputed a barely less aged man, whom he identified only as 'one of the college servants', to be their guide to Professor Masterson's office, and they set off with him across the quadrangle.

'The professor's round in Foster Court,' said the servant in the stolid tone of a man much put upon by life. 'That's where the Faculty of Laws is – or at least where it was until the war started. The students have all gone off somewhere else now.'

Ahead of them, all the windows to the left and right of the central portico had been blasted out. Most were now patched up with what looked like kitchen-floor linoleum, but through the few that weren't Jago could see only sky and the charred remains of a few roof timbers.

'I see you've had a visit from the Luftwaffe,' he said.

'Yes, sir,' said their guide. 'More than once. That was back in September. They hit the Great Hall, the gym and the college library – pretty much destroyed them. A hundred thousand books went up in smoke, or so they say. Not much of a reading man myself, but they can't get enough of it here.'

'It must've been devastating for everyone.'

'I dare say it was, sir. They made a right mess of the place. These bits here with the windows gone – that's what we call the cloisters, and very pretty they were too. Nothing much left of them now, though, is there? And behind that wall everything's been completely wrecked.'

He trudged on in silence, leading them through a door in the far right-hand corner of the quadrangle and on through a small open space and a couple of tunnels until they came to an enclosed modern-looking area that seemed to have escaped the bombing. 'Here you are,' he said. 'Foster Court.' He led them up some stairs to the first floor, knocked on a door, waited until Jago and Cradock had identified themselves to the professor and been admitted, then trudged off again.

'Good afternoon, gentlemen,' said Masterson closing the door behind them, 'and welcome to what's left of University College London, or UCL, as we call it. Take a seat. I assume this is to do with what's happened to poor dear Rosemary.'

'I'm afraid it is, sir,' said Jago, sitting down. 'You've obviously already heard.'

'Yes, a fellow called Nadelmann told me. He's a mutual acquaintance – a German refugee she'd helped.'

'So I gather – we've met him. It was Mr Nadelmann who told us you were a close friend of Mrs Webster, and that's why we wanted to meet you. I understand you're a professor here at the college.'

'That's right. In the Faculty of Laws – I'm a professor of international law.'

Jago immediately felt out of his depth. As a detective inspector in the Metropolitan Police he was trained and experienced in everything a police officer in England had to know in order to uphold and enforce the criminal law of England, but what the law might be in Siam or Timbuctoo he neither knew nor needed to know. And as for laws that applied to every country in the world, he wasn't even sure he could say hand on heart that he knew what that meant. After all, the laws in England were made by parliament, but there was no parliament to make laws for the whole world, and if that's what the League of Nations had been set up for, it clearly hadn't worked. He was aware of things like the Geneva Convention, because that had impinged on his own life in 1936, when Britain had put on a ban on exports of arms to Spain. He'd been sent to Spain to liaise with the French police working to stop weapons smuggling, but that didn't exactly make him an expert. All he knew was that if there was any international law to stop one country bombing and invading another, it wasn't working very well, and he found it difficult to believe it ever could. As an English police officer he was sworn to preserve the King's peace in England, but the idea of some international policeman knocking on Mr Hitler's door and arresting him for causing a breach of the whole world's peace seemed more like something out of a George Formby film. 'Really?' he said. 'That must be . . . er . . . interesting.'

Jago's reply felt very lame, but Masterson seemed either too polite or too absorbed in his own vocation to notice. 'It certainly is for me,' he said. 'I love what I do, although it does make for a very busy life, what with teaching, writing papers and supervising postgraduate researchers, not to mention all the administrative work. I'm an adviser to the Home Office, and I also get co-opted onto all sorts of working groups and committees where the powers that be think I can make a useful contribution. And now, of course, there's the additional complication that we're in the middle of what people are calling the Second World War – the college has been bombed, the students have been evacuated, and frankly we don't know whether we're coming or going.'

'But you're still based here, in Bloomsbury?'

'Only partly. When war broke out the students were all evacuated to other parts of the country because of the risk of air raids, and the buildings here in Gower Street were taken over by the War Office for the duration. The evacuation was a big job for us, I can tell you – we even had to evacuate the dead.'

'The dead?'

Masterson laughed. 'You must forgive me, Inspector – it's a sort of private joke. Do you know Jeremy Bentham?'

'I'm afraid I don't.'

'Well, he's our illustrious predecessor, a philosopher and, I'm pleased to say, originally a lawyer – not the founder of the college, but such a tremendous influence on its creation that we think of him as our patron saint. He's been dead for more than a hundred years, but in his will he left instructions for his body to be preserved, dressed in his clothes, and seated on one of his chairs. Eventually it came into our possession, and it's been here ever since, sitting in a special glass case in the library, albeit with his skull lying at his feet and his face replaced with a wax effigy. Unfortunately over the years its condition deteriorated and it was quite literally a decaying moth-eaten old relic, so much so that shortly before the war started we asked our colleagues in the Department of Egyptology to get it completely restuffed, repadded and restored to its original glory – they did a grand job. But now even he's had to be evacuated. We're just thankful that we managed to get him to a place of safety before he could be blown to bits by those dreadful bombs.'

'So you put him on a train to somewhere with all the students?'

'No – I'm sure they would have liked that, but we thought it might be safer to entrust his welfare to the Provost of UCL himself and the administrative staff. They've been evacuated as well, to Hertfordshire, so that's where he's residing now, safe and sound away from London. But I can't give you his precise address – it's a closely guarded secret. It was a labour of love, of course, but it was an added burden of responsibility for the college authorities on top of having to find accommodation for teaching as well as organising lodgings for all the students, which I can assure you was no easy task, and then notifying them all of the arrangements.'

'How many students was that?'

'Around twelve hundred in all – about seven hundred and fifty male and four hundred and thirty-odd female, plus of course the teaching and administration staff. Quite a headache, but as you can see from the damage here since then, it was a wise decision. The largest group of students moved to Aberystwyth, including the Faculty of Laws, but then later on the accommodation we were using was required for the RAF, so we had to move again. Happily, at about that time – last July in fact – the War Office suddenly decided they didn't need our buildings here any more and handed them back to us, so we thought we could just come home. We had everything planned to move back here to London last autumn in time for the new term, which was good news for all the people running boarding houses and renting out lodgings in Bloomsbury, but then of course we had the devastating air raid in September, and that put the whole idea of returning out of the question. The students were dispersed again to various parts of the country, and the Faculty of Laws ended up unexpectedly moving to Cambridge instead. We're one of the smaller faculties, and even smaller than we were before the war – this year our students number just thirty-two men and three women – but even so I have to spend a lot of my time up there, although I retain this office because I'm still involved in various things in London.'

'Mr Nadelmann mentioned your work with a society of some kind in Gordon Square that helps refugee lecturers like him.'

'Yes – the Society for the Protection of Science and Learning. But it's not in Gordon Square any more – like everything else, it's been evacuated. Luckily for me it's in Cambridge now – it's been taken in by the Scott Polar Institute, but still doing the same work, helping people like Nadelmann.'

'From what he told us, you must've both been in Aberystwyth at the same time – he mentioned that he'd been evacuated there at the beginning of the war, like you.'

'That's right – he was sent there by the British Museum, to the National Library of Wales. We kept in touch, and the society and I were able to help him when the government interned him.'

'Yes, he mentioned that too – he said he was indebted to you.'

'Oh, it was nothing – I was just doing what any decent person would do. It was a simple favour from one academic to another.'

'Speaking of Mr Nadelmann, it's been suggested to us that there was some sort of trouble between him and Mrs Webster. Do you know anything about that?'

'Not that I recall, no – he's a very mild-mannered sort of chap, so I'm surprised to hear that. I'm sorry I can't be of more help.'

'Well, if you do recall anything, please let us know.'

'Of course.'

'To get back to Cambridge for a moment, we met someone recently who's a student at the London School of Economics, and she's been evacuated to Cambridge too – Claire Bowman, Mrs Webster's niece. Do you know her?'

'I met her once, here in Bloomsbury, when I was visiting Rosemary and she dropped in, and I did bump into her recently in Cambridge – the London School of Economics students have their headquarters in a big old house called Grove Lodge in Trumpington Street, and our University College law students also tend to hang out there, as they like to say, so I look in occasionally. I can't really claim to know her, though.'

'Do you know her family?'

'No. Rosemary never talked about them, and I didn't pry. I formed the impression they weren't particularly close, but I could be mistaken.'

'Thank you. Just one more thing, if you don't mind. As I said earlier, we've been told that you and Mrs Webster were close friends. Is there anything you can tell us about her that might shed any light on why someone should want to harm her?'

Masterson shook his head slowly. 'No – it doesn't make any sense. I can't imagine why anyone would want to do that. She was a gentle person, and she had a wonderful smile that would melt the hardest of hearts. She had energy, commitment and a passion to see people treated fairly, but I'm not aware that she had any enemies. Is it possible that it was just some unfortunate accident?'

'One could say that anything's possible, but we're treating it as suspected murder.'

'I understand – but surely there'd have to be a reason for that? I mean, there are people who'd disagree with her for giving shelter to aliens like Nadelmann or helping people who've fallen on hard times, but they wouldn't kill her, would they?'

'I'm afraid people sometimes do the cruellest things for the slightest of reasons, Professor, as I'm sure you'd agree – that's why we have laws, isn't it?'

'Yes, of course, but when it comes down to a particular case it can still be baffling, especially when it concerns someone you know so well.'

'Were you particularly close to Mrs Webster?'

'What do you mean?'

'I mean was she more than just a friend?'

Masterson seemed to be thinking before he answered. 'In one sense yes, and in another no – by which I mean there was no understanding between us, as you might say, but I did regard her as more than just another friend.' He paused again. 'She was a remarkable woman, Inspector, and to be perfectly honest, I adored her. Nothing would have given me more joy than to spend the rest of my days with her.'

'You mean marry her?'

'Yes, I do.'

'Did you propose marriage to her?'

'No, but I should have done – I might have been able to protect her from this terrible fate. I intended to ask her, but she was taken from me before I could.'

'Taken from you by death, or by a rival for her affections?'

'By death, certainly, but as for a rival, I'm not aware of anyone. All I know is someone killed her, but they can't have loved her or even respected her.'

'Do you have any idea who might've been responsible for her death?'

'No. All I think is that it must have been a stranger – no

one who knew her could have wanted to punish her like that.'

'Punish? Why do you say that?'

'Because it was cruel – it just seems so vindictive for someone to strike her down in her own home.'

'You know how she was killed, then?'

'Yes – Nadelmann told me she'd been hit with a poker.'

'I see. So if someone was punishing her, punishment for what?'

Masterson was silent for a moment, his eyes seeming to fill with anxiety. 'I don't know – all I can think is that she was punished simply for being herself.'

He waved Jago away as if he couldn't say anything more for fear of bursting into tears and put his head in his hands.

'So,' said Jago as he and Cradock retraced their steps to Gower Street, 'the list of male admirers seems to be growing. First Buckleby, and now Masterson – Rosemary Webster seems to have had a knack for making men fall in love with her, don't you think?'

'Certainly looks that way, guv'nor,' Cradock replied. 'But then some women do, don't they?'

'I'm afraid I wouldn't know, Peter, but I'll take your word for it. I was even beginning to think Nadelmann might've had a bit of a crush on "dear Rosemary", as he called her. A case of the damsel riding to the rescue of a knight in distress, perhaps, if you get my drift.' Cradock's face suggested he didn't, but Jago carried on regardless. 'After what Susan Ingram said about him taking advantage of Mrs Webster, though, I'm not so sure.'

'Me neither, sir. But if Nadelmann was what you might call a rival for her affections, that Professor Masterson didn't seem to know about it, did he – if he was telling the truth, of course.'

'Indeed. And we don't even know whether Rosemary herself was aware of Masterson's feelings for her – we've only got his word for it that he intended to propose to her.'

'So we need to keep digging?'

'Yes, Peter, we do.'

CHAPTER TWENTY-FIVE

The Metropolitan Police prided itself on deploying modern technology in its fight against crime, and during the previous decade it had built a network of police boxes and posts that enabled the local police station to be in contact with its officers on the beat by telephone, and which also gave the public a way to contact the station in an emergency. An additional benefit was that the boxes gave those officers somewhere to eat their sandwiches. There had been complaints initially, because the boxes were so cold that the men said they preferred to eat outside, but eventually electric heaters were provided, affording a modicum of comfort as well as privacy. There were now hundreds of such boxes across London.

And so it was that as Jago was driving along Gower Street, he had the unusual experience of being flagged down by a uniformed police constable. He pulled in to the kerb and got out of the car, followed by Cradock. 'Yes, Constable?' he said.

'Detective Inspector Jago, sir?' said the constable.

'That's right.'

'PC Staunton, sir,' he said, saluting, 'from West End Central. This is my beat. Sorry to disturb you, sir, but we got a call from the station this morning at the police box telling us to look out for you, and I spotted your car and registration number. I was to give you a message from the inspector at the station. He said a couple of our lads brought a young lady in last night, drunk and disorderly with two blokes, students apparently. They'd been caught shining a flashlight onto a wall, trying to find out what street they were in – said they were lost – and they must've known that was an offence under the Lighting Restrictions Order, so we nicked 'em, and on the way back to the station she kept saying "Don't tell my parents, and don't tell Detective Inspector Jago." It turns out she was related to that woman who was murdered in Guilford Street, and she'd met you.'

'And her name?'

'Claire Bowman, sir. She seemed to think she was in a lot of trouble, not just with us and her mum and dad, but with you too.'

'Have they been charged?'

'Yes, sir, with using a hand torch that wasn't properly screened – probably just a ten-bob fine if she's lucky, and maybe a bit more for being drunk and disorderly. She took it very bad, though – crying, she was. But that's not all. Thing is, the station sergeant put them in the cells overnight, and when she turned her pockets out they found a little ball of something that he reckoned was hashish – you know, that Indian hemp stuff.'

'You mean marijuana?'

'That's it, sir. Just a little bit, but it's still illegal, isn't it? Anyway, the inspector bailed them this morning, and her mum came to take her home. She'll be up before the magistrate tomorrow morning. He thought you ought to be told.'

'Yes, thank you, Constable – well done.'

'Thank you, sir,' said Staunton, looking pleased to be appreciated.

Jago and Cradock drove straight to the Bowmans' flat, where Helen Bowman opened the door to them.

'Good morning, Mrs Bowman,' said Jago. 'May we come in?'

A pained look came into her eyes, and she nodded silently, stepping back to let them in. 'This won't take long, will it? It's just that I didn't sleep a wink last night and I've had a very busy morning.'

'We'll be as quick as we can – and while we're here, could I ask you a quick question about Monday morning? I'd just like to know where you were between eight and ten o'clock.'

'By all means. I was here. We're fortunate to have a basement shelter in this block of apartments, and I'd been sleeping as best I could down there as usual, not without interruptions, of course, and I came back up here for breakfast at about half past eight. I was in for the rest of the morning.'

'And your husband?'

'He'd gone off to work before I got back up here – he starts early. That's usually the case, but you'll have to ask him if you want to know when. But that's not the only reason you've come here, is it, Inspector?'

'No, it isn't. I know this can't be easy for you, but the fact is I understand you've brought your daughter home from West End Central police station this morning. Is that the case?'

'Yes, it is.' Her voice was despondent. 'Come this way, please.'

They followed her into the drawing room, where they found Claire Bowman hunched in a chair and avoiding their gaze.

'I'm so sorry, Inspector,' said Helen. 'I don't know what came over her. She's never been in any trouble with the police before.' She paused and looked at her daughter. 'You haven't, have you, Claire? Up in Cambridge? Is there anything you haven't told us?'

'Oh, Mother, why do you always have to think the worst of me? Of course I haven't.'

'You know it's only because I love you and worry about you. I don't know what your father will say.'

'Miss Bowman,' said Jago, 'I understand you were charged with being drunk and disorderly last night.'

'Yes, that's correct. But it was nothing serious – just horseplay. I was with a couple of friends from the LSE. We're all feeling a bit bored being at home for the vacation, missing our social life, so we got together for the evening. One of them had got a bottle of whisky from somewhere, so we shared it and I think we probably had a bit too much. We went out for a walk in the blackout and got lost, so one of my friends . . . er, well, I'm afraid he got his flashlight out and was climbing up one of those Belisha beacons to get a better look at the name plate on the wall at the corner of the street when two of your colleagues happened to come along. They, er, took a dim view of it, as you might say.' She offered them a meek smile as if to seek a show of sympathy, but Jago's face remained impassive.

Helen Bowman, by contrast, looked shocked. 'Claire, how could you? You didn't say anything about a Belisha beacon – you weren't stealing the globe, were you? I've heard about young ne'er-do-wells all over London who do that and then smash them or play football with them, but that's not how we brought you up, is it?'

'We weren't stealing or smashing Belisha beacon globes or doing anything like that,' Claire replied in a tone of mild exasperation.

'So I should think. But look at you – you're at university. You're not stupid, so what possessed you to get drunk with two men?'

'There's nothing to worry about, Mother dear. Times have changed. If you must know, I was drowning my sorrows. I'd been telling my friends about what happened to Aunt Rosemary, and I was feeling very sad. So yes, I got a bit tipsy, but I was missing her. She always understood me.'

Jago took this to be a rebuke to her mother, because Helen Bowman's face flushed.

'But I understand you too, darling – I just worry about you and want the best for you.' She turned to Jago. 'I'm sure you can see it was indeed just a case of innocent horseplay, as my daughter said. Surely there was no need to charge her – can't you just give them all a talking-to and let that be the end of it? My husband is engaged in essential work for the Canadian government, and this will be embarrassing for him.'

'I'm sure that's very important, Mrs Bowman,' said Jago. 'But there's also the matter of the other charge.'

'What other charge?'

'Being in possession of a dangerous drug. That's a criminal offence that the courts take very seriously.'

Helen Bowman's voice exploded. 'What?'

'My colleagues at West End Central found a small quantity of marijuana in your daughter's pocket.'

'Claire! What were you thinking? Dangerous drugs?'

'Don't panic, Mom – I wasn't going to use it. It was just a little present I'd been given. I'd been carrying it round in my coat pocket for a week and pretty much forgotten it was there.'

'Who gave it to you?'

'My cousin – Jack. He said he was using it for the pain he's been in since he was shot down and he thought I might like to try a bit – he said it might help me. He knew I'd been under a lot of stress, what with the war, the bombs, and having to be evacuated to some weird place full of posh boys, but I haven't used it, not even since . . . since what happened to Aunt Rosemary . . . She was like—' Claire bit her lip. Jago thought she was about to say 'like a mother to me', just as Susan Ingram had, but she didn't complete the sentence. Instead, she started it again. 'She was a friend to me – probably the best friend I've ever had.'

'Did she know about this? That her son was supplying you with drugs?'

'I don't know. If she did, she never mentioned it.'

'She probably approved of it.'

'How can you say that, Mom?'

'Please excuse us, Inspector – I don't like to discuss family matters in public, but the reason why I say that is that Claire's aunt had some very liberal views, not the kind of thing my husband approved of, and I agree with him. She'd grown very lax in her opinions and attitudes – probably because of the people she mixed with, but I think it was there in her from the start. Ask my husband – he'll tell you. He's her brother, after all, although only by adoption, not by blood. She was from very different stock, and I think that's where the trouble began. Suffice it to say that she and my husband and I have always moved in rather different circles.'

Claire rolled her eyes. 'That bit about different circles is definitely true, Inspector, but I think my mother's annoyed because she and my father know which circles I prefer.'

'Including a cousin who's a drug pusher?' said Helen. 'This is what comes of living in Bloomsbury – an intellectual hell-hole packed with overeducated people who think their "values" are so enlightened. A friend of mine told me last week she regarded Bloomsbury as next-door neighbours to Hades, and I think she's right. Jack Webster is a bad influence on you, Claire, and it was a case of like mother, like son. People seem to have got it into their heads that she was some kind of angel, but she wasn't – and you know it.'

'I think that's being disrespectful to Aunt Rosemary, Mother.'

'Disrespectful? You're the one who's been disrespectful. Do you think your brother would ever have sunk so low as to dabble in dangerous drugs? Harold was a fine young man, and pure in heart, and now he's given his life for his country. Everyone seems to think Jack Webster's a hero, but I tell you he was never a patch on your brother. Why can't you be more like him?'

She began to cry, but Claire looked unmoved. 'We can't all be perfect, Mother.'

CHAPTER TWENTY-SIX

'No love lost there then,' said Jago as they left the mother and daughter to deal with their conflict as they saw fit. 'I suspect Mr and Mrs Bowman might have to try keeping young Claire on a tight leash for the time being, although what chance there is of that when she goes back to living fifty miles away is anyone's guess.'

'Living the life of Riley, as far as I can see. I wouldn't mind being a student myself – it sounds like quite a lark.'

'I don't think you need to worry about that happening, Peter. University's not for the likes of you and me – you've got to have money to do that, and it's not the kind of money people like us have when we're that age. If you want to do that, you have to plan ahead and make sure you're born to the right parents, like our own dear prime minister.'

'Toffs, you mean?'

'That's right. It makes a difference. Mr Churchill and I have something in common, which is that we've both been to Oxford, but the difference is that he went to Eton and then studied at the university, while I just got the train from Paddington and had a day out looking round the place, then came back to West Ham. It's all about choosing the right family to be born into.'

'Thanks for the tip, guv'nor. Mind you, that Claire Bowman doesn't seem to have chosen a very happy one, does she?'

'My sentiments entirely – and as for Cousin Jack, maybe I spoke too soon when I said he was an officer and a gentleman. The uniform certainly says officer, but I got the impression his Aunt Helen would struggle to vouch for his credentials as a gentleman.'

'Too true. And maybe that explains what the friction was that Claire said she'd picked up between her dad and Mrs Webster. It'd be interesting to hear whether he feels the same way as his wife, wouldn't it?'

'Yes, but not now. I think it's time we found out a bit more about that other friction – what Susan Ingram said about Nadelmann being involved in something dishonest and putting Rosemary in a nasty position. She said she'd got the story from Mrs McCready, so let's pop round to Guilford Street and see if our Annie's in. If there's any time left after that we can go and have a word with Gordon Bowman.'

'Good afternoon, Mrs McCready,' said Jago when the housekeeper opened the door. 'I hope we're not disturbing you. Could we have a quick word?'

'By all means. I'm busy, but it's nothing that can't wait. Come in.'

They went into her room and sat down. Jago noticed

a photograph on a bookshelf, showing a man in army uniform standing beside the standard photographer's prop of a potted plant on a stand. 'Your husband?' he asked.

'Yes,' she replied. 'I think I mentioned he was gassed in the war. I don't have many photos of him, and I like that one because it was taken when he was young and strong. When he came back from the war he was never a well man, and in the end the gas did for him. Still, there's plenty worse off than me. I've got my health, a job and somewhere to live, and that's all I need. Now then, can I get you a cup of coffee? I don't think I've got any tea at the moment.'

Jago and Cradock both accepted her offer, and she went away to make it. When she returned with the drinks, she also brought a large round tin that seemed to Jago to have captured Cradock's undivided attention as soon as it appeared.

'Would you like a slice of Dundee cake?' she said, opening it. 'I used to bake my own, to remind me of home, but it's too much trouble trying to find all the ingredients these days. I managed to get a shop one, though – it's not the same, but it's better than nothing.'

'Just a small one, please,' said Jago, attempting to forestall too enthusiastic a response from Cradock. 'We don't want to eat you out of house and home.'

She complied with his request, slicing the cake thinly, and Jago observed that if Cradock was disappointed, at least he tried hard to conceal it.

'So what brings you back?' she said. 'Something to do with Rosemary, presumably?'

'Yes. It's just that Susan Ingram said she believed

there'd been some trouble between Mrs Webster and Mr Nadelmann – some business about him being involved in something dishonest and putting her in a difficult position. She said that was all she knew, but when I asked her who'd told her, she said you, so we wondered if you might be able to tell us more about it.'

'Well, I'll certainly tell you what I know, but whether it's of any help you'll have to judge for yourselves. All I know is that Rosemary told me she'd recently overheard Nadelmann on the phone in the living room as she was passing – the residents are allowed to use the phone and they're expected to note their calls in the book and pay for them at the end of the month. It sounded quite heated, like an argument, she said, and she could only hear one end of it, of course – but she said it sounded like they were arguing over the price of something. And that's pretty much all I know about it.'

'So what made you say he was involved in something dishonest that put Mrs Webster in a difficult position?'

'Because that's what she told me. But she didn't go into any more detail.'

'Do you know of anyone else she might've confided in?'

'Well, if you want to know more, I suggest you talk to Mr Masterson. Him and Rosemary, they were very friendly, and if she told anyone about something like that, I reckon it would be him.'

'Were they particularly close?'

'I don't know about that. He used to come round here, but as far as I could tell it was always about work – things to do with refugees and suchlike. They always seemed to be quite businesslike when I saw them, nothing more than that, but I think she trusted him – he was probably the kind of person she could confide in if she ran into trouble. And she certainly had her fair share of that – I suppose it was inevitable. That other fellow, for example – that must have been trying for her.'

'Who was that?'

'The businessman with no business – Concrete Charlie, that's what I call him.'

'Mr Buckleby?'

'That's right. I think she'd had a bit of a set-to with him as well. He was short of cash as usual and thought she'd lend him some, but she turned him down. I don't think she told him why – she had her pride – but I suspect she just couldn't afford to subsidise him any more. I think they had words about it, if you know what I mean.'

'You mean an argument?'

'Oh yes, what we call a real collieshangie where I come from – a proper run-in, no holds barred.'

'Well, thank you, Mrs McCready. You've been most helpful.'

CHAPTER TWENTY-SEVEN

The University of London's Senate House in Malet Street, home since the outbreak of war to the government's Ministry of Information, offered a forbidding prospect as they walked up to it. The sight of the soaring skyscraper brought to Jago's mind what Dorothy had said the evening before last about the nickname it had acquired: the Bloomsbury White Elephant. This unofficial title must surely have been intended to be derogatory, but whether or not the implication of uselessness was appropriate, as far as size was concerned it was spot on: the building dominated the whole area and was a picture of strength and solidity. He wondered, though, why it also had such an intimidating air. As he gazed up at its tower he was struck by the thought that the university must have envisaged it standing as an inspiring beacon of confidence, ambition and academic freedom, but now that it was reborn as the headquarters of the government's total grip on information and its chief generator of propaganda, that very strength and solidity made it seem like a grim bastion of unassailable power.

The entrance to the building was sandbagged against bomb blast, and a soldier with a rifle over his shoulder stood guard. On arriving, they discovered that all visitors were now required to show a pass with a certified photo of the holder before being admitted, so it was only by a combination of producing their national identity cards and Metropolitan Police warrant cards and getting Gordon Bowman to come down and vouch for them that they were allowed in. He apologised for the inconvenience and took them up several floors to his office.

'Thank you for sparing the time to see us,' said Jago once they were seated in the sparse modern room. 'We'd just like to ask you a few questions.'

'You're very welcome,' said Bowman. 'It's always a pleasure to assist the police, although I'm glad to say that's a pretty rare experience in my case.'

'Thank you. It's quite a place, this, isn't it?'

'It is – very grand. But I guess basically it does what it was designed to do – create a space for a lot of people to do a lot of work.'

'Yes, I've heard a lot of people work here – and apparently some say too many. Is there any truth in that?'

Bowman smiled. 'That's not for me to say, Inspector. I haven't counted them.'

Jago had come away from their first meeting with Gordon Bowman with the impression that he was a smooth-talking character. Now he found himself wondering whether he'd get much in the way of straight answers out of the Canadian, so decided to test the water. 'I was talking to a journalist the other day who said the ministry had a rather unenviable reputation for being amateurish and inefficient,' he said. 'Is that right?'

'I couldn't possibly comment on that, Inspector,' Bowman replied. 'There may have been a few teething troubles at the beginning, but the important thing is we're all pulling together to win this war.'

Diplomat by trade, diplomat by nature, thought Jago. Bowman's answer was as politely evasive as he'd expected. 'A comedy of errors, that's what the journalist called it,' he added, as a final test.

Bowman's expression remained placid. 'That's easy to say if you're not responsible for getting a whole new government department on its feet from nothing almost overnight. I wouldn't pay too much attention to journalists' idle chatter if I were you.'

Jago's suspicions were confirmed, and he wondered what Dorothy would have said if she'd been in the room with them. She'd probably have asked decidedly more incisive questions than he had, and he smiled to himself as he pictured the scene.

Bowman glanced somewhat theatrically at his watch, and Jago moved on.

'Yes,' he said, 'I'm sure you're right. Now, you told us a little about the time when Rosemary Webster became part of your family as a child, but I wonder if you could tell us how that whole adoption went, from your point of view.'

'Well, I think I mentioned that I was ten and she was only six. I remember my parents telling me I was going to have a new sister, but she wasn't a baby, she was a little girl, and we were all to love her and look after her.'

'What did you think when they told you that?'

'Not much – what I mean is, in those days, at that age things just happened. You didn't necessarily understand them, and you certainly didn't have any choice about it – you just accepted it. I don't remember thinking deeply about it – I thought this must be something that just happens, like everything else, and I accepted it.'

'How did the two of you get on?'

'So-so. Four years is quite a gap when you're ten, so to me she was just a kid – she could be annoying, but I just ignored her. I can't remember us playing together much, but that might well have been the case if we'd been natural siblings too – I had no way of knowing what was normal and what wasn't. I don't think I loomed very large in her life, and she didn't in mine.'

'And that remained the case right up to her unfortunate death?'

'I think it did, yes. I've been very busy with my work ever since I arrived in London, and she seems to have had a finger in a lot of pies with all those little projects of hers too. We didn't spend time together, but that didn't bother me much, and as far as I'm aware it didn't bother her. That's about all I can say, really.'

'Thank you. I was struck by something your daughter, Claire, told us – she said Mrs Webster had liberal views you don't approve of. Could you tell us more about that?'

'Yes. We're just different – we see things differently.'

'Because you're from different stock?'

'What makes you say that?'

'They were your wife's words.'

'I see. Well, yes, you could say that. And it's not

just our backgrounds, it's a question of experience and temperament. I've worked all my life in the Canadian civil service, and now here in London as part of the High Commission I'm representing Canada. That's a very serious position, with important decisions to make, and people expect someone in that position to be sober-minded, consistent, not swayed by romantic notions or emotional responses. Rosemary was the opposite – she just went whichever way her heart or her imagination led her, like some kind of well-meaning butterfly.'

'A lot of people seem to have admired her for her work.'

'I'm sure they did. All I'm saying is in my work I can't be like that – questions and issues arise every day, and I can't respond to them emotionally. I have to remain detached, because that's my job. As a civil servant, I have to work for governments of any political shade and be impartial. And that was the difference between me and Rosemary – I was impartial, but she was committed. And not just in our work – in our lives too. She could be maverick, but I cannot. She could be angry, but I cannot. She could afford to offend people, but I cannot.'

'Who did she offend?'

'I don't know of any individuals, still less their names, but we can be sure that not everyone agreed with everything she said and did. And then there'd be the people she'd let down.'

'Let down?'

'Yes, I mean she was idealistic, wasn't she? And when you're idealistic you can promise the moon – but can you deliver it? I wouldn't be surprised if she left a whole trail behind her of people who thought she'd solve all their problems but then she let them down. It's inevitable, isn't it?'

'And you said "maverick" – is that what she was?'

'I'd say emotionally and intellectually she was, yes. People who thought like her might call it being free or spontaneous, but I call it capricious and sometimes ill-considered. In a place like this we have to give serious consideration to the implications of our actions.'

'Your wife told us she thought your sister had grown very lax in her opinions and attitudes – would you agree with that?'

'Yes, I would. It's the same thing – her admirers would say she was tolerant, but I'd say she was irresponsible. She held some quite unorthodox views. Now, you might say it's a free country, and she's entitled to her opinion, but that's not the point. Some people these days laugh at the idea of being respectable, and I think she'd be one of them, but I do not – and in my work I have to be respectable, because professionally I'm representing my country.'

'So you don't take kindly to the idea of your daughter being found in possession of a dangerous drug?'

'Ah, yes,' said Bowman cautiously, 'that unfortunate business – indeed I do not. My wife telephoned me earlier this afternoon and told me. The whole thing is deeply embarrassing for both of us, and I'm just hoping it doesn't get into the papers. But it's simply the foolishness of youth – my daughter's behaved very unwisely, but I sincerely hope she'll learn from this and not do it again.'

'You and your wife are of one mind on this matter, then?'

'We are, and I'm thankful I married someone who thinks the same way as me. If I'd been married to Rosemary, I'd have . . . well, I don't know what I'd have done.'

'Would you say your sister was a bad influence on your daughter?'

'Not in the sense that she deliberately set out to corrupt her, no. I just think that when Claire grew up and became, let's say, increasingly radical in her views, she found a sympathetic ear in my sister, and that encouraged her down that road. Losing her aunt like this has shocked her, but I hope this might be the beginning of Claire coming to a more mature approach to life.'

'And your nephew? Is he a bad influence?'

'Undoubtedly – I mean I know everyone admires him as one of our brave young pilots, but the fact is he supplied my daughter with a dangerous drug. If that's not a bad influence I don't know what is. I want her to stay away from him, and as far as I'm concerned, the sooner she goes back up to Cambridge and resumes her studies the better. This isn't a good place for her.'

'Thank you. And speaking of places, could you tell me where you were on Monday morning between eight and ten o'clock?'

'Eight and ten . . . Let me see now. Ah, yes, I started work at eight-thirty as usual, and I always walk here from home – it takes about ten minutes, so I probably set off at about ten past eight. Then I'd have been here in my office until ten, because that's when we have our daily departmental briefing and co-ordination meeting.'

'Can anyone confirm that?'

'The meeting, certainly, and if someone happened to see me on my way here, possibly yes, but I don't know who they would have been, so that's the best I can do. Is there anything else you'd like to know?'

'No, I think that'll be all for now, thank you.'

'You're welcome. I hope your visit has been useful, and that my family and I will soon be able to put this whole sorry business behind us. In the meantime, allow me to walk you down to the entrance and see you off myself – I wouldn't want one of our guards to discover you don't have an official pass and arrest you . . . or me. As I said, in here we have to think carefully about the implications of our actions.'

CHAPTER TWENTY-EIGHT

Jago came out of the Senate House, followed by Cradock, and strode off down Malet Street towards Montague Place. When they reached the corner, with the stone façade of the King Edward VII Galleries at the back end of the British Museum facing them, he pointed across the street. 'There's one,' he said.

'One what, sir?' said Cradock.

'A public call box – let's get over there before someone else nabs it.'

The door of the red telephone box was heavy to pull open, as always. 'Here we are,' he said. 'You wait here for a moment, Peter. I need to make a quick call.'

The door swung shut behind him, and Cradock stood outside, stamping his feet against the cold while he watched Jago through the glass searching for a couple of pennies in his trouser pocket and making the call. He couldn't hear what it was about, but to his relief it was brief, and Jago re-emerged onto the street.

'Success, sir?' he said.

'Yes,' Jago replied. 'I would've asked Bowman if I could use the phone in his office, but I didn't want him listening. I just wanted to call the Yard.'

'Oh – why's that?'

'I've had a couple of things on my mind, and one of them's drugs. I want to pick someone's brains on the subject, and I reckon there won't be many more useful to pick than the brain of Chief Constable, CID, so I just called Mr Ford to book a few minutes of his time. He said six o'clock sharp today, in his office.'

'And the other thing?'

'The other thing that's been on my mind is kindred spirits.'

'Sir?'

'It's what Arthur Murray said. So if he's in at that place of theirs in Gordon Square we should be able to have a quick word on our way to Scotland Yard.'

'Oh, right, yes – kindred spirits,' said Cradock, baffled.

'Good afternoon, Mr Murray,' said Jago when they arrived at 4 Gordon Square. 'I hope you won't mind us interrupting you, but there's something I'd like to check with you.'

'By all means,' said Murray, leading them into the house and up to the room they had used on their previous visit. Jago noticed it still had no fire in the grate.

'Go ahead,' Murray continued, shutting the door behind them. 'There are days when it feels like my whole life is one long interruption, and today's one of them, so I don't suppose one more's going to matter.'

'I'm sorry to hear that, but I suppose your work must be a bit unpredictable.'

'Indeed it is – in fact you could say unpredictability is the only predictable thing about it. I think it's because all our work is reactive – bombs fall from the sky and we have to respond, people need help and we have to give it. Not that I'm complaining about that – it's precisely why we're here. But it takes its toll – those night shifts I told you about are hard work, but even when I'm on the day shift I sometimes get out of bed in the morning feeling exhausted before I start. But then I think I should be grateful I've got a bed to get out of, and that I'm alive for another day. I suppose it must be like that in the police sometimes too.'

'You could say that, yes.'

'Valerie Palmer was telling me recently about how it works in the auxiliary ambulance service. She's full-time, so she gets paid a bit, but she said there are thousands of part-timers and they don't – they might work a twelve-hour shift in a factory in the daytime and then get called out three or four times a week for ambulance duties in the night, up against the worst the Luftwaffe can throw at us, but they're not paid a penny for it. At least I'm only doing one job, and I receive a little pocket money. When they're doing their ambulance duty they don't even get food. You can't go on doing that for ever, not even in a war.'

'I'm sure we all hope it'll be over soon and things can get back to something like normal.'

'Yes, but the question is, what will that normal be? That must be on everyone's minds. I mean, how much is it costing us to fight this war? By the time we're through it, the country'll be broke, on its knees. There's nothing I want more than an end to it, but I can't help wondering what I'll do for a job when it's all over. Drive a peacetime ambulance, perhaps? That's about all I'm good for.'

'What'll become of the Friends' Ambulance Unit when the war ends?'

'I don't know. I imagine our work in this country will wind up, but maybe there'll be needs elsewhere – wars in foreign countries, for example. I'm not sure I'll have the energy left to do that, though, after Finland and Norway and now the air raids here. I think Valerie Palmer's in the same position – the Spanish Civil War and now the Blitz. It's all right when you're in the first flush of youth, but neither of us can claim to be quite that now. So ask me anything you like about the past or the present, but please spare me from having to think too much about the future.'

'It's the past that interests me, Mr Murray. I've been thinking about what you said, about kindred spirits – you said you thought Mrs Webster felt that's what you and she were. At the time I thought you meant you were both interested in the same kind of work and had a shared outlook, but of course when people talk about a man and a woman being kindred spirits that's not always all what they mean. They're talking about attraction too – romantic attraction. Was that the case between you and Mrs Webster?'

'You mean were we "involved"?'

'I suppose I do, yes. You told us yourself last time we spoke that you were very fond of her, so if she felt you were kindred spirits, I'm wondering whether on her side at least there were stronger emotions at play. Is that how it was?'

Murray seemed to be uncertain how to reply. 'What I said was true – I was very fond of her, but not in that way.'

'But what about her feelings?'

He hesitated again and cleared his throat. 'There were times, just now and then, when I thought perhaps she was being a little over-affectionate, but I put that down to her big-hearted nature.'

'A little over-affectionate? What does that mean?'

'All right – she was being very forward. I began to feel as though she was pursuing me.'

'But you didn't reciprocate whatever feelings she may've had?'

'If you're asking me did I give her any encouragement, no, I didn't. The fact that I was fond of her didn't mean I was looking for a more intimate relationship, and it actually made me feel rather sad, because I thought her attachment to me might spoil our friendship.'

'So what did you do about it?'

'I didn't want to hurt her, so I tried not to reciprocate but without obviously spurning her.'

'And did that work?'

'I hope so – but I don't know. I didn't want to end our friendship, because that was what I thought "kindred spirits" meant.'

'So how would you describe your relationship with Mrs Webster?'

'I'd say we had a lot in common, although our backgrounds and experiences were very different. She used to say she'd had a hard start in life and felt driven to do whatever she could to help other people going through a difficult time. Her heart went out particularly to people like her German lodger Mr Nadelmann, hounded out of their job, their home and even their country for no reason except that they'd found themselves living in a place where there were people who hated them – and those people had power, while their victims had none. It left her with very ambivalent feelings about people in authority – even policemen, I suspect. She respected the law, but not if it oppressed people. She cherished freedom, but she knew how fragile it was in the face of malevolent authorities. If we were kindred spirits, it's because I share a lot of that vision she had. That's why I'm a pacifist – not because I love the Nazis, but because I don't believe in killing anyone, even if they're out to kill me. They want to control the world, and do it by force of arms, but I don't want to force my views on anyone. I want to show there's a different way of living, and the only way I know to do that is to start with myself and live differently.'

'That must feel like an uphill struggle, to say the least. All the pacifism in the world wasn't able to stop this war we're in. So what keeps you going?'

'My dream, I suppose, and I think maybe that's why Rosemary felt we were kindred spirits, because she had a dream too.'

'And what's your dream?'

'To live my life in a way that brings hope to people, not despair, that makes their life better, not worse, that encourages and supports them, doesn't use and abuse them. And maybe it's just to increase the amount of love in the world, by loving them. I'm sure that sounds very soft to you, and I'm sure it wouldn't cut much ice with a sergeant-major in the British Army, but I'd rather have an impossible dream than live with the certainty of a hardened heart. It's not something I talk about to everyone, but what I liked most about Rosemary was that when I told her that's how I felt, she didn't laugh at me or look down her nose at me – she encouraged me to pursue it.'

'You told us you thought there was nothing sentimental about Mrs Webster. Doesn't that rather contradict the way you've just described her apparent feelings for you?'

'No – when I said that I just meant she wasn't a soft touch, and she called a spade a spade when she thought it was called for.'

'I see. By the way, when we were here before, you said Miss Palmer had mentioned some trouble between Mrs Webster's nephew Harold and his parents, but you didn't know what it was. We've spoken to Miss Palmer now, and she said it was about him wanting to be a conscientious objector, and she thought it was probably due to the fact that Mrs Webster would've been sympathetic to Harold's ideas when his parents weren't. Does that ring true to you?'

'Yes, from what I know of Rosemary I can imagine she'd support Harold even if it meant crossing his parents.'

'Miss Palmer said Mrs Webster had very strong principles. Would you agree with that?'

'I would, yes.'

'And Miss Palmer also said she had strong principles herself.'

'Yes, I think that's true too. And so do I, for that matter, but I think the difference between them and me is that they were both what you might call "action" women, whereas I'm like some of my colleagues in the Unit, inclined to get a bit too theoretical sometimes and spending too long worrying about whether what we do is a faithful reflection of our principles and values.'

'And would that mean Quaker principles and values?'

'Yes. For me they're summed up by the story of the Good Samaritan. There are some pacifists – we call them absolutist objectors – who won't do ambulance work for wounded soldiers in a war zone because it's tainted by its association with the military. But we say that's like the priest and the Levite in the story who declined to help an injured man who'd fallen among thieves. My conscience may forbid me to kill another man or inflict wounds on him, but that doesn't mean I shouldn't bind up his wounds. It's our duty before God to be a Good Samaritan to anyone and everyone who needs humanitarian help.'

'So do you feel you're succeeding in doing that?'

'To be honest, I'm not sure. When I was in Finland I knew I was making a real difference, saving lives, and it was an adventure too. But when I came back here I was disappointed, because I found they didn't need me to drive an ambulance, and when I look at Valerie I think she's making a huge difference – she's saving people's lives. When I think about the work I'm doing now, I know it's important to help people in the shelters and rest centres, but I can't help feeling it's not making the same difference as what I was doing in Finland. I feel a bit superfluous, and feeling superfluous isn't an adventure.'

'What did Rosemary think about that? Did you ever talk to her about it?'

'Yes, Rosemary was the kind of friend who tells you what's real even when you don't want to hear it. She understood, and she cared, but she didn't pull her punches, and after what she said I could see that there was something missing in my life – it was that sense of purpose and adventure that I'd had in Finland and that I could see in Valerie. I need a purpose and I have a taste for adventure, and I'm frustrated because I don't think I'm finding either in what I'm doing now.'

'So what did Rosemary say?'

'She told me the truth, and I had to face it. She said if I want those things, I have to take life by the scruff of the neck and make it happen – and be prepared to fail if it doesn't work out. She said when you're surrounded by needs, being indecisive is a curse and a waste, and it doesn't change anything – I ought to just knuckle down and take control of my life and my future. And now that she's gone, it feels as though my duty to her is to do exactly that. The trouble is, I can't think of anything else I can do.'

CHAPTER TWENTY-NINE

Jago had worked for men who'd insisted their door was always open to their staff but who'd then proved surprisingly inaccessible. With Chief Constable Ford, however, it was different. He'd never made such a sweeping promise, but instead had taken action, making it known to those who needed to know – including Detective Superintendent Hardacre – that while Jago was seconded to Scotland Yard he'd have direct access to Ford whenever he needed it. The fact that the chief constable was head of the entire Metropolitan Police CID made this a privilege that Jago valued highly but used sparingly. Ford's other virtue was that he knew how to run a meeting and keep it short, which meant he was always on time for an appointment. The only drawback to this was that it didn't pay to be late, so Jago made sure that he and Cradock arrived in time to knock on his door at precisely six o'clock.

'Hello, John,' said Ford, welcoming them into his

office. 'Take a seat. How's your Bloomsbury case going?'

'Decent progress so far, sir,' Jago replied as he sat down, 'but I'd like to pick your brain on something for a moment.'

'By all means – on what subject?'

'Dangerous drugs, sir.'

'Carry on, then.'

'Thank you, sir. The thing is, we seem to have run into a bit of illegal drug dealing and we suspect some of the people we've been talking to in the course of our inquiries are involved in it in one way or another. I haven't had to deal with many drug offences in the past, but I know the law and regulations well enough to nick someone when I need to. The thing I'm not very well up on, though, is how they get the blasted stuff into the country in the first place, and I thought you'd probably know a lot more than I do about that.'

'Well, I'll do my best. The first thing to bear in mind is that it's a growing business. When I was a young copper you didn't come across it much, which is probably why we didn't have a Dangerous Drugs Act until 1920. Are you talking about a particular drug, or just drugs in general?'

'Both, I suppose, but marijuana in particular.'

'Right, well, marijuana didn't feature in that act – it was mainly to do with opium, but the more recent regulations include it, which I suppose reflects the growth in its use. During the thirties it became a big business, with more people trying to bring more of it into the country, and that means smuggling. A lot of marijuana's grown in Mexico, and before the war the Mexican stuff would come across the Atlantic in ships to Antwerp, where a lot of the smugglers were based. Another major source was

Morocco – the marijuana from there would be smuggled into southern France, and we suspected there was a supply chain operating before the war from France through Spain and Portugal to England, and quite possibly there still is. Our colleagues in what the press likes to call the "Scotland Yard drug squad" keep observations on various clubs in the West End and make the occasional arrest, but the big problem is catching the smugglers. The truth is, it's always been too easy to bring things like that into the country without anyone knowing. The smugglers were using small private yachts, taking them into little ports on the south coast and saying they'd just come from some other place a bit further up the coast, because even if there was anyone official in the port he'd only be required to inspect the boat if it had come from somewhere foreign.'

'Presumably the war's put a stop to most of that, though?'

'I think it's certainly slowed the trade down. For one thing, shipping things across the Atlantic isn't as easy as it used to be, and some of the countries the drugs used to pass through are occupied now, so the trade will have been disrupted. And I imagine some of the methods that seemed clever before the war don't look so appealing to the crooks now. Five or six years ago there were small planes flying into Yorkshire with drugs and landing in some lonely spot in the back of beyond near the mouth of the Humber – until a customs officer caught one of them in the act. They'd have a job trying to do that now. Apart from anything else, the Air Ministry banned all private flying when the war started, and I imagine anyone trying to pull that trick these days would come a cropper pretty quickly – either brought down by anti-aircraft fire or shot down by an RAF fighter on his way in, or, if he did manage to land, finding himself at the mercy of the local Home Guard patrol. And who's going to take a chance on landing a boat somewhere quietly on the south coast when the whole country's geared up to fight off an invasion?'

'But are some drugs still getting in?'

'I'm afraid the answer has to be yes – where there's money to be made, someone's going to take the risk. And the consequences can be deadly. There was that case over in your old manor in West Ham just before the war, wasn't there – do you remember? In Barking, wasn't it?'

'You mean the bloke who hijacked a car?'

'Yes, that's the one. You weren't there, were you?'

'Thankfully not, otherwise I might not be here. Unfortunately for him, he picked a car being driven by an off-duty detective constable, who deliberately crashed it into a lamp post outside Barking police station. Then when the bloke made off, three of our men chased him, but he produced a gun and started shooting at them. It was a miracle no one got killed – he just seemed to go mad.'

'That was drugs, though, wasn't it?'

'Yes – when his case got to the Old Bailey, his defence was that he'd been smoking marijuana and that it causes excitement and hallucinations.'

'That's putting it mildly – not my idea of excitement.'

'No, and I don't think it impressed the judge very much – he gave him ten years' penal servitude for shooting with intent to murder.'

'Are you seeing any similarities with this murder in Bloomsbury?'

'I'm not sure, sir – I'll have to think about that.'
'Will that be all, then?'
'Yes, sir – thank you very much.'
'In that case I wish you a pleasant evening.'
'You too, sir – and goodbye.'

CHAPTER THIRTY

The evening was cold, but Jago had every expectation that it would be pleasant. Dr Gibson had invited him to come over for a drink at his serviced flat in Knightsbridge, and past experience told him it would be warm there, so he had gladly accepted. Thanks to Chief Constable Ford's skill at not letting his meetings overrun, he'd had time to drop Cradock back at the section house and still be sitting in Gibson's living room by a little after seven. Minutes later they were eating a light meal brought up from the kitchens below, after which they relaxed in the doctor's comfortable armchairs.

'Thanks very much,' said Jago. 'That was a very welcome change from boiled beef and carrots in the police canteen.'

'I'm glad to hear it,' said Gibson. 'And now I've got a little surprise for you – I think you're going to enjoy it.'

'That sounds appealing. I don't get too many nice surprises in my life – most of them are in the line of duty, and they're not usually the kind I enjoy. What is it?'

'Just wait here for a moment and you'll find out.'

Gibson left the room and returned moments later with one hand behind his back. 'Here,' he said triumphantly, sweeping it round before him. 'Take a look at that.'

Jago nodded approvingly – it was a bottle of whisky.

'Glenfiddich pure malt,' said Gibson. 'A Christmas present from my sister – she's in the Wrens, stationed up in Scotland at Crail, where the Fleet Air Arm trains its torpedo bomber pilots. I don't know how she got it, and I didn't ask, but it arrived in the post on Christmas Eve. In the nick of time too, perhaps, because she's told me since then that two days later there was a big fire at the Glenfiddich distillery. I hope it hasn't stopped production. Anyway, as you can see, I've taken a nip or two just to check it's the real thing, but the rest I've saved for an evening of agreeable company. I hope you'll sample it with me.'

'I shall be only too pleased to assist,' said Jago.

Gibson poured a generous measure into two glasses and handed one to Jago, who sniffed it approvingly.

'Your good health,' said Gibson, raising his glass.

'And yours too,' Jago replied.

Gibson put his glass down on a small side table. 'So how are you getting on with your inquiries?'

'Inching forward, I'd say, and finding myself getting entangled with matters on which I'm not expert.'

'Such as?'

'Dangerous drugs.'

'Ah, I see – anything I can help with?'

'Possibly – I'm sure you'll know a lot more than I do. I don't need to know much – the law says what's dangerous, not me, and all I need to do is bring people to book if they've broken the law. But one or two of the people we've met during those inquiries have been indulging in substances listed in the Dangerous Drugs Regulations, so I'd be interested in what you can tell me about the effects the drugs can have.'

'What drugs are we talking about?'

'Marijuana mostly – what people call reefers.'

'Well, I won't go into the pharmacology unless you want me to, but it can affect both the mind and the body. People have been using marijuana therapeutically for centuries, especially in the East, and for about the last hundred years in the West too.'

'So is it helpful for things like pain relief or stress?'

'Some people would say its effect on the mind can be helpful, yes, and a doctor can prescribe its use as long as it's for medical treatment.'

'And are there less helpful effects?'

'Yes, and that's why there's been concern about marijuana cigarettes. They've only been around for about thirty years, but their use for non-medical purposes has grown rapidly on both sides of the Atlantic. There's the problem of addiction, of course, but also other effects on the mind – hallucinations, for example, which can be dangerous in some circumstances.'

'Dangerous enough for the person hallucinating to kill someone?'

'In principle yes, I suppose.'

'Thank you – that's very helpful.'

'Is that enough medical advice?'

'Yes, thanks. I don't think I'll be trying it myself.'

'Nor I. So, apart from chasing drug-crazed suspects and an unknown murderer round the back streets of Bloomsbury, how's tricks?'

'Well, I'm not sure what to say, really – the way things are at the moment, there doesn't seem to be much time for anything except work. I imagine it's the same for you.'

'Married to the job, you mean? Yes – it's a bad habit. I suppose that's something else we got used to in the war – whether it was the infantry for you or the medical corps for me, your time was never your own, was it? Always on duty in one way or another, and no family to go home to at the end of the day, even if you had one.' Gibson looked down into his glass thoughtfully and swirled the liquid round. 'That war,' he said. 'It was hell, wasn't it?'

'Yes,' Jago replied. There was nothing more to say, and mercifully no need to: Gibson had been there and knew.

It was the doctor who broke the silence. 'You know, when that whole miserable business finally ended, all I wanted was a quiet, ordinary life, and peace, and perhaps a family. Normality, I suppose. It didn't work out quite like that, of course – I haven't got a family, and my life's not exactly quiet, but I would say I'm contented, and I'm very thankful for that. Would you say you're contented?'

'I enjoy my work,' said Jago, 'and I think it's worthwhile, so that's good, but I'm not sure I can say I'm contented. I often find myself wondering what it's all about – life, that is. I sometimes wish I'd had a family too – it feels like there's something missing. Not children, necessarily – I mean, what kind of world is this to bring children into?'

'I'll tell you what I miss,' said Gibson. 'It's someone to share it all with – the good times, the bad times, the ups, the downs. I have friendships that I treasure, and I appreciate these occasional chats of ours because I know you've been through some of the same things as I have, the things you can't talk about with people who weren't there. But I'd love to have someone in my life who's closer to me than any other, someone I can say anything to and know that I'll be understood and accepted. I suppose it's what people always say – the love of a good woman. Do you feel that too?'

Jago envied the way Gibson could talk so freely about his thoughts and feelings, something he found so difficult for himself. 'To be honest, I suppose I do, but love hasn't featured very much in my life – I've always felt a bit out of my depth. Do you think it's something to do with the war? Our war, I mean.'

'In what sense?'

'Well, we all saw terrible things, and perhaps even did terrible things. Sometimes we were pushed beyond the limits of what any man should have to endure, and either you went mad or you just bottled it up. That's what we did, isn't it? We bottled it up. The fear, the shock, the disgust – it's all bottled up inside us, and we daren't let it out.'

'And do you think perhaps that makes us afraid to let love in?'

'I don't know – maybe. It's an emotion, isn't it? When you've spent years doing everything you can to lock your emotions down, how do you handle something like that? People talk about being an emotional cripple, don't they? Perhaps that's what we are, men like us – scared of love because of what else might come out if we open the door to it. We've learnt to keep our defences up against any kind of emotion. Does that make sense to a medical man like you?'

'I think it probably makes sense to any man who was there and experienced it all at first hand. "Emotional cripples" just about sums it up. We all know men who lost an arm, a leg, their sight, even their mind, and we're grateful if we came through it pretty intact, but I wonder whether nearly all of us lost something in our heart. Do you know what I mean? There must be thousands of them out there. Men who look fine on the outside, but on the inside their hearts have been hardened, turned to stone, and they hurt the ones closest to them because they've forgotten how to show affection, and they can't enjoy the simple pleasures of life because of the guilt they feel – even guilt at surviving when so many didn't. I see it in myself – I'm a doctor, and I survived, but for every man whose life I may have saved a dozen more died in front of my eyes. Emotions can be dangerous things. I think I let something like a callus grow over my heart to stop me feeling, so what hope is there of me ever falling in love? I'm not sure I could risk the pain if it didn't work out.'

Jago nodded slowly but said nothing: he wasn't sure he wanted to go where this train of thought might be leading. Gibson, however, seemed to have got the bit between his teeth and ploughed on.

'So what do we do? No offence, but I don't want to spend the rest of my days sipping whisky with a pal and bemoaning my fate. You said men like us have got too used to keeping our defences up. Do you think you need to keep those defences up even against the love of a good woman?'

'I don't know. The stakes are so high – it's a scary prospect.'

'I know how you feel. I don't think I've met a woman yet that I'd want to take that risk for – but I'd like to. Wouldn't you like to have a woman in your life who you'd trust, who you could talk to, share your deepest pain and joys with, someone you knew would accept you just as you are and love you and stand by you?'

'If you put it like that, I suppose yes, I would.'

'Do you know anyone like that?'

Jago paused and cleared his throat nervously. 'You doctors swear to keep secrets, don't you?'

'You're talking about the Hippocratic oath, I suppose. Yes, we swear not to divulge what ought not to be divulged, whether that's in our professional life or outside it, so if you're about to tell me something in confidence you have nothing to fear – I won't tell tales out of school. So do you? Know anyone like that, I mean.'

'To be honest with you, until recently I'd have said no, but now I think perhaps I do.'

'Then I'd say if you do, don't let her go – don't let her slip through your fingers. You're a grown man, after all. You're a free agent, and sometimes you just have to take decisive action, make things happen.'

Jago was silent. He drained his glass of whisky in one gulp and put it down. 'You're right, you know,' he said quietly. 'But that's easier said than done. For one thing, how can you really tell? It's a big thing, isn't it?'

'I'm probably not the man to ask, having never found myself in that position, more's the pity. But I suppose in the end you just have to take a good hard look at her and ask yourself "Do I love this woman?" And if you find yourself saying "Yes, I do", that's probably all you need to know. There – the advice of a man who knows nothing.'

Jago laughed. 'As much of an expert as I am, then. Maybe you're right. I'll keep your advice in mind and I'll let you know if your prescription works. Just don't expect to get a progress report any time soon.'

'I'm sure it doesn't pay to hurry these things – but don't forget there's a war on. We're living in uncertain days, and the future's not as predictable as we'd like it to be. *Carpe diem*, that's what the Romans used to say – seize the day.'

'Yes, but I'm not a Roman.'

'*Carpe* whisky, then – may I refill your glass?'

'That's very kind of you, but I think I'd better be running along. That job will still be waiting for me tomorrow morning, and I need my sleep if the Luftwaffe will let me have any. I'll say good night – and, er . . . thank you, Doctor.'

CHAPTER THIRTY-ONE

Jago's night was broken, not by the sirens, bombs or guns for once, but by a disturbing dream. He was lying on a slab in the mortuary, dead, but conscious in the way that's only possible in dreams. Dr Gibson had carried out a dramatic incision from neck to navel and now loomed over him in silent concentration, busily examining his heart, lungs and other vital organs. He struggled to ask the pathologist to stop, but he couldn't speak and realised he'd just have to put up with the intrusion. The distress persisted, however, and he woke up suddenly with an aftertaste of anxiety haunting his mind. It was some time before he got back to sleep, and when he finally got up the dream was still vivid in his mind. He shook it off and washed, scrubbing at his face as if to erase it.

It had still been in his thoughts when he picked up Cradock at the section house, but he'd kept it to himself, and now, as they drove north in the direction of Bloomsbury, it began at last to fade.

They had just passed the bombed remains of Leicester Square Theatre, with a mile or so to go to their destination, when Jago spotted a woman in a uniform of full-length dark-blue coat and matching ski cap waiting to cross the road on a pedestrian crossing and pulled up, signalling her to cross. She stepped onto the road and turned to acknowledge his stopping with the customary raising of her hand, but then leaned forward and gave a more vigorous wave. As soon as she did, Jago recognised her: it was Valerie Palmer. He gestured to a point beyond the crossing and pulled in to the kerb.

'Hop out, Peter,' he said, 'and see if she'd like a lift.'

Cradock duly got out of the car and, having ascertained that she would, brought her back and climbed into the rear seat of the Riley, leaving the front passenger seat for her.

'Thank you so much,' she said as she settled in. 'I was just about to get the Tube up to Russell Square to go to work, but a ride would be lovely. I was visiting a friend near here yesterday and stayed a bit later than I'd intended to, and then the sirens went off, so she suggested I stay the night.'

'A sensible decision in the current circumstances,' said Jago, rejoining the traffic and heading up the western side of Leicester Square.

'I suppose it is, yes,' said Valerie as they passed the wreckage that had once been the famous Thurston's billiards hall. 'Normally I wouldn't bother, but I think Rosemary's death has affected me more than I thought. To be honest, I'm still struggling to grasp the fact that she's not here any more – she was so full of energy and life, and now someone's taken her from us. It's not just that she's been killed – I mean, we're all in the same boat these days, aren't we? It just depends on where the bomb lands, and I'm well aware that with the work I do, going out in the air raids while others are taking shelter, I could die tonight, and whatever hopes and dreams I might have would die with me. But somehow it's different when it's murder – someone stood in front of her in her own home and took her life, and I'll never see her again. She was unique, you know.'

'So I gather. How would you describe her in one word?'

Valerie thought for a moment. 'That's easy. I'd say "driven" – not in the sense that I'm being driven right now, of course, but you know what I mean.'

'Of course. Driven by what?'

'By her sense of duty – that was the strongest thing I saw in her. When I was a child I joined the Girl Guides. I had to learn the Promise – *I promise to do my best, to do my duty to God and the King, to help other people at all times, and to obey the Guide Law.* And the Guide Law said a Guide's duty is to be useful and to help others. I don't think I necessarily understood it, but we had to learn it to be enrolled, and I think it was always there at the back of my mind as I grew up. I don't know whether Rosemary was ever a Girl Guide, but if ever there was a woman who seemed to have bound herself to doing her duty, it was her.'

'Hence all the good deeds people have been telling us about?'

'Exactly – I think it was all motivated by that sense of duty. If I look at my own life, I think I'm the same – on a smaller scale than her, of course, but then I didn't have all the natural advantages she had.'

'What do you mean?'

'I mean she was more gifted than me, and had more money than me, and more social connections, so she could make more of a difference than I could. But I like to think I've done what I could. Sometimes when I'm driving my ambulance around London and the bombs are falling, I get to thinking. I might be taking the injured survivors to the hospital or gathering up body parts and taking them to Billingsgate, but whatever it is, every so often my mind goes back to when I was in Spain, with the Spanish people in their war, and it feels as though I've spent the best years of my life rubbing shoulders with jeopardy, danger and death. That feels like a privilege, but it doesn't stop me thinking about what might have been. I sometimes wonder whether Rosemary thought like that too.'

The traffic ahead of them had come to a halt, and Jago stopped. 'In what way?' he said, keeping his eyes on the vehicle in front in case the queue started moving again.

'I'm not sure,' she said. 'It's just that I saw something of myself in Rosemary, and I think she saw something of herself in me. She'd done so many good things, helped so many people, but I don't think she was necessarily happy. Happiness is such an elusive thing, isn't it? We tend to think if we had enough money we could buy it, but we can't, can we? I don't think we can obtain happiness – it just seems to be something out of our control that sort of turns up. Or doesn't. I've been thinking about what I said to you when we were talking the day before yesterday. I think I must've been out of sorts, a bit gloomier than

I had any right to be, perhaps. Do you remember? I was being grumpy, saying I'm on the shelf, too old to marry and settle down, and I wanted to find a man who'd still got a thirst for adventure in him instead, as if the two things were mutually exclusive. I just want to say I think that was self-pity speaking, and I've no right to talk like that. I said I'd probably end up an old maid living on her fading memories, but I take that back. I won't let that happen. I'm going to be like Rosemary, and make my own future, and if I should end up marrying, I'll look for the adventure in that and find it. To be perfectly honest, if I ever manage to find the right man, I rather like the idea of settling down in a nice little house.'

'I suspect Mrs Webster would've seen more in you than just a reflection of her own unhappiness. Did she ever talk to you about that?'

'I don't recall her ever saying to me that she was unhappy – it was something I sensed. She was always busy, and I suppose that could have been because she wasn't happy, but I think it was just because of that strong sense of duty she had. She once told me she admired me because I was doing my duty, not shirking my responsibility to the world but taking life seriously and being useful.' She paused, as if recalling that moment with Rosemary. 'I appreciated that, because I admired the same attitude in her.' Her voice caught, and she sniffed. Jago glanced round at her and saw a distant sadness in her eyes. 'But the thing is,' she said, wiping away a tear, 'it's good to be useful, like the Guide Law said, but I don't want to be just useful . . . I want . . . I want to be happy before I die.'

CHAPTER THIRTY-TWO

Jago dropped Valerie Palmer off at the auxiliary ambulance station in Woburn Place and said goodbye. As he pulled away from the kerb, he looked back and saw that she hadn't gone in: she was standing on the pavement watching them go, and as the car picked up speed she raised her right hand and gave them a brief, restrained wave. He settled back into his seat and turned left at Tavistock Square, heading for Gower Street and University College, where he hoped to find the answer to a question.

Now that they were familiar with at least part of the University College site, the two detectives made their own way to Foster Court and found Professor Masterson in his office.

'Good morning, Professor,' said Jago. 'I'm sorry to disturb you so early in the day, but there's something I'd like to ask you, and it won't take long.'

'That's all right, Inspector,' said Masterson. 'I was just sitting at my desk here working – there's always so much paper to get through. When I was a young man I played tennis, I ran, I was always active and on my feet, probably as fit as a policeman, but I'm at an age now where I spend most of my time sitting on things. I'm a magistrate, so I sit on the bench. I sit on committees, I sit on tribunals. At the Society for the Protection of Science and Learning, I sit on the advisory council. Sometimes it seems all I do is sit on things, and then if I have the good fortune to come up with bright ideas to change anything or improve anything, there's always someone higher up who sits on them. And of course I'm a professor, so what does that mean? It means the university gives me a chair.' He laughed heartily. 'So they seem to know I can only do my job if I've got something to sit on – just like Jeremy Bentham.'

Jago recalled Masterson's description of the ancient moth-eaten remains of Jeremy Bentham and thought the academic was doing himself a disservice – he looked lean, fit and strong, more than capable of giving a policeman a run for his money. He smiled politely as Masterson continued.

'Can I get you some coffee?'

'No, thank you. It's just a quick question.'

'OK – fire away then.'

'Thank you. It's just that since we spoke to you yesterday we've been told that Rosemary Webster had apparently overheard Mr Nadelmann having a heated argument on the telephone shortly before her death. I'd be interested to know more about that, and the person who told us suggested that we talk to you, since you and Mrs Webster were very friendly with each other.'

'Why don't you ask Nadelmann?'

'If Mrs Webster were still alive I'd be talking to her first, to establish exactly what she heard, and then I'd decide whether it was something I needed to pursue with Mr Nadelmann. Unfortunately she's not, but if she happened to tell you anything about it, I'd like to know what she said.'

'I see. Right, well, she did speak to me about it, because it was a rather sensitive matter. She said she'd accidentally overheard Mr Nadelmann speaking to someone on the phone, and although she only heard one end of the conversation, of course, it disturbed her. Do you know about the work Nadelmann's been doing here since he had to flee from Germany?'

'Yes – he said you'd had a word on his behalf with the Keeper of Prints and Drawings at the British Museum and helped him get some work with them updating their catalogues, and you'd also put a good word in for him with Faber and Faber.'

'That's right – he loves the museum, and that cataloguing was the perfect job for him in times like these. It was the least I could do to help the poor man. It was Rosemary's idea, of course – she'd met him through her work with refugees and wanted to help him get back on his feet.'

'He seemed to be very appreciative of what you'd both done for him when we spoke to him. Very fond of Mrs Webster too, I thought.'

'Yes, well, she had a lot of admirers.'

'But you said what she heard of him on the telephone disturbed her. Did she tell you why?'

'She did – she was rather shocked, because she said it

sounded so out of character, or rather so at odds with the impression she'd formed of his character, which of course is not necessarily the same thing. How much do you know already?'

'Only that she apparently said it sounded as though Mr Nadelmann was arguing with someone over the price of something.'

'That's what she told me too – but what shocked her was that from what she could hear, she got the impression he was arguing over something he'd stolen, talking about the risks he'd taken and what it was worth.'

'Did she know what the something was?'

'She said she couldn't be sure, but it sounded to her as though he might have been stealing old drawings from the British Museum's collection.'

'Really? I imagine that certainly would've shocked her. Did she hear anything else?'

'She said she'd heard him say he was only putting a wrong right – that's all.'

'Did she report all this to anyone?'

'No, not as far as I know.'

'And did you?'

'Well, no. I must admit I found myself in a difficult position when Rosemary told me what she'd overheard, because I knew the man and liked him. I didn't want to go behind her back and get him into trouble, especially if it meant going against her wishes – I valued my friendship with her too highly. But even if I'd wanted to, you know as well as I do that my telling you what Rosemary told me she thought she'd overheard someone saying on the telephone to an unknown person would be of no value as evidence, especially as she's sadly not here to confirm it now – it's pure hearsay.'

'You've told us Mrs Webster was shocked by what she heard. You know Mr Nadelmann too, so what was your reaction to what she told you?'

'Like her, I find it difficult to imagine him stealing – he seems like an honourable man. But he's been through a terrible time, losing everything, so who knows what that kind of strain can do to you? Do you know about how the Nazis confiscated his personal collection of drawings?'

'Yes – and he claimed that some of those items had since turned up in the museum's collection, presumably sold by the people who'd stolen them from him.'

'Precisely – and that's why I find it difficult to believe he'd steal from the museum himself. It would mean he was acting no better than the Nazis.'

'Could he have been stealing those items that used to be part of his collection? He told me himself that he wouldn't stand idly by while someone cheated him out of what was rightfully his. He might've seen it as nothing more than getting his own property back.'

'That's what Rosemary said – it might seem an obvious explanation, but she couldn't imagine he'd then try to sell them. Apart from the fact that they were so precious to him, she had the same reaction as me – if he stole them and sold them, he'd be doing to his beloved museum what the Nazis had done to him.'

'So did she say what she was going to do about it?'

'No, and I don't really know what she could have done. Maybe she was going to tell the police, but she's always been one to give other people the benefit of the doubt, and I'm not sure she could have brought herself to do that. Knowing her, she'd have been more likely to tell him frankly what she thought of it and then leave it to him and his conscience. If you want me to guess, I'd say she probably intended just to have it out with him face to face.'

CHAPTER THIRTY-THREE

'He's a dark horse,' said Cradock.

'Who? Professor Masterson?' said Jago.

'No, I mean that other bloke. The German – Nadelmann. I mean, one minute he's a shy little academic poring over a pile of dusty old catalogues probably in some dingy basement in the museum that nobody ever goes to, and next minute he's on the phone to some shady crook flogging priceless old drawings that he's nicked from the British Museum.'

'According to Professor Masterson.'

'Well, yes – but there's no smoke without fire, is there?'

'In my experience, Peter, when people are providing information to the police, smoke without fire is too often exactly what we get – and it's usually smoke they want to get into our eyes. I'm not saying he was necessarily lying to us, but he said it himself – all we've got is his account of what he says Rosemary Webster told him about what she overheard Nadelmann saying on the phone. We'd be skating on thin ice if that's all we had to take to the magistrate. And if we're basing our suspicion that Nadelmann's some kind of crook on the professor's testimony, don't forget in virtually the same breath he told us his impression of Nadelmann was that he was an honourable man, which a sceptic might say was at best contradictory and at worst evidence of unreliable judgement.'

'Oh, right. I see what you mean, guv'nor. But we still ought to put the heat on Nadelmann and see if we can get the truth out of him, shouldn't we?'

'Put the heat on him?'

'Sorry, sir. I mean, er, question him further with a view to establishing the facts of the matter?'

'That's better – and yes, we definitely should.'

When they arrived at Russell Square, the leafless trees were swaying ominously, helpless against the onslaught of a biting wind. They hurried into the Faber and Faber building and found Nadelmann at work in his room. It was cold and draughty, but after the square outside it felt at least a little more comfortable. Jago's eye went to the tiny desk in the corner, where the papers and books had been pushed to one side to accommodate a large and ancient-looking typewriter.

'Ah,' said Nadelmann, 'I see you've noticed my new equipment. My office has been modernised. I suppose it was kind of them to provide me with a typewriter, even though this one looks as though it should be in a museum – and indeed, perhaps it was. But I am a bad typist at the best of times, so I'm trying to avoid using it, and it has an English keyboard, not a German one, so the Y and Z keys are the other way round and it doesn't have the special keys for the vowels with umlauts – you know, the little dots over the top. I'm hoping to discover some other employee here whose need is greater than mine so I can donate it to them.' He gave a fleeting smile. 'So, once again I apologise that there's nowhere in here to sit, not even on the desk now. How can I help you?'

'Well,' said Jago. 'I'll get straight to the point. We're here because there's something important we need to ask you. It's been suggested to us that Rosemary Webster suspected you of being involved in the unlawful disposal of items from the British Museum's collection, and I want to know if that's true.'

'What on earth do you mean? What is "unlawful disposal"?'

'In this case it means taking something that's the property of the British Museum and giving it or selling it to someone who's not entitled to possess it.'

'So you mean I was stealing?'

'That's what we've been told.'

'By whom?'

'I can't tell you that.'

'And what were these items that this mysterious person says I've been stealing?'

'Valuable old drawings – the kind of things you specialise in, I believe.'

'I do, but I don't specialise in stealing them. And you're saying my dear Rosemary thought I was involved in doing that – involved in a crime?'

'Yes.'

'But how could she imagine that? It's ridiculous. Have

you forgotten it was I who had my own collection stolen by the Nazis – do you think I'd do the same thing? It's not possible.'

'You told us yourself you'd discovered some of your items confiscated in Germany had been bought by the museum. Were you planning to steal them back? Or had you in fact already done so?'

'No, absolutely not. I had raised the question of the provenance of those items with the museum's authorities and was trusting them to investigate it and do the right thing. I can assure you categorically that I did not steal anything from the museum, nor was I going to. How could I? It was the museum that had helped me by giving me work. I am in their debt, Inspector – I'm not going to steal from them. In my language we say you do not bite the hand that feeds you – you know that expression?'

'Yes, we say the same thing.'

'Then you'll understand what I mean – it's not what I would do. And another thing – poor Rosemary is dead, so she clearly didn't tell you this. So how is she supposed to have come to the conclusion that I was involved in theft?'

'It's been alleged that Mrs Webster heard you arguing with someone on the phone in her house, and she formed the impression that you were stealing Old Master drawings from the museum.'

'What?' Nadelmann sounded both shocked and pained. 'But that's awful. You mean she really believed that?'

'That's what we've been told by someone who knew her.'

Nadelmann shook his head slowly. 'That is a tragedy. She was precious to me, and I valued her opinion greatly, including her opinion of me. It's just appalling to think she might have gone to her grave believing I was a thief. If it's true that she did, she was completely mistaken. I am not a thief, Inspector.'

'So what were you discussing in that telephone call?'

'I'm afraid I cannot tell you that.'

'But it's very important if you want to dispel the suspicion that's hanging over you.'

'I'm sorry, but it was a confidential conversation, and it must remain so until such time as I am at liberty to divulge it.'

'Even if you may face a criminal charge?'

'Yes, even if I may. I'm very sorry, Inspector, but I repeat, I am not a thief.'

CHAPTER THIRTY-FOUR

'He didn't deny it, did he?' said Cradock as they emerged from Faber and Faber to brave the wind again. 'I mean he wouldn't say what the call was about, but he didn't say it never happened – he just said he couldn't tell us. It must be something important, or he wouldn't clam up like that. So what's his guilty secret?'

'I don't know – perhaps it's a guilty secret, or perhaps it's just a secret. He strikes me as the kind of man who'd keep a confidence as a matter of honour, so maybe it's someone else's guilty secret. Maybe he feels under a moral obligation not to betray it.'

'Right . . . Well, whatever it is, he's clearly decided to keep his mouth shut.'

'Yes. So we'll need to find something we can prise it open with, won't we? He may or may not've been flogging off old drawings, but right now I'm more interested in who's been dealing in dangerous drugs, so we're going to call on Charles Buckleby and see if we can find out who's telling the truth, him or Webster.'

In view of what Buckleby had said about giving up on life the last time they'd seen him, Jago would not have been surprised to find him still in bed when they arrived at Rosemary Webster's house in Guilford Street. The one-time businessman was in fact, however, up and dressed, although whether this signified a renewed strength of purpose or merely the resumption of an old habit it was impossible for Jago to tell.

'Mr Buckleby,' he said, closing the door behind them as they entered his room. 'This won't take long. I'd just like to check something you mentioned yesterday when you were talking about marijuana cigarettes.'

'Don't worry,' Buckleby replied, sounding tired. 'I've got all the time in the world. What was it you reckon I said?'

'You said Mrs Webster's son had sold them to you, but we've spoken to him and he denies that.'

Buckleby stared at Jago and snorted. 'He's lying, then.'

'He says they were a gift, to help you deal with the troubles you'd been through.'

'Yes, well, he would say that, wouldn't he? I'm told they all start like that, those people. "The first one's free," they say, and maybe even the second or third, but it's always just enough to get you wanting more, and then you have to start paying. It's how they get you onto the stronger drugs, and once you're hooked, the price goes up and up. He was trying to dupe me, stringing me along, just like the government.'

'What do you mean?'

'Those contracts I told you about – that was just a ruse by the perishing government. I should never have trusted them. They promised me the moon, but I don't think they had any intention of building more than a handful of those acoustic mirrors. I can't prove it, but I know. It was a conspiracy against me, and once I'd served my purpose they left me high and dry, without a business.'

'But why would the government conspire against you, a concrete contractor?'

'To fool the Germans, of course. I used to think it was a bit odd when I'd see a little article in the newspaper before the war, just occasionally, saying the Air Ministry was testing some new secret weapon that would hear enemy planes coming. I mean, why would the government allow that sort of thing to be published if it was true? I thought the idea of the Official Secrets Act was to keep secrets out of the papers, not to tell the whole blinking world about them. No – I reckon that was just to cover up the fact that they were working on that other thing that was the real secret. Governments always have secrets, don't they? They know things that we don't, and knowledge is power. There's no doubt about it – it was all a ploy to mislead the Germans, and to fool them, they had to fool me. The fact that my whole life was ruined means nothing to them – I'm just a victim, another minor casualty of war. They don't give a damn.'

'And Jack Webster?'

'He's just the same – doesn't give a tinker's cuss. Jack Webster was trying to trick me into using drugs, and that's the plain truth – I'm sure of it.'

'Why? To make money out of you?'

'Maybe, but I think the real reason was different. It was to turn Rosemary against me. He must've been able to tell there was something special between Rosemary and me, and he wanted to stop it. Maybe he was jealous, wanted her all to himself.'

'Do you have any evidence of that?'

'Yes. She'd changed – she wasn't as friendly to me as she used to be. She'd always been so sympathetic about my problems – I knew she really cared, but she'd started saying maybe I should think about getting a job, some war work perhaps, in a factory or something, and finding somewhere else to live, by myself. She said it was about helping me get back on my feet, but I think Jack was talking to her behind my back, poisoning her mind against me – probably telling her I was a drug addict. Don't believe what he tells you, Inspector – that's all I'm saying.'

'I base my judgements on evidence, Mr Buckleby, and evidence alone – you need have no fear about that. And let me assure you also that when I have evidence, I act – without fear or favour. Do I make myself clear?'

'Er, yes,' said Buckleby, with a flash of anxiety in his eyes. 'You do.'

CHAPTER THIRTY-FIVE

As Jago and Cradock left Buckleby's room, they saw Claire Bowman approaching down the corridor, and she saw them. She jumped. 'Oh,' she said, sounding disconcerted, 'I didn't expect to bump into you here.'

'Good morning, Miss Bowman,' said Jago. 'And I didn't expect to see you here today either. How are you?'

'As well as can be expected,' she replied gloomily. 'I've just been to see Annie McCready – I've had a rather demanding morning.'

'I'm sorry to hear that. Would I be right in assuming that was to do with your appearance at the magistrates' court?'

'Ah, so you know about that, do you?'

'Yes, I do. What was the verdict?'

'I've been let off with a fine on both charges. My parents are angry about the whole thing, but they've said they'll pay the fines for me. My father says at best it'll make him a laughing stock at the High Commission, at worst it'll tarnish his reputation for moral probity and ruin his career. I think what really worries him is that his job means he's meeting journalists every day, and one of them might get wind of what's happened and write something that'll either make fun of him or humiliate him. I feel really bad about it – he may be a stuffed shirt and all that, but he's still my dad. It won't surprise you after what you saw of me and my mother at home yesterday that I disagree with my parents on just about everything, but I do love them.'

'I'm sure they know that.'

'I hope so. I didn't think about any of that when I was out with my friends, but now it makes my cry when I remember it. I even cried in court when the magistrate looked at me over the top of his glasses and gave me a dressing-down. My friends Eric and John – the boys who were arrested with me – were there too, of course, and Eric said afterwards he thought that was a very cunning move, playing the penitent daughter and turning on the crocodile tears to tug at the old fool's heartstrings and make him go easy on me. But it wasn't like that at all – I really felt terrible about how I'd hurt my parents. I hated the way Eric could be so cynical, but he's like that – very clever and witty, but cruel with it. He's got more money than sense, and he was the one who got us all drinking that night. It all seemed like tremendous fun at the time, clowning around, but then it does when you've had one too many, doesn't it?'

'It does indeed,' said Jago, thinking of his own youth and chastened by the sudden thought of how old he must appear to be in her eyes. 'But we learn from these things.'

'Well, I certainly have. I want to achieve something in life, make my mark on the world – maybe write a book, like Susan Ingram.'

'You know Miss Ingram?'

'Yes, Rosemary introduced us – she thought we'd get on. I told my father she worked at the same place as him in some lowly job, but one day she'd be famous, just to see his reaction, but he turned very frosty. I got the impression he knew her but didn't like her.'

'Did you tell Miss Ingram?'

'No – it was none of my business. But I learned from Susan that doing something worthwhile like writing is a serious matter. I realised this morning that those boys and I were the only fools in that courtroom, and that's not what I want to be. I may have been a fool when I was drunk, but I saw today that Eric's a fool when he's sober too. When he found out Jack had given me that marijuana, he wanted to know if he could have some for free too, so I don't think he'd learned anything.'

'Did you ever ask your cousin if he could supply some to your friends?'

'No, I didn't. When Jack gave me that little bit he said it was free, but that was because I was family. He said if any of my friends wanted some, they'd have to pay for it. I never mentioned that to Eric, though, because he can be so irresponsible, and I didn't want to be the one who'd helped him get a supply of drugs – he's got parents too, and I didn't want to cause them grief.'

'Have you seen your parents yet?'

'Not my father – he went to work. But my mother came to the court with me, which can't have been easy for her. She hasn't said anything about it – I think she finds the whole thing humiliating, but at least she was there with me, and I appreciate that.'

'So how are you feeling now?'

'I feel bad about what this whole business has meant for my parents, but do you know, I think I care more about what my Aunt Rosemary would have said. That's why I came to see Annie – she's the next best thing I have now that Rosemary's not here. She's always listened to me, like Rosemary did, and she never has a go at me or talks down to me – she's been through a few scrapes in her time, and she's always got good advice. We've just had a good chat, and she was very kind and understanding, and I actually discovered something I'd never known.'

'Really? And what was that?'

'I've always known Rosemary didn't drink, whereas Annie does – I know she's partial to a drop of Scotch from time to time, but she mentioned that Rosemary hadn't touched it for years, and then told me why. It was to do with her husband, my Uncle Elliot. I never met him, because they lived in Canada until he died, but Annie said he used to get drunk and hit my aunt, and she swore she'd never drink alcohol again.'

'I recall your cousin Jack saying he'd died in a fall – is that right?'

'I believe so, yes. It's what my parents told me, and Aunt Rosemary too – she said he'd fallen down the stairs.'

'Did your aunt ever suggest that he fell because he was under the influence?'

'Of alcohol, you mean?'

'Yes.'

Claire thought for a moment. 'Yes, she did – just once. She said something like he'd died, and that was something she'd never be able to forget, but it was a mercy, and she had no regrets. I thought that was strange, and perhaps I was too young to understand, but you know, I had the strangest feeling when she said that.'

'In what way?'

'Well, at first I assumed she meant it was a mercy for him because the alcohol was ruining his life, but then I thought no, she means it was a mercy for her, because it freed her from his violence. But ever since then I've had a thought at the back of my mind that perhaps she pushed him – that perhaps she killed him. Do you think that's possible? I mean, she was such a good person.'

'In my experience anything's possible, but that doesn't mean everything that's possible actually happens. It's all a question of evidence – do you have any evidence to support the idea?'

'No, I don't – and it's not something I want to think about unless I find some one of these days.'

'Quite. But to return to something more tangible, I'm interested in what you've just said. You said your Aunt Rosemary always listened to you, and that you cared about her opinion, so I'm just wondering – when you told us yesterday that you didn't know whether she was aware of Jack supplying you with drugs, and that she'd never mentioned it, was that true?'

Claire looked bashful. 'It, er, wasn't entirely accurate. Actually she did know he'd been supplying drugs to people, and she did tell me, but I didn't want to drag her name into that conversation we were having, not with my mother there, especially as poor Aunt Rosemary wasn't there to defend herself.'

'Did your aunt tell you how she'd reacted when she discovered her son was involved with drugs?'

'Yes. She said she'd been shocked, and sad, and angry, and she told him so. She said they had a big row.'

'I see. Thank you very much, Miss Bowman, that's been very helpful. I expect you may have some work to catch up with, so we'll leave you now. I wish you every success and happiness in your studies.'

CHAPTER THIRTY-SIX

'So Claire wasn't telling us the truth when we spoke to her yesterday, was she?' said Cradock when they were back out on the street. 'She said she didn't know whether Rosemary Webster was aware that her son had been supplying her with drugs, but now she says she did know and she'd had a big row with him. Supposing that wasn't the only argument they had – maybe they had another one later. And I was thinking of what Mr Ford said, about marijuana giving you dangerous hallucinations – that doesn't sound good if you end up in a row, even if it's with your mum.'

'Yes, I was chatting with Dr Gibson about marijuana yesterday evening, and he mentioned the risk of hallucinations too. But there's something else Claire said, isn't there – she said when Jack gave her that little bit of marijuana he said it was free, but that was because she was family, and if any of her friends wanted some they'd have to pay for it. So it looks as though our fine young officer hasn't been telling us the truth either.'

'And what about that thing he said about Buckleby – having a screw loose. I mean, the government conspiring against him, and Jack Webster too? Sounds a bit odd, doesn't it?'

'It does, yes, but we can't exactly go and question the government and ask them whether they were conspiring against some bloke with a concrete business, can we?'

'No, sir, but we could have another crack at Jack Webster. We still don't know how those drugs ended up in his mum's bedroom, do we? And another thing – I was thinking about what Mr Ford said.'

'Yes, and what in particular?'

'About those drug smugglers, flying small planes into Yorkshire without being noticed. He said they wouldn't be able to do it now, because they'd probably get shot down, but I was just thinking, there's one sort of plane they wouldn't shoot down, isn't there? An RAF plane. Supposing Jack brought some drugs back from France? Mr Ford said there was some sort of supply chain from Morocco into France, didn't he? I don't suppose Jack popped home every weekend when he was fighting, but I'm wondering whether there was some way he could've got them over here. Do you think we need to find out?'

'Yes, Peter, I think we do. Let's go.'

'Not you again,' said Webster when they tracked him down at the RAF station. 'I've told you everything I know. I do have work to do, you know.'

'I do,' said Jago, 'but I've got some important questions for you to answer. First of all I must tell you that your cousin Claire was arrested yesterday and charged with being in possession of a dangerous drug. Were you aware of that?'

Webster's face registered dismay. 'No, I wasn't – poor kid. What's going to happen to her?'

'It's already happened – she was fined at the magistrates' court this morning.'

Webster let out a slow sigh. 'And are you going to suggest I sold it to her?'

'It's more a matter of what she said – she's told us that you gave it to her for nothing because she was family, but you also said that if her friends wanted some they'd have to pay for it. That sounds very much like the words of a man selling drugs for money, which means you haven't been telling us the truth.'

'No, no, it's not like that,' said Webster, his voice rising in anxiety. 'I admit I did say that, but I meant in general, because I didn't have any to give away – I meant they'd have to pay a dealer, not me. You've got to believe me, Inspector – it's the truth.'

'We'll see about that. And another thing – she's told us that when your mother found out you'd supplied some drugs to Mr Buckleby, she was angry and had a big row with you. Is that true?'

'No – it was nothing like that. I told you before – my mother didn't like the idea or condone it, but we didn't have a row. I think she was more sad than angry.'

'Did you have an argument with her on Monday morning?'

'What? No, of course not – I told you I was here on Monday morning.'

'Yes – in a field across the road, on your own, with no

witnesses. You could've been anywhere – especially when you've got a nice little MG that goes like a rocket, as I recall you mentioning. And you told us yourself you can come and go pretty much as you please here.'

'Look, I was there, walking in that field. I was not with my mother on Monday morning, and I did not have a row with her. And for the last time, I am not dealing in drugs. You can search me if you like – you won't find any drugs in my possession.'

'Perhaps not, but what about the drugs in your mother's bedroom? Can you explain that?'

Webster hesitated before replying. 'Ah, well,' he said, 'that was what you might call a family matter.'

'And?'

'As I told you, I did have some reefers for my own use, and my mother . . . well, you know what they say, once a mother, always a mother. She came across them one day and, er, jumped to the wrong conclusion. To put it bluntly, she confiscated them – she told me later she'd put them in the garbage can. They're quite harmless, of course, whatever the law may say, but she didn't know that.'

'And cocaine? There was some of that too – is that harmless? Have you been dealing in cocaine?'

'Of course not – I bought a tiny amount when I got the reefers, in case they didn't work, but they did, so I never had to use it. Look, I can see how this must look to you, but I'm afraid you've got hold of the wrong end of the stick. The fact that a tiny bit of cocaine may have turned up in my mother's bedroom is precisely because I was neither using nor selling it. And as for the special cigarettes, well, it's not a very serious matter. I mean if someone wants to get a little relief by smoking a reefer, what's the problem? It's not going to hurt anyone else, is it?'

'I wouldn't be so sure about that, Mr Webster – I may not be an expert on marijuana, but I do know it's listed as a dangerous drug under the Dangerous Drugs Act regulations. Whatever you think about those cigarettes, selling them is an offence under that Act, and you could be fined if you're caught in possession of them.'

'Lucky I'm not, then, isn't it?'

Jago gave no response, and Webster continued. 'So when is this alleged trade of mine in dangerous drugs supposed to have happened?'

'In about June of last year.'

'Well, I wasn't here then – I was in France, fighting the Germans.'

'Yes, I know. And did you ever have occasion to fly back to England during that time?'

'Once or twice, yes.'

'And I don't suppose your Hurricane was searched when you did, was it?'

'No, of course not. But are you suggesting I was flying this marijuana stuff back to Blighty and hawking it?'

'I'm considering the possibility. So did you?'

'Of course not – what do you take me for? Besides, a Hurricane's not an airliner – it doesn't have space for luggage, you know.'

'I assume there would've been some larger aircraft coming and going, though – bombers, transport planes? Those ATA planes you told us about?'

'Yes, of course, but I wasn't flying them, was I?' Webster was beginning to look tired. He gripped his wounded leg and sighed. 'Look, Inspector, I won't pretend the odd irregularity doesn't occur in the RAF, any more than it does in the navy or the army, I imagine. No need to name names, of course, but I know there were one or two chaps who'd take a bottle of French brandy home with them if they got the chance, and I dare say there might even have been the odd rascal buying exotic cigarettes from Morocco in France as presents for the folks back home.'

'And would you count yourself as one of those?'

'Hypothetically I could have been, but if I had I could only have brought a tiny amount home, not enough to start a drug-dealing business. Now, I'm still in pain, you know, and I'm pretty certain you don't have any evidence, so why don't we leave it at that? It seems to me you don't have a very strong case. Besides, what magistrate's going to look at me, a young pilot in uniform risking his life every day to fight off the country's deadly enemies, and take the word of some convicted criminal like Buckleby against me? I really think you're wasting your time, Inspector.'

'We'll see, Mr Webster – we'll see. You may be hearing from us again on this matter.'

CHAPTER THIRTY-SEVEN

Unlike their previous visit, this time there had not been even the slightest whiff of an invitation on Jack Webster's part to join him for lunch. Jago was not surprised, because their conversation must have been at the very least disgruntling to the pilot, but he knew the lack of food would certainly have disgruntled Cradock.

'Sorry, Peter,' he said as they left. 'No time for lunch today – we need to get back.'

Cradock did his best to hide his disappointment. 'Never mind, sir. Where are we going?'

'Well, having heard what Claire Bowman told us, I think we should pay Miss Ingram another visit. There's an interesting discrepancy I'd like to explore with her.'

'Really? What's that?'

'You'll see when we get there.'

'Oh, all right.'

Jago drove east, concentrating on the road, while Cradock gazed absently out of the window as the anonymous suburbs of Middlesex gave way to the more familiar streets of West London. Eventually they reached Mecklenburgh Square, and Jago parked the Riley outside the fire-gutted remains of the house next door to the aspiring author's home. As they waited for her to come to the door, he wondered idly whether the occupants had found themselves in the care of Arthur Murray and his friends at the Taviton Street rest centre, or whether in one fatal instant they'd been added to the growing list of Londoners who'd perished in the air raids. He put such thoughts out of his mind when Susan Ingram let them in.

'How's your brick wall?' he said as they squeezed past the furniture in her bed-sit.

'I'm sorry?' she replied.

'In your plot – you told us yesterday you'd run up against one in your plot.'

'Ah, yes – I finally fixed it, but it meant I was up half the night redrafting three chapters – I sometimes think I must be spending half my income on paper and ink. But what brings you back here?'

'Something you said. Yesterday you told us about your work with the Small Pig-Keepers' Council and said that you're now working part-time at the Ministry of Information. I mentioned Mr Gordon Bowman, since he works there too, and you said that although you were aware of that, because Mrs Webster had told you, you didn't actually know him and you don't come into contact with him. Is that correct?'

'Well, I don't remember exactly what I said.'

'Perhaps it's fortunate, then, that I do. Now, the reason why I'm reminding you of this is that we've just been speaking with his daughter, Claire, who says she knows you. She also said that when she mentioned you to Mr Bowman, she got the impression that he knew you and didn't like you. He turned very frosty, she said. Now, you'll understand that the discrepancy between what she told us and what you'd said earlier sparked my curiosity, so I wonder if you'd care to explain to us what the true nature of your dealings with Mr Bowman is.'

She looked uncomfortable, then shrugged her shoulders. 'OK, if it's that important to you. I just wasn't aware that it mattered that much. It's true that I didn't know him personally, and I was only aware of him because Rosemary happened to mention that he worked there. I'd never met him, but one day a couple of the girls in my department were gossiping and mentioned his name. I didn't say I knew who he was – it wasn't as though we were friends or anything – but the way they were talking was quite shocking.'

'In what way?'

'They were making out he was some sort of spy.'

'Did you believe it?'

'No, I didn't – it all sounded a bit far-fetched to me, the sort of thing I might write in a thriller, if I wanted to write that kind of thing. But I have to admit, there are some odd types in that building, and it is the Ministry of Information, after all – and spying's all about information, isn't it? I mean, it's only a few weeks since those two Germans were hanged in Pentonville Prison for trying to send information back to Berlin by short-wave radio. The paper said they were expecting to be rescued when the invading army arrived, but it didn't, did it? And the government said we should all watch out for enemy agents hanging around in pubs and trying to pick up bits of information from what we're saying to each other.' She laughed. 'Which is ironic, isn't it, since that's precisely what the ministry's own social survey reporters do. No wonder people call them the MoI's army of spies. But seriously, it's the ministry's job to censor the press, and that's to make sure no information leaks out that could be useful to an enemy, but that means the people who work there know what that information is, so it would be a very good place for a spy to work.'

'Are you aware of any evidence that that's actually happening?'

'No, I'm just talking hypothetically.' She laughed again. 'There was a joke going round the office the other day. A Canadian soldier in Bloomsbury asks a policeman what the big building is. "The Ministry of Information," says the policeman. "Ah, yes," says the soldier – "I reckoned the ministry would have to be about that size, to store all the information they never give away."'

Jago responded with no more than a hint of a smile, out of politeness, and she continued, 'Look, I'm sorry if I sound frivolous, but all I'm saying is that a civil servant working in the MoI could have far greater access to information that could be useful to an enemy than the average man or woman in the street.'

'Did you report your colleagues' comments about spying to any of the senior officials in the department?'

'No. Perhaps I should have, but I didn't. The thing is, you see, I wasn't a friend of his or anything, but he was Rosemary's brother, so I felt a kind of loyalty or obligation to him. I decided to write him a little note – not a proper memo through the internal mail, but just a handwritten note in a sealed envelope that I marked "Personal" and left on his desk.'

'And what did this note of yours say?'

'Well, I didn't want to repeat what I'd heard, just in case some nosey person opened the envelope and read it, so I just said something like "I thought I should let you know there are people in the office spreading rumours about you, saying you're a spy. Please see me if you want to know more." I was just trying to be helpful, and I must confess I was also interested to see what kind of response I got – although when I thought about it later I was a bit worried he might think I was trying to blackmail him. I wasn't, but by the time I thought that, it was too late – when I next passed by his desk, the envelope wasn't there. Anyway, he never came to see me, but the next day I found a similar personal note in a sealed envelope on my desk. He hadn't signed it, of course, but it was obviously from him.'

'Can you remember what he said?'

'Yes, I can. But better than that, you can read it for yourself – I've got it here in my handbag.' She pulled an envelope from her bag and handed it to Jago. 'There you are.'

Jago opened the envelope and took out the single sheet of paper it contained. He read it silently.

Dear Miss Ingram,

I'm obliged to you for bringing to my attention the matter to which you alluded. It's not uncommon for people in large organisations to start this kind of rumour, often for reasons of petty spite, mischief or jealousy, and they are usually baseless. I can assure you that the insinuations you report are precisely that: baseless and mischievous. I appreciate, however, the discretion you have shown in your communication, and I shall keep in mind what you have said. In conclusion, I have one request: if you come across any other such malicious gossip, whether directed against me or any other member of staff, please keep me informed on a confidential basis.

Jago passed the note to Cradock, who read it for himself. 'Sounds a bit pompous,' he said, folding the note back into its envelope and handing it back. 'Is that how they all talk in the ministry?'

'I think they have a certain style of writing,' said Susan. 'And you're right – not exactly racy, is it? I don't think I'd get very far if I wrote a novel in that style.' She paused and looked at Jago with a glum expression. 'But then I haven't got very far with a novel in any style, have I?' She shrugged her shoulders. 'But never say die, eh? Anyway, I hope that might be of some use to you.'

'Thank you for letting us know,' said Jago, returning the note to its envelope and holding it out towards her.

'No, no,' she replied, putting her hands up to stop him. 'You keep it. I've no use for it.'

'Very well,' said Jago, 'and please let us know if you receive anything else in the same vein or hear any more of these rumours.'

CHAPTER THIRTY-EIGHT

'Do you reckon Bowman really could be a spy, sir?' said Cradock as they settled back into the car. 'I mean, that Susan's got a good point about all that information and stuff.'

'I don't know,' said Jago. 'Anyone could be a spy, I suppose, and the whole point about spying is that no one should be able to spot you. But it could all be just a rumour, office girls sensationalising something they've overheard, when all the time he's doing something perfectly legitimate, keeping the Canadian government briefed on the mood of the nation, morale in Britain and that kind of thing.'

'But presumably someone in his position could possibly be passing sensitive information about Britain to the enemy, couldn't they?'

'Yes, it's certainly possible, in principle at least, but we haven't seen any evidence that Bowman is. He could equally have been passing information about Canada to the enemy, but there's no actual evidence of that either, is there?'

'No, I suppose not.'

'We could ask him, but all we can really do, I think, is let Mr Ford know about it, then he can have a word with Special Branch if he thinks it's justified. I expect it'll turn out just to be office gossip by people he's annoyed, but you never know – better safe than sorry.'

'Good idea, sir – catching spies is more up their street, isn't it?'

'It is. But tell me, what did you make of that note Bowman wrote to Miss Ingram – apart from the fact that it was a bit pompous?'

'Well, that's about it really – his daughter said he was a stuffed shirt, didn't she, and that's what he sounded like. A typical stuffed shirt. Is there something else I should've noticed?'

'I'm not sure. But what struck me was this.' He reached into his pocket and pulled out a card. 'It's this postcard that we found in Rosemary Webster's handbag. I can't be certain, but the handwriting in that note from Bowman that Susan Ingram showed us reminded me of this – they both look similar to me, but I'm thinking perhaps we should get an expert to look at them.'

'You mean a graphologist, sir?'

'I do – Miss Beryl Stevens. Come on – I want to catch her before she shuts up shop for the day.'

Jago drove as quickly as safety permitted to ABC Introductions in Museum Street, where he was pleased to find Beryl Stevens still at her desk.

'Miss Stevens,' he said. 'I'd be very grateful if you

could give us the benefit of your graphological wisdom on two samples of handwriting I've got here.'

'Is this police business?' she replied.

'Yes.'

'In that case there'll be no charge – I'm always happy to assist the police. May I take a look?'

Jago handed her the note and the postcard. 'Are these both written by the same person?'

She placed them side by side on the desk and scrutinised them carefully.

'Yes,' she replied. 'There are some very clear similarities. For example, the overall slant, the way he forms the capital letter *I*, and the length of the loops on his lower-case *g*.'

'You're confident it's a man, then?'

'Undoubtedly. And an educated man, I'd say – you may have noticed yourself that in both samples there are no errors in spelling, grammar or punctuation. Would you like to know what this handwriting says about the character of the writer?'

'No, thank you – I haven't got the time right now, and I can form an impression of his character in other ways. But there's another sample I'd like your view on before we go, if you don't mind, and in this case I'd like to know everything you can tell me.'

'By all means.'

He pulled a smaller piece of paper out of his pocket and handed it to her.

'My pleasure,' she replied, taking it from him.

'Well,' she said after perusing it, 'this is quite different to the other two. They were written by a mature and serious man of a sober and rational make-up. This one, however, strikes me as a feminine hand, a less mature person, someone volatile and impulsive, at risk of making bad decisions – what one might categorise as a flighty young girl.'

'That's a lot to deduce from a few words on a scrap of paper.'

'So it may seem to you, Inspector,' she said, handing it back to him, 'but not to an expert. I'm not claiming to be infallible, of course – handwriting can be deliberately crafted to deceive, for example, or injury can distort it – but here at ABC Introductions my insights have proved very fruitful, so I just hope what I've said helps to shed some light for you.'

'Well, thank you very much, Miss Stevens – that's been most illuminating. We must go now, but thank you for your time.'

Jago picked up the note and postcard from the desk and bade her farewell. She watched as they headed back down to the street door, their steps clattering on the bare wooden stairs.

CHAPTER THIRTY-NINE

'I've been thinking, sir,' said Cradock as Jago pulled away from the kerb and headed north up Museum Street in the direction of the British Museum. 'All that talk in there about writing got me wondering about something Susan Ingram told us. Do you remember what she said about Rosemary advising her to write romantic fiction to pay the bills?'

'I do,' said Jago. 'What about it?'

'Well, I was just thinking about those two letters we found in Rosemary Webster's flat – in the envelope addressed to that ABC Introductions mob. Do you think maybe she was thinking of writing a bit of romantic fiction herself? I mean, maybe she'd got some idea of a story about a woman who meets someone through one of those agencies and falls in love with him, but he turns out to be someone else or a liar or something. Maybe she wrote those letters for that and was planning to show them to the agency to see whether they were like the kind of letters they get, to make sure they were realistic.'

'Hmm . . . Sounds as though you've been reading some of those romantic novels yourself, Peter. I suppose what you're saying is as plausible an explanation as any other, but I've been thinking along more prosaic lines and I'm beginning to smell a rat – and it may be a rat up there in Hadleigh Mansions.'

'You reckon there's something fishy going on in ABC Introductions, then?'

'Not necessarily. It may be that it's all above board and tickety-boo, but the thing is, there's been a long history of fraud in the matrimonial business. There was a big scandal one of the old coppers told me about when I was new to the job. It was about a matrimonial agency in London and it all happened way back before my time, but I reckon he thought he was putting me wise with a cautionary tale in case I was thinking about using one to find myself a wife. He said this agency seemed like a professional set-up and provided glowing testimonials about its success, but actually it was a fraud.'

'Not something Mr Hardacre would approve of, then.'

'No indeed. I imagine he'd have come down on them like a ton of bricks.'

'So how did it work?'

'Well, as I understand it, the whole thing revolved around the fact that the agency channelled all the correspondence between the men and women on its books through what it called its negotiator, working in its office. In those days the clients were all men looking for a wife, and there was no trouble until it turned out that in one case the letters the negotiator wrote to the client on Miss so-and-so's behalf and the letters he claimed Miss so-and-so had written herself were both in the same handwriting. And then the same thing happened to another client, who received letters from a woman with a different name but in the same handwriting. What's more, in both cases the women later stopped corresponding with the client because they suddenly had to move abroad – and both to the same location. A suspicious coincidence, eh?'

'So you mean the men thought they were hearing from women who might be interested in marrying them but the women didn't actually exist?'

'Exactly – the letters from the women were all just faked by the agency. And the men who'd been duped were very reluctant to come forward as witnesses in court, because they were scared they'd be a laughing stock. Now, as I say, it may be that ABC Introductions is a reputable establishment without spot or blemish, and you might think people are more savvy and sophisticated nowadays, but you know what they say – a fool and his money are soon parted, and all a good confidence trick needs is a gullible victim. In this particular case, one of those victims eventually came forward. He'd shelled out his hard-earned cash to the agency, and when he couldn't get a reply from the lady concerned he went to the police. A detective searched the premises and found that the same name had been used for replies to several clients, but their description and their income varied. It was clearly a huge case of fraud.'

'And the verdict?'

'Guilty – five years' penal servitude for the ringleader, three years for his pals.'

'Interesting.'

'It is, isn't it? Now, you're right about Susan Ingram saying Rosemary had advised her to write romantic fiction to pay the bills, and I agree that maybe Rosemary took her own advice. But I'm not thinking she was writing a romantic novel – I think she'd found a much easier way of making a bit of money on the side. You remember Beryl Stevens told us the record card said her colleague had come to a mutually advantageous arrangement with her? I'm wondering whether that meant she'd cooked up some scheme with Rosemary to supply ABC Introductions with fake letters that they could send to their clients.'

'But if they were in the same handwriting, wouldn't that be a giveaway, just like in that old case?'

'Maybe, but if Beryl's such an expert on handwriting, perhaps she just made sure those letters went to men at opposite ends of the country, or perhaps she got someone else to copy them – after all, I imagine the skill's in composing a letter that'll do the trick and hook a client, not in the handwriting.'

'You mean Beryl and her mates are crooks?'

'I mean I think we should take a closer look into that business.'

'But if they are, that would make Mrs Webster a crook too, wouldn't it?'

'It would.'

Cradock concentrated on his own thoughts for a moment. 'And if someone else knew what she was up to, they could turn that to their own advantage, couldn't they? Maybe blackmail her. But she doesn't seem to have been the kind of person who'd take that lying down – so it could've ended up nasty. Trouble is, we don't know if anyone else actually knew, do we?'

'No, we don't, but what you're saying is quite possible. In the meantime, though, we've got the matter of the note to deal with – the one Miss Ingram gave us – and that postcard. We'd better step on it and have a little word with Gordon Bowman before it gets too dark.'

CHAPTER FORTY

It was twenty to six, and the blackout had just started. The streets that had been bustling with people hurrying home from shops and offices were now shrouded in darkness and littered with hazards for the unwary. Jago and Cradock parked the car in Goodge Street and picked their way as quickly and carefully as they could past a row of shadowy houses until they spotted the sign on Daventry Mansions glimmering faintly with reflected moonlight. Once they were inside, they found themselves in the sudden glare of electric light and headed briskly to apartment 7, where the door was opened to them by Claire Bowman.

'Good evening, Miss Bowman,' said Jago. 'Is your father at home?'

'Yes, he is.'

'We'd like to have a word with him, please, if it's not too much trouble. May we come in?'

'Er, yes, I suppose so. He's in the drawing room – follow me.'

She led them to the room in which they had previously met Gordon Bowman and his wife. Both were present again, but this time there was a third person: Charles Buckleby. He was standing by the fireplace with a glass in his hand and turned round to face them as they came in.

'Mr Buckleby,' said Jago. 'I didn't expect to see you here.'

Bowman spoke before Buckleby could reply. 'Charles is an old friend of the family,' he said with a smile. 'We've known each other for years.'

'Yes,' Buckleby added awkwardly, as if embarrassed to be found there. 'I believe I mentioned that I knew Gordon and his family.'

'Indeed you did,' Jago replied.

'Won't you sit down, gentlemen?' said Helen Bowman. 'And can I get you something to drink?'

'Thank you,' said Jago. 'We'll take a seat, but not a drink, thank you very much.'

She cast an enquiring glance in the direction of her husband, but he declined with a quick shake of the head.

'Actually,' Jago continued, 'when I said I was surprised to see Mr Buckleby here in your home, Mr Bowman, my surprise was more to do with you.'

'What do you mean?' said Bowman.

'I mean I've been told that you care about your reputation and you're anxious not to see it tarnished. And yet here you are entertaining Mr Buckleby in your own home – an old friend, yes, but nevertheless a convicted criminal. That does surprise me – from what people have told me about you, it seems somewhat out of character.'

'I don't think I need any advice on who I choose to

associate with in my own time, Inspector,' said Bowman calmly. 'Now, why are you here?'

'I'll come to that in a moment. But since we have Mr Buckleby with us, there's something I'd like to know first. Mr Bowman, you and your wife and daughter all know about Jack Webster's involvement with dangerous drugs, and so do you, of course, Mr Buckleby, but I'd like to establish what part Rosemary Webster played in that.'

'But she wasn't involved,' said Buckleby. 'She'd never get mixed up with drugs.'

'So I understand. But what I'd like to know is how much she knew about it. Mr Bowman, she was your sister – what can you tell us about that?'

'Not a lot, I'm afraid. Some weeks ago Buckleby and I were chatting, just the usual kind of "How's things" conversation, and I happened to mention I was experiencing quite a lot of stress at work. He said he'd been smoking marijuana cigarettes and recommended them – he said he'd got some from Jack and suggested I do too.'

'And did you?'

Bowman looked horrified. 'Certainly not. I was pretty shocked, and I told Rosemary what Jack was doing. So she definitely knew then.'

'And Mr Buckleby, you'd had some drugs from Jack Webster yourself, but did you know he'd also given some to Claire?'

'Yes – he mentioned it to me.'

'When was that?'

'About a week ago.'

'Did you report this to her parents?'

'No.'

'But you're their old friend – surely you would've told them their daughter had a dangerous drug in her possession?'

Buckleby shifted nervously on his chair. 'Yes, but... I didn't, because I thought they might use it against Rosemary. To be quite honest, I don't think they cared about her as deeply as I did, and I couldn't stand by and see her name dragged through the mud.'

'Did you mention this business of the drugs to Mrs Webster?'

'No – I was still trying to decide whether to tell her when she died.'

'That doesn't sound like a man who cared deeply for her. She and Claire were very close – did you really find it that difficult to tell Mrs Webster what was going on? Or did you perhaps have plans to use the information for some other purpose? You told me yourself that knowledge is power, and you had some knowledge you could use to your own advantage.'

Buckleby looked baffled. 'I don't know what you mean.'

'There was a scandal brewing around Jack Webster and Claire, with careers and reputations to be ruined. Did you intend to blackmail Jack Webster, or Mr and Mrs Bowman for that matter? Or even Rosemary Webster? I understand you'd tried to borrow money from her and she'd turned you down. Mrs McCready told us you had a big row about it – no holds barred, she said. Perhaps you thought you could persuade Mrs Webster to change her mind.'

'No!' said Buckleby. 'It wasn't like that.'

Gordon Bowman looked Jago in the eye. 'Inspector, I can't speak for Rosemary, of course, nor for her son, but I can assure you that Mr Buckleby has made no attempt to blackmail me or my wife.'

'That's right,' said Buckleby. 'I didn't blackmail anyone.'

Bowman pulled the cuff of his left sleeve back and checked the time on his watch. 'And now, Inspector,' he said, 'this is all very interesting, but I've told you everything I know about these alleged activities of my nephew, and that's only what Charles here told me, so I don't think I can be of any more help to you. I know there's a war on and we're all having to cope with extra work and no sleep, but I've got some very important matters to deal with at the ministry tomorrow, so if that's all, may I suggest you continue your discussions with Mr Buckleby later and let us all get to our beds?'

'I'm sure we could all do with more sleep, Mr Bowman,' Jago replied, 'but actually there's another matter of interest that I'd like to ask you about, and it concerns you personally. So I'm afraid we'll have to intrude upon you for a little longer.'

'Very well, but let's try to be quick about it, shall we?'

'By all means. It concerns a Miss Susan Ingram, who knew your sister and who works at the Ministry of Information. You know her?'

Bowman pulled a face that suggested he had never heard of her, but said nothing.

'Well,' said Jago, 'she may have quite a humble role in the ministry, but it seems she's had some dealings with you.' He reached into his pocket and pulled out a sheet of paper. 'Here,' he said, passing it to Bowman. 'I expect you'll recognise this.'

Bowman made no response, and Jago continued. 'According to Miss Ingram, she heard two colleagues talking about you in a way that suggested they believed you were involved in some kind of espionage activity.'

Helen Bowman looked up, startled. 'But that's— It's absurd, Inspector.' She turned to her husband and added nervously, 'Tell him, Gordon.'

'It's nonsense,' said Bowman.

'I'm not saying Miss Ingram believed it, Mr Bowman, but she said that because she knew Mrs Webster and knew that you were her brother, she felt a sense of loyalty to you, so she wrote a personal note to let you know and left it on your desk. And then she received a reply from you – unsigned, but she was sure it was from you. Is that the reply you left for her?'

Bowman scanned the note. 'Yes, it is. But what of it?'

'Were they right? Are you involved in spying?'

'What a preposterous idea – of course not. Look, the truth is that part of my job is to write reports and briefings on how Britain's coping with the war – not for a foreign power or an enemy nation, but for the Royal Canadian Mounted Police. They're responsible for all Canadian counter-intelligence and security matters, and the information I provide is purely for background, to help equip them to deal with any subversive activity that could damage the war effort – our war effort and yours. My reports are confidential, but they don't involve any spying. I suspect some ill-informed busybody in the junior ranks at the ministry has got wind of this and blown it up out of all proportion – that's usually how rumours start, isn't it? When the garrulous meet the credulous. I can assure you there's nothing in it.'

'Did your sister know about this allegation?'

'I couldn't say.'

'Do you think her strong principles would've found the idea objectionable?'

'What are you getting at?'

'It's just because of this.' Jago produced the postcard he and Cradock had found in Rosemary Webster's handbag and showed it to Bowman. 'We've had the handwriting examined, and it's the same as the handwriting in that note you left for Miss Ingram. This postcard to your sister was from you, wasn't it?'

Bowman gave the postcard a cursory glance. 'Yes, I guess it was. What of it?'

'I'll remind you of what it says.' Jago read out the message on the card. '"No one's going to bully me. Best thing is for you to keep quiet. These things have a nasty habit of blowing back in your face, and we don't want that, do we? I recommend you don't breathe a word. If you do, you'll regret it – trust me."'

He looked for a reaction on Bowman's face, but there was none. 'That sounds like a threat to me. Were you afraid that your sister would expose you as a spy?'

'Of course not – I've told you there's no truth in those so-called rumours. How do you know this Ingram woman wasn't just making the whole thing up to discredit me? No, Inspector, I freely admit I sent this postcard to my sister, but it wasn't about that. It was about my nephew –

her son – and his involvement with dangerous drugs. When Buckleby told me about that, I knew I had to let Rosemary know, so I wrote her a letter.'

'How did she react to that?'

'I guess the best way to describe it would be forcefully. She wrote back in strong terms warning me not to reveal it to anyone.'

'And did you?'

'What, reveal it? Of course not. I had no intention of revealing it, because of the scandal it would cause for both Jack and Rosemary – and even possibly myself, since I'm related to them.'

'Did you tell your wife?'

'No.' Bowman cast a careful glance at his wife. 'I didn't. Helen was already suffering a lot of emotional stress because of our son's tragic death, and the last thing I wanted to do was put the idea of taking dangerous drugs into her head.'

'And Claire, your daughter?'

'No. I never dreamed Jack would try to introduce his own cousin to those dreadful substances – and I didn't want to put the idea into her head either. I knew Jack respected his mother and I thought he'd listen to her, more fool me.'

'Did Mrs Webster explain why she was warning you not to reveal it?'

'Yes. She said if I did it would ruin Jack's career – as if I didn't know that. Obviously it would, and I had no intention of betraying him. But I don't think she trusted me. She said if I said anything about it, she'd let the world know one or two things about me.'

Jago scanned the faces before him to check their reactions. Buckleby's expression was impassive, Claire seemed to be listening intently and Helen looked increasingly distressed. 'About you spying?' he said. 'But you've just told us you weren't doing that.'

'I wasn't,' Bowman replied. 'But mud sticks, as they say, and whether she was referring to that or any other malicious gossip I have no idea. Whatever it was, I felt she was trying to bully me into silence quite unnecessarily. When I sent her that card, I was annoyed about that, yes, but I was keen to reassure her that family secrets were safe with me. No one was going to get information about Jack's private life out of me, and I was only concerned that she should keep the whole business of him and his drugs under her hat too. I was just as keen not to see Jack's career ruined as she was.'

'But you have a career too, Mr Bowman, don't you? And a successful one at that, I gather. I can imagine you'd be anxious not to allow either your sister or her son to say or do anything to jeopardise your own future.'

Helen Bowman jumped to her feet. 'That's not fair, Inspector,' she said indignantly. 'You're the one who's trying to bully my husband. Are you trying to suggest—'

'Now, now, my dear,' said Bowman soothingly, 'there's no need to worry. Just sit down quietly. Everything's going to be fine.'

She looked defeated and sat down meekly on the sofa. Jago could see tears brimming in her eyes.

'But Gordon,' she said, 'it's so unfair. He's trying to make out you're . . . something I know you're not. It's too much. I can't bear the thought of anyone trying to ruin you, to destroy your career and your good name – not on top of losing poor Harold.'

'I'm sorry, Inspector,' said Bowman. 'The last few weeks have been torture for us. I have a job to do and I sincerely hope it'll help us win this war, but at least it occupies my mind. For my wife, though, the agony . . . well, it's relentless – she has nothing to fill her thoughts except the loss of our dear son. I hope you understand.'

'Yes, I do.'

'My sister was a good woman, and our son was a good young man. But now Jack's lost his mother, just as we've lost our son. There must be thousands of people quietly mourning the loss of a loved one in this war already, but that doesn't make it easier for anyone. Our hearts are eaten away by grief, but it's the price we pay for war.' Bowman moved to his wife's side to comfort her. 'Come now, my love.'

'Oh, Gordon,' she replied through her tears. 'You said she was good, but I still can't understand it – how can someone who's good do such a bad thing?'

'What do you mean, my dear?'

'You must know what I mean. You knew her – she wasn't what people took her to be, was she? That smile of hers – that beautiful smile that everyone loved so much . . . so kind, so sympathetic. But how could it be sympathetic when she had blood on her hands?'

Jago noticed the puzzled look on her husband's face. 'What do you mean, Mrs Bowman?' he said quietly.

'I went to see her,' she said, her voice strained. 'I couldn't bear it any more. I had to speak to her . . . I told her I couldn't cope with the strain. I thought she'd understand, but that smile she gave, that self-satisfied grin on her face . . . She told me that war's a terrible thing, and we have to look into ourselves and find the strength to go on. Such a patronising hypocrite. So I said to her "What do you see when you look into yourself?" She acted like she didn't know what I was talking about, so I said "Inside yourself – what is there, Rosemary? Is there a heart, or is there just a cold stone? You and your cold, hard principles." She just looked at me, as though she felt sorry for me because I was weak and she was strong. I could see she thought I just wasn't coping and I should be, but I said "You – it was you. You killed him."' Helen turned her tear-stained face towards her husband. 'She did, Gordon, she did.'

Bowman looked shocked. 'What are you saying, my dear?'

'She could have saved him. She knew – she could have saved him.'

'I'm sorry,' said Jago, 'but could you explain what you mean?'

'The tribunal,' she replied, leaning forward. 'The London Conscientious Objectors' Tribunal. When our son Harold was hauled up in front of it, she knew one of the people sitting on it. He was a friend of hers – that man Masterson. She could have persuaded him to make them uphold Harold's appeal, couldn't she? As a favour to a friend if nothing else. It's not much to ask when a young man's life is at stake. But she didn't lift a finger, because of those principles of hers – those fine, cruel, murderous principles. She sent him to his death because she wouldn't compromise her fancy principles, not even for her own family. She wouldn't make that friend of hers exempt him, and he sentenced my son to death. But it was her fault. He was doing his job, but she could have changed the verdict and chose not to.'

She sank back into the sofa and sobbed quietly.

'Tell me what happened, please,' said Jago.

'I don't know – we had an argument, and I slapped her. All I remember is it felt like a huge wave of grief and anger welling up inside me and overflowing me. I tried to hit her again, to punish her for her wickedness, for sending Harold to his death and finishing my life, but she stepped back and I missed her. I grabbed something from the fireplace – I think it was the poker – and lashed out with it. She fell down and didn't move.' She paused and took a deep breath. 'I never meant to kill her – I just wanted to make her face up to what she'd done. But I wanted to hurt her too. Was that wrong?'

She looked up pleadingly into her husband's eyes. He said nothing, but moved closer to her side and put his arm round her.

Jago placed his hand on her shoulder. 'You're under arrest, Mrs Bowman,' he said.

Silence descended on the room, broken only by the quiet sobs that began to rack her crumpled body.

CHAPTER FORTY-ONE

'I suppose that's all sewn up, then, guv'nor,' said Cradock cheerily the next morning. We've got a confession, so now it's just the paperwork. Any chance of knocking off early, do you think?'

'We'll see, Peter. There's a few loose ends we need to tie up first.'

'Yes, of course, sir. Now you mention it, I've got one of my own, actually. It's to do with that Beryl Stevens at ABC Introductions.'

'Is this a personal loose end or a professional one?'

Cradock looked aggrieved. 'Professional, sir – I don't think I want her poking about in my personal life.'

'Quite. So what is it?'

'Well, sir, it's just that apart from the two letters we found at Rosemary Webster's place and the postcard, and that note that Susan Ingram got at work, I don't remember us finding anything else that might be significant as far as handwriting's concerned. So what was that other bit of paper you asked her to take a look at yesterday? I was lying in bed last night trying to puzzle it out.'

'Oh, that – yes. Actually it was a note to the milkman, written by me yesterday morning. It said "No milk today, thanks, but an extra pint on Wednesday please."'

'But you haven't got a milkman, sir – you're living at Rochester Row nick.'

'Yes, you're quite right, but believe me, I've written a lot of notes to the milkman in my time. So you might say that like Beryl Stevens, I have a lot of experience in the skill.'

'So why did you ask her to analyse it?'

'It was what I believe scientists call a control experiment, to test the claims she'd made about her remarkable intuitive gift.'

'Oh, right, I see . . . I think.'

'So how remarkable do you reckon this gift of hers is?'

'Er, not very, sir. You tricked her then?'

'Indeed I did. So there you are – we've tied up one loose end already, and the day's barely started. Any more?'

'Yes, sir. It's about ABC Introductions again. What are we going to do about them?'

'A good question. A sweet little trio of well-meaning young ladies, or a bunch of swindlers? We need to go back there and get to the bottom of whatever's going on in that office – if they're working some kind of racket, we may end up making one or two arrests, but I think I'd better check first with Detective Superintendent Hardacre whether he'd prefer to pass that particular investigation on to some of our colleagues – he might have more pressing duties lined up for us. If he does, though, I'll advise him not to send any single young men of marriageable age.'

'Definitely, sir – they'd have those boys signed up and parting with their cash faster than you could say "psycho-whatever-it-was profile".'

'I think you're right. Is that all?'

'Not quite, sir. When we were with the Bowmans yesterday, I was expecting Gordon Bowman to start shouting about diplomatic immunity. Isn't that what foreigners always do when they work at an embassy here in London and get nicked for something?'

'That's true, Peter, but Canadians aren't foreigners – they're British subjects, even the High Commissioner. That's why Canada House is the Canadian High Commission, not the Canadian Embassy. I'm no expert on these matters, but I would've thought that meant that none of the Canadians who work there have diplomatic immunity – not even the High Commissioner himself, nor his wife. Of course, Mr Hardacre did say the powers that be don't want any complications to mess up our relationship with Canada, so there might be some sort of high-level shenanigans between our government and theirs if we stir up trouble, but that won't stop me charging her. What happens later is somebody else's business.'

'And Jack Webster, sir – I don't suppose he's high up enough to cause any trouble between our government and theirs, but what are we going to do about him and those drugs?'

'Well, I fear he may be right – we haven't got a very strong case against him. I remember one we had a couple of years ago back in West Ham. Our boys thought they'd got a bloke fair and square on possession of some hashish, because they'd seen him drop a little packet of it on the floor. We reckoned we had a pretty cast-iron case against him and charged him, but the magistrate dismissed the case owing to lack of evidence. You wouldn't credit it, would you? So I think we need something more before we charge him – especially if he's going to turn up in court in his RAF pilot's uniform.'

'I see, sir – yes. But it'll certainly mess things up for him if he gets a conviction, won't it? He won't be the golden boy hero then.'

'I don't suppose he will – carpeted by his commanding officer, more likely.'

'There's something I keep thinking about, though – that thing Mr Spindle said.'

'Which particular thing?'

'That bit he quoted from the Bible, by the bloke with the same name as him.'

'Obadiah, you mean?'

'That's the gent, yes. I can't remember exactly what he said – it was all in that old-fashioned talk – but it was about someone going up as high as an eagle, and then God saying he was going to bring him down again.'

'You remember it? I'm impressed.'

'Yes, well, when he said that, it felt like I could see it happening. But then Jack Webster said what it was like flying his plane – he said you soar up into the sky like an eagle looking for its prey, didn't he? And I was just thinking what a fool he's been. I mean, he was like that eagle, and he'd most likely have got medals for it, but now he'll probably end up like Mr Spindle said.'

'Or like the other Obadiah said.'

'Yes, that's what I mean – he's been flying right up into the sky like that eagle, but now if he's not lucky he'll crash right back down to earth and he'll be finished. Not literally, of course – I don't mean he'll get shot down again, just that he'll find his career and reputation are destroyed. It's like you said yourself, sir – how the mighty are fallen. Do you think God'll do that to him – bring him down, I mean?'

'I'm afraid you're asking the wrong man for a question like that, Peter – even detective inspectors don't know the answers to everything. I can't tell you whether God's got a hand in it, but I'm pretty sure if young Webster finds himself in trouble with the court it'll be because he's the architect of his own misfortune, as they say. If he comes a cropper he's only got himself to blame. All we've got to do is decide whether we've got enough evidence to charge him, and then we can leave it to the magistrate to decide what happens next. I think it's safe to say that what anyone else higher up might think about it, even the Almighty himself, isn't strictly our concern. Is that the lot, or do you have any more questions that I'm competent to answer?'

'Just one, sir – what do we do with Nadelmann?'

'Ah, yes – our tight-lipped academic. I think we'll have to see if we can persuade him to come clean about that whole business of the phone call and the drawings – either that or find enough evidence to nail him. But given that it looks like he wasn't our murderer, Mr Hardacre may prefer to pass that little case to someone else too, in which case it's not our problem any more. All done?'

'Yes, sir. Thank you, sir.'

'Good. And now there's something I want an answer

to. Don't worry – not from you. I've got a question for Professor Masterson – I want to know whether what Helen Bowman said yesterday was right. What I mean is whether he knew her son was related to Mrs Webster when he came up before the tribunal. We'll make Foster Court our first call of the day.'

'Good morning, gentlemen,' said Masterson when they arrived at his office. 'You've timed your visit well – I've just arrived and haven't plunged into my work yet, so my mind is completely at your disposal. What can I do for you?'

'We've had some developments in the case since we last saw you and we've now charged someone with Mrs Webster's murder. I wanted to let you know.'

'That's very considerate of you, Inspector. May I ask who it is that you've charged?'

'Yes – it's her sister-in-law, Mrs Helen Bowman.'

'Ah, I see. So was it over some family issue?'

'It was, yes, and there's something I'd like to ask you about it.'

'Please do.'

'You told us that in addition to your academic responsibilities, you find yourself called upon to sit on various committees and tribunals, but may I ask whether they include one of those tribunals that judge claims for exemption from military service by conscientious objectors?'

'They do – they've been set up in various parts of the country, and I'm a member of the South East Local Tribunal, which sits at Bloomsbury County Court.'

'And they're set up by the government.'

'Yes, under the National Service (Armed Forces) Act 1939. Each one must have a chairman and four other members, all appointed by the government, and the chairman must be a county court judge. I think professors are the kind of people the authorities like to have on them, but they make sure the members are a mix, so a typical tribunal might include a professor, a trade union official and a former town councillor or similar type of person, to try to make it fair. Why do you ask?'

'I ask because Mr and Mrs Bowman's son appeared before that tribunal, and yesterday evening Helen Bowman told us that she knew you were a friend of Mrs Webster's and you sat on that tribunal, and she believed Mrs Webster could've persuaded you to uphold his appeal. So I'd just like to know this – did Mrs Webster try to do that? When that young man came up before you at the county court, did you know he was related to her?'

'No – I had no idea. As I think I mentioned before, Rosemary never talked about her family, and I didn't pry. If I had known, I would have recused myself from that hearing – if you'll pardon a lawyer's inevitable quoting of the letter of the law, the Act says that local tribunals must be made up of impartial persons, and as a member I'm expected to withdraw if I have any personal interest in a case.'

'And Mrs Webster definitely didn't make any attempt to influence you?'

'No, she didn't – and I would suggest that the fact that I was part of the tribunal that rejected his claim for exemption from military service confirms both my impartiality and her integrity.'

'Quite. Does it surprise you she didn't tell you her nephew was coming up before the tribunal?'

'Not at all. Rosemary was a woman of principle – that's one of the things I admired her for. I don't think she'd ever try to pull strings to benefit a friend or relative, let alone try to subvert the proceedings of a lawfully instituted tribunal. She believed in supporting and encouraging people to plough their own furrow in life. She was a very compassionate woman, but she was nobody's fool. She'd come from a poor background, you see, and life hadn't rolled the dice kindly for her – she'd had to find her own way through all the challenges, and that's what made her the wise and wonderful woman she was. She knew it's the hard things in life that make us strong, and she believed in helping people to face those challenges and overcome them, not just to dodge them. So no – I think she would have felt that if her nephew had a strong enough conviction and a good enough case, he'd win his appeal, and if he didn't, it would be his responsibility to deal with it. It was how she'd brought up her own son, and I don't think she would have applied one rule to her own flesh and blood and another to other people.'

'Even if the consequences could prove to be so tragic?'

'No – I don't think even that would have swayed her from doing what she was convinced was the right thing. She knew that principles sometimes come at a cost, but she wouldn't flinch. It's an awful thing to think about, but I suppose in the end she paid the ultimate price for doing what she believed was right. I just hope the end came swiftly for her.'

'I'm told it did.'

'Then that's all she would have wanted for herself, I'm sure of it. Thank you for taking the trouble to let me know, Inspector. Nothing can bring Rosemary back now, but to know there's a prospect that justice may be done is a comfort to me, and not just as a lawyer.' He paused. 'Will you be telling Nadelmann you've made an arrest? I believe he was rather attached to Rosemary in his own way, and this whole business seems to have been quite distressing for him. I think he'd appreciate knowing before he reads about it in the paper.'

'Yes, we'll do that,' said Jago. 'We'll be on our way now, but I'd just like to say I'm very sorry for your loss, Professor, especially in view of what you said about your own affection for Mrs Webster.'

Masterson smiled. 'Thank you. She's gone now, and all I can say is that I loved her with all my heart, and I hoped only that she would love me too. There – you may think me a sentimental old fool, but that's the truth of it.'

'I don't think you're a sentimental old fool, Professor,' said Jago. 'I think you're a man who's found what's most precious to him and had it stolen from him. I'm very sorry that's how your story has ended.'

Masterson nodded his head with a sad, awkward smile of acknowledgement, and Jago fell silent. There was nothing more he could say.

CHAPTER FORTY-TWO

Jago was in two minds about how to approach Nadelmann. He was still annoyed by the German academic's refusal to disclose what he'd been talking about in his suspicious phone call, but at the same time he'd taken a liking to the man and felt sympathy for the way his life had been turned upside down by malevolent politics. Unfortunately, however, his job didn't allow any such sympathy to be stretched as far as giving Nadelmann the benefit of the doubt. When they arrived at his office, Jago spoke with restrained politeness.

'Good morning, Mr Nadelmann. We've come to tell you that we've arrested someone on suspicion of murdering Mrs Webster. Professor Masterson was keen that we should let you know.'

'Ah, yes, he's a kind man,' said Nadelmann, 'and very thoughtful. Rosemary's death must have been devastating for him.'

'So you knew about his feelings for her?'

'I suspected them. When you've studied the art of the Old Masters for as long as I have, you learn to appreciate how much they expressed through the eyes of their subjects. When Masterson spoke about Rosemary, I could tell from his eyes that he cared for her. He will be desolate without her. But tell me, the person you've arrested – who is it?'

'It's her sister-in-law, Mrs Bowman. Did you know her?'

'No, I've never met her. I suppose if it was murder she must have had her reasons, but I'm not sure I want to know what they were. I'd rather think about my good memories of dear Rosemary, not her death. Ignorance is bliss, yes?'

'Sometimes it is, yes. But sad as this news is, I must remind you that you've been doing your very best to keep me in ignorance of what you've been up to with regard to the old drawings that Mrs Webster believed you'd been stealing from the British Museum. I hope you've had time to reconsider your position since then, otherwise things will get very serious for you.'

'There's no need to threaten me, Inspector. I have some experience of being threatened, including by the Gestapo, and I like to think I've built up a certain resistance to threats from anyone. I assume you are planning to arrest me, but I must reassure you that when I made that telephone call that you were so interested in my intentions were entirely honourable.'

'Do you deny that you were offering to sell items from the British Museum's collections to whoever it was you were talking to?'

'I do not.'

'Right – now we're getting somewhere. And what were those drawings worth?'

'The ones we were discussing were altogether worth about two hundred pounds.'

'That's a lot of money – especially to someone in your position, I'd imagine. And I suppose this other fellow's got clean away with them now, has he?'

'Yes – he did get away with them, but that was not the end of the story, and I believe I can now tell you what the content of that telephone conversation was.'

'Really? So what's changed?'

'What's changed, Inspector, is that earlier today I was informed that the man I was speaking to is now enjoying the hospitality of your colleagues in the Metropolitan Police.'

'What? Do you mean he's been arrested?'

'I do. I'm surprised you don't know already. I have the impression that you London detectives are not as good at keeping each other informed as I assumed you'd be. Perhaps I should explain.'

Jago was beginning to feel exasperated by the academic's punctilious manner. 'Yes, I think you should.'

'It's quite simple. For some months now the museum's been conducting what it calls an internal investigation – that means one that doesn't involve the police. I'm afraid it was all my fault – I was at the root of the problem, as you might say. I was working my way through the old catalogues of the museum's collections to check their accuracy and update them, and to my surprise I found that some items that were listed in the catalogues appeared to be missing. Now, it's possible for individual items to get misfiled in an institution as huge as the British Museum, but I began to see a pattern to these losses. They seemed intentional – I began to think perhaps they'd been stolen. These things can happen in a museum, of course – sometimes an unscrupulous person whose position gives them access to rare and precious objects wants to possess them for their private pleasure, and sometimes they just want or need to get money, so they take them and sell them. I have bitter experience of that in my own life. I know quite a lot about the market for Old Master drawings in this country, so I began a little research project of my own – studying what was being bought and sold on the open market. I found that some of the drawings that had been traded appeared to match ones that had gone missing from the museum – not the most famous and valuable ones, which would attract too much attention, but lower-ranking, less conspicuous pieces. I became convinced they'd been stolen.'

'Did you go to the police?'

'Not at that stage, no – I went to the director of the museum. He decided that we should test my theory by setting a little trap. We began to make discreet enquiries in the market and eventually learnt of a new dealer who was active in buying and selling Old Master drawings. To cut a long story short, we found out who he was and where he lived, and I wrote to him under a false name and offered to sell him some – as the director put it, to see whether he'd bite.'

'And from what you've said, I assume the items you were offering were from the museum's collections?'

'Indeed. But I did so with the full knowledge and

permission of the director – in fact, literally under his direction. It was perfectly straightforward, you see – as he explained to me, when the British Museum was founded nearly two centuries ago, it was set up as a trust, and the man who founded it, Sir Hans Sloane, said in his will that the trustees must ensure that its collection was preserved, as he put it, "whole and entire, without the least diminution or separation". That meant they were allowed to buy exhibits, but not to sell them. Parliament later granted the museum some discretion in the matter, so it was allowed to dispose of items that were duplicates or that it considered unfit for its collections, but even so, the law required that seven or more of the trustees must agree to authorise such disposals. So if anything from the museum's collections appears on the open market without the knowledge and approval of the trustees, it must be an unauthorised sale, and if anyone tries to buy items belonging to the museum they are clearly doing so illegally. The director decided we could use some items of relatively low value as bait, knowing that when the dealer took the bait, the police could take him.'

'So by this stage you'd got the police involved?'

'Yes. No one else in the museum knew what we were doing, of course, and I suppose the fact that you haven't heard about it yourself does mean that the essential secrecy of the operation was maintained. The director informed the police of where I'd arranged to meet the man and at what time, and after I'd handed over the drawings and taken my leave they followed him and arrested him. I understand that your colleagues are also questioning the dealer's client – the man who wanted to add those drawings to his own collection and knew that he could only get them if they were stolen.'

'I see.'

'So I think you'll agree there's no need for you to arrest me, Inspector. Our little operation has been a success, and we hope the museum will get at least some of its missing items back. I'm sure the museum will also be reviewing its procedures to make sure this doesn't happen again.'

'Yes, but how did these drawings get out of the museum in the first place – before you laid your trap?'

'That is an important question. The director and I believe we have identified a member of staff who had access to the collections and the opportunity to remove items without anyone knowing.'

'And that's because only someone who was checking the records as closely as you were would notice?'

'Precisely. His name is now in the hands of your colleagues too, and I expect they'll be taking the appropriate action when they see fit.'

'So who is this thief? And who's the client behind the thefts?'

'Forgive me for not giving you names, Inspector, but the officer investigating the case swore me to secrecy, and even though you are a fellow officer, I imagine it's more appropriate for you to get them from him than from me. I think it's safe for me to tell you, however, that the client, the man behind the theft, as you put it, is a man of considerable wealth. I'm not personally acquainted with him, but I happen to know that before the war started he was the leader of a particularly vicious and ugly group in the British fascist movement – in other words a Nazi.

You will remember me telling you that my own collection of valuable drawings was stolen from me in Germany by Hitler's Nazis. Those people are of course beyond the reach of British justice, even if, as I hope, only for the time being, but it is a sweet consolation to me to know that one of your own home-grown Nazis should soon be spending some considerable time behind bars.'

'A successful day for you and the museum, then.'

'Yes, it is. But that success is outweighed by the great sadness I feel, that dear Rosemary's life was cut short with her thinking that I had betrayed her trust. That will always weigh heavily on my heart.'

CHAPTER FORTY-THREE

On the way out of the Faber and Faber building, Jago remembered that at their first meeting with Arthur Murray, the young Friends' Ambulance Unit man had requested that they let him know who had killed Rosemary Webster if and when they found out, so he decided to add the FAU headquarters as the final stop on their itinerary. When he and Cradock arrived at the house in Gordon Square, they found Murray in the hall, lifting one end of a large box from the floor. The other end was held by Valerie Palmer.

'Ah, hello, Miss Palmer,' said Jago. 'I didn't expect to see you here.'

'Hello, Inspector,' she replied, as she and Murray deposited the box on the table. 'Blankets,' she added, by way of explanation. 'I don't know where they're all coming from, but it seems everyone needs blankets these days. I haven't defected to the FAU, by the way – I just popped in to see how everyone's getting on here. Carrying on Rosemary's good tradition, I suppose – I think I mentioned that she used to call in from time to time, and I thought that was very nice of her. A little encouragement doesn't cost anything, but we all like to know someone cares, don't we?' She glanced at her watch. 'My word, is that the time? You'll have to excuse me, gentlemen – I really should be running along now. I have my own tasks to attend to, so I need to get to the little post office down the road and buy some stamps before it closes for lunch.' She flashed a smile at Murray. 'We'll continue that conversation later, shall we? It sounds like a good idea to me. Two heads better than one, eh?'

With that, she strode to the door and was gone.

'Busy girl,' said Murray. 'But better to be busy than idle at times like this – at least it makes you feel you're doing something to help. Anyway, I'm all yours. Sorry if that sounded a bit cryptic, by the way – it's just that Valerie and I have been talking business. But what brings you here?'

'We've just dropped in because I told you I'd let you know the outcome of our investigation.'

'Ah, I see. Shall we go somewhere a bit more private, then? Follow me.' He took them down the corridor to an empty office. 'So,' he said when they were all seated, 'what can you tell me?'

'Just that we've got someone under arrest.'

'Who is it?'

'We've arrested Mrs Helen Bowman and charged her with murder. She'll be appearing in the magistrates' court tomorrow morning, and the magistrates will decide whether to commit her for trial at the Old Bailey.'

'Harold's mother . . . well, that is a surprise. I barely knew his parents, though, so I suppose there's nothing for me to say. But was it anything to do with Harold's death?'

'There could be a connection, but I'm afraid I can't go into any more details.'

'Of course. Well, I'm not part of the family, so I guess it's none of my business. I'm just glad it wasn't Valerie you arrested – we're planning to go into business, you know.'

'Really? I didn't know you were a business-minded person.'

'I don't suppose I am – not yet, anyway. But I've been thinking about what I'll do when this war's over, as I sincerely hope it soon will be. I can't honestly say the end looks near, but when it comes I want to be able to earn a living. I've had an idea, and when you arrived I was just telling Valerie about it, to see what she thought of it. It turns out she's been thinking along similar lines – how to earn a living when this is all over – and she's rather interested in joining in, making it a joint venture.'

'So that's what she meant by two heads being better than one, I assume?'

'Exactly. The thing is, you see, I want to make some money – a lot, preferably – but the only practical skill I've got that I could make a business out of is driving. So as I said, I've had an idea. I reckon when the war ends there'll be army surplus trucks going cheap, so my plan is to buy one, or maybe more if I can borrow the money, and start a transport business. All I need is a bit of capital to get things started. It's the kind of thing Rosemary might have helped me with, if she hadn't been taken from us – she was generous like that. But it's too late to ask her now – I'll just have to knuckle down to it and earn what I need by the sweat of my brow, and I don't mind doing that.'

Jago smiled to himself: he knew precisely how much Murray stood to gain from Rosemary Webster's will, but he wasn't at liberty to disclose it. He was sure, however, it would come as good news when her bequests were made known: it should be more than enough to buy a decent-sized truck, and possibly even two.

'I wish you well, then. But forgive me for saying this – I wouldn't have imagined you as the sort of person who wanted to make a lot of money. How does that fit in with your principles?'

'A very fair point, Inspector. But it's a question of why. I've got a bit of a dream – and it's to do with Harold. He died too young to fulfil his dreams, but I believe if he'd lived he'd have made the world a better place. What I'd like to do is make enough money to set up a fund – a scholarship fund to enable a promising young man or woman with the same kind of vision that Harold had to study at UCL and then go on to make the difference he wasn't able to. It would be like a living memorial to him – not a dead statue, but a living person who can carry on his dreams and make them come true. I'll call it the Harold Bowman Scholarship. And if I could do that using old army lorries left over from the war, well, it would have a touch of "swords into ploughshares" about it, wouldn't it? I think Harold would have liked that.'

'That sounds like an admirable project, Mr Murray. And I imagine you'd like to think Mrs Webster would've liked it too.'

'Yes – I think she would. And I hope she would have approved of Valerie being part of it with me – especially if she'd never thought of Valerie having a heart of stone in the first place.'

'And what about Miss Palmer being clever but cynical? That was something you told me Mrs Webster definitely had said about her.'

Murray laughed. 'A good question, Inspector. Rosemary didn't mince her words, but that didn't mean she was always right. I actually told her at the time she was wrong – I said Valerie may talk like a cynic, but deep down she's as warm and tender-hearted a woman as any man could hope to meet. Not that I've ever said that to Valerie, of course – it might sound a bit forward, mightn't it?'

Jago remembered what Valerie Palmer had disclosed last time he'd seen her, about her recently conceived interest in finding the right man and settling down. He wondered whether when Murray became aware of Rosemary Webster's bequest he might settle for one truck instead of two and use the rest as a deposit on what Valerie might regard as a nice little house. He smiled to himself again but made no comment.

'Mind you,' Murray continued, 'she's quite a girl, isn't she? I do admire her, and I'm wondering whether I should . . . you know, tell her how I feel about her. Pardon me for asking, but you're an older man, and you strike me as wise.' He paused. 'What do you think? You've seen us both, together and apart – to put it bluntly, do you think I should marry her? My mother always used to say "If you're not sure which way to go, ask a policeman."'

Jago was briefly lost for words. He was also conscious that Cradock was watching him intently, as if hanging on to whatever might tumble from his mouth when he found a reply to give. 'I'll grant you I am a policeman,

Mr Murray,' he said cautiously, 'and I have the power to arrest people, but I don't think my job or my age qualify me to advise you on affairs of the heart. All I can say is that I recently had occasion to become acquainted with the work of a matrimonial agency – in a purely professional capacity, that is, in the course of my inquiries. I wouldn't necessarily advise you to use one of those places, but the woman running it gave me a piece of advice I can pass on if you like.'

'Of course – what is it?'

'She said it's all about identifying the qualities you're looking for in a life partner and then finding someone who has them. An agency like hers helps you to make a list and then they look for a match for you. She said there'll always be someone out there, but the challenge is to find them.'

'That sounds sensible, I suppose.'

'Perhaps it is – she claimed to be an expert, but she's still basically running a business that'll charge you plenty of money to help. But be that as it may, she did say "Happy is the man who finds her for himself", so I suppose if you can do that without professional assistance you'll be saving yourself a good bob or two. I'm definitely not an expert, but it sounds to me like you may be getting a bit happy already – and if you can make her happy too, well, I'm sure that would be a very good thing. I didn't know Mrs Webster, unfortunately, but from what you and others have told me, I think if she were here she'd say to you "Follow your dream."'

Murray laughed again. 'I think you may be right, Inspector. Thank you very much. I might just act on your advice – and on Rosemary's.'

CHAPTER FORTY-FOUR

Jago had been brought up by his father never to keep a lady waiting, so he'd taken pains to ensure he was at the pub where he was to meet Dorothy for lunch well before she arrived. It was an old-fashioned place in Great Portland Street, and she'd suggested it because she'd be working nearby in the morning and because it wasn't far from Bloomsbury. Business seemed to be brisk in the public and saloon bars, but the snack bar upstairs was a little quieter, and he managed to secure a corner table where he reckoned they'd be able to talk without having to raise their voices over the general hubbub. He went back downstairs just in time to meet her coming in through the door from the street.

'Sorry I'm late,' she said, a little breathless. She looked as though she'd hurried to get there.

Jago glanced at his watch. 'Only by three minutes,' he said. 'I don't think that counts as late. Besides, it's a lady's privilege, so no need to apologise. Let me get you a drink – lemonade as usual?'

'That'd be just fine, thanks.'

He got her drink and a pint of mild and bitter for himself, and they took them up to the snack bar.

'Have you been here before?' he asked as they took their seats.

'No – it was recommended to me by some of my fellow American journalists at the Savoy. They said they liked it because it's traditional and the food's good, especially the sandwiches – I think some of them have put considerable time and effort into exploring London's pubs.'

'Valuable research, I'm sure. Let's see if they're right about the food – I enquired when I got here and they said they did a range of sandwiches, nothing too fancy, but fresh and tasty, and with the bread cut nice and thick. They can do cheese, pork, liver, herring roes, coleslaw or mock crab.'

'Mock crab? What's that?'

'That's what I said. The man at the bar said it's grated cheese and margarine, with just a dash of anchovy paste to give it a taste of the sea, on account of actual crabs being scarce at the moment. He didn't know whether that's because the crab fishing season's ended or whether the fishermen were a bit wary about catching mines instead of crabs, but either way mock crab is as good as it gets wherever you go. I was thinking I'd prefer plain cheese myself, but then he said they do Cornish pasties as well, and they have the advantage of being hot.'

'That sounds like a good idea on a day like this. I've heard of them but never eaten one, so I think I'd like to try one.'

'Very well, Cornish pasties it shall be, and I shall think

of my Cornish ancestors as I eat it.'

'Ah, yes, I remember you mentioning your people were Cornish when I first met you. That must be four months ago now, mustn't it? A lot of water's flowed under the bridge since then – and there's been a lot of change around here. I had no idea how long the air raids would go on for back then, and I don't suppose you did either.'

'Certainly not. And judging by what's happened since Christmas, they don't look likely to stop any time soon.'

Jago went to the bar and brought back two Cornish pasties. Dorothy took a tentative bite from hers and breathed in sharply. 'Wow,' she said, 'that *is* hot.' She ate the mouthful she'd taken carefully. 'But very tasty – yes, I like that.'

'Good,' said Jago. 'People say the old tin miners in Cornwall used to take them to work to eat. They're basically meat and potatoes spiced up with pepper in a pastry case, so for them a pasty was a whole meal in itself, and you didn't need any cutlery to eat it, which made it easier to handle down a mine. I like to think maybe some of my ancestors used to eat them.'

'Were they tin miners?'

'I don't know, but a lot of men were in the old days. They probably lived on pasties – and squab pie, of course.'

'And what's that?'

'It's a meat pie made with mutton and apples, pepper and salt, and onion too. I remember when we all had to start using our ration cards last year there were people saying it was the ideal recipe for rationing, but of course that was when you could still get onions. They're a bit hard to come by now.'

'Yes, I know. And why do they call it squab pie?'

'I'm not sure. I think a squab's a young pigeon, so maybe that's what they used to make them with in the old days. My dad told me the Cornish people used to make pies out of anything and everything, and he said there's an old story down there that the devil's never been to Cornwall because he was afraid if he did, they'd make him into a pie.'

Dorothy pulled a face. 'I can't see that being much of a hit on a London pub menu, with or without onions.'

Jago laughed. 'No, indeed – and I doubt whether they'd serve us a glass of black-strap at the bar over there if we asked for one.'

'I suppose that's what they drink in Cornwall, right?'

'So I believe – my dad said it was the fishermen's favourite. It was two parts gin and one part treacle, and they liked it because it warmed them up. I have to say I've never tried it myself, though.'

'Neither have I, although my American ancestors may have – it may surprise you to know that people used to drink black-strap back in the old days in America too, although I think they made it with rum or whisky instead of gin.'

'Well I never.'

'We do have some history in America, you know.'

'Ah, yes. My turn to apologise – forgive me.'

'You're forgiven.'

'Thank you.' Jago sipped his beer. 'So tell me, what was the work you were doing this morning that brought you to this neck of the woods?'

'I had an appointment in Harley Street.'

'With a doctor? That's where all the expensive ones are, isn't it?'

'With a psychologist.'

'Really?'

'Really – but not as a patient. I was interviewing him for an article I'm writing for the paper. He was a fascinating man.'

'And what makes him interesting for your American readers?'

'He wrote a book about his reflections on the first few months of the war, and it was published here and in the States. It generated some interest over there, and my editor in Boston asked me to do an interview with him. The other thing that's interesting about him is that he's a man of many parts – he's a medical doctor and a psychologist, but he's also a journalist and a broadcaster on the BBC. And another thing – on top of all that he's a successful author of crime novels.'

'Really? What's his name?'

'Anthony Weymouth. Do you know his books?'

'No, I'm afraid I don't, but then I'm not a big reader of murder mysteries – I have enough of my own to solve in real life.'

'Of course. And have you discovered who killed that woman you mentioned, in Bloomsbury?'

'Yes – we've made an arrest and charged someone with murder, so now it'll be up to the magistrates to decide whether to commit her for trial at the Old Bailey.'

'It's a woman then?'

'Yes, it is.'

'So what happened?'

'Well, the murdered woman had a nephew who'd tried to register as a conscientious objector but was turned down by the tribunal. That meant he was then called up into the army and unfortunately got killed in action.'

'And that's why she was killed?'

'Yes. It seems she died because she could've tried to influence the tribunal to register him and saved his life, but she chose not to. She must've sympathised with him and his pacifism, because she had a passion for peace, but she also had a passion for duty.'

'So she was torn.'

'Yes, she must've been, and I'm guessing in the end she knew it was her duty not to interfere in the legal process, not to use her own influence to get him out of that situation, so that's what she did. It was a matter of principle, and maybe she paid for that principle with her life.'

'What a sad story.'

'Yes, and it seems she was quite a woman – she helped refugees and took people into her home when they were going through hard times. One person we spoke to described her as an angel of mercy.'

'She sounds like an interesting lady.'

'I think she was, but let's talk about something else.'

'OK – did you meet any other interesting ladies?'

'I did – several, in fact, including one who'd be right up your street. She's a writer, although with all due respect to your Mr Weymouth, I think she'd regard writing detective stories as rather beneath her dignity. She wasn't interested in writing what she called sentimental tosh, by which she meant popular fiction, although I would've thought if you're writing fiction you'd want it to be popular. Still, what do I know?'

Dorothy laughed. 'So what does she write?'

'Well, she seemed to think she was going to write the defining portrait of British life in the 1930s, but given that we're into 1941 now and she hasn't had any success finding a publisher, I'm wondering whether she might've missed the bus. She said she was a serious writer and talked about how she wanted this new book of hers to shine in the firmament, but I couldn't help feeling a lot of it was just wishful thinking, poor woman.'

'That's interesting – it's one of the things Anthony Weymouth talked about. Wishful thinking, I mean, not her book – I don't imagine he's ever heard of her. He was talking about the British character and how it affects the way you look at war.'

'You mean we wished for it? I don't think many people would agree with that.'

'No, he was talking about how we make decisions in our everyday life – he said they're often just based on wishful thinking, because when we're making decisions we let our emotions sway our judgements. He said British people's feelings told them war was too awful to contemplate, and so they decided there wasn't going to be one, despite what the plain facts said. What we should do is keep our feelings out of it and just make rational decisions, but he thinks British people aren't very good at that.'

'Well, he's the expert, I suppose.'

'He did have something positive to say, though – he said that although you British people are too prone to wishful thinking, you do have an enviable ability to laugh at misfortune.'

'That's something, I suppose – and we've had plenty of misfortune to laugh at over the last year or so, haven't we? I'm not sure the young lady I'm talking about was very good at laughing at misfortune, though – I got the impression she thought the world was conspiring against her to frustrate her ambition, as if being a success was her destiny and she was being cheated of it. Still, who am I to judge?'

'Would you say it's true of British people on the whole, though? True of you? Wishful thinking, letting your emotions get in the way of the facts so you make bad decisions?'

Jago was silent: this theoretical discussion had suddenly become personal. He responded to her question carefully. 'I'm not sure. My life is my job, and my job's about assessing the facts and making decisions on the basis of evidence, so that means the answer should be no, I don't let my emotions affect my decisions. But as soon as I say that, I remember the whole reason why I do this job is because of the feeling I had at the end of the last war – I wanted to make life safer for people, and that was an emotional reaction to everything I'd seen when I was fighting in France. So looking at it that way, everything I am and do now is the result of that decision I made, based on my feelings – so that would make my answer yes. What about you?'

'I think it's not so complicated for me – I follow my feelings, simple as that.'

'Then I envy you.'

She smiled. 'If it's any comfort to you, Anthony Weymouth said he was uncertain too. He said sometimes he'd believed war was coming, but sometimes he didn't, and in the end he reckoned he was a victim of wishful thinking – he was convinced all the facts pointed to bloodshed, but then he'd tell himself that that simply couldn't be.'

'In that case I don't feel so bad about not being able to give you a straight answer. Sometimes life just isn't as simple as we'd like.'

'Yes, and I've just said following my feelings is simple, but emotions can actually be dangerous things.'

'That's funny – a doctor said exactly the same thing to me just a couple of days ago.'

'What, that emotions can be dangerous?'

'Yes. It came up in the conversation when I was having a chat with him.'

'As a patient?'

Jago laughed. 'No, not as a patient, just like you with your Dr Weymouth. And the doctor wasn't a psychologist either – it was Dr Gibson, the pathologist who works with us on these murder cases of ours. Not a job I envy him, I must say – cutting up bodies all day long.'

Jago's voice was light, but as he said these words they seemed to summon up the dream he'd had after that evening, and once again Gibson was silently cutting into his body, revealing his heart and lungs. He drove the image out of his mind. 'We spent the evening jawing about this and that over a good glass of whisky. We probably spent too long reminiscing about the old days, but it was a pleasant time.'

Dorothy looked at her watch. 'Speaking of time,' she said, 'I'd better be going – I have to get back to work and start writing that article. Thanks for a very nice lunch – I've had a lovely time.'

'Thank you,' he replied, smiling at her. 'So have I – I always enjoy being with you.'

'That's kind. But if ever you feel you've had enough of spending time together, you only have to say. I don't want you to feel obliged to – you're a free agent. You know that, don't you?'

Jago paused as the memory of his evening with Gibson replaced that of his dream. He said nothing, but took a good hard look at Dorothy across the table, then quietly, as if to himself, said just three words.

'Yes . . . I do.'

ACKNOWLEDGEMENTS

When war broke out in 1939, Bloomsbury was a focal point of London's cultural and intellectual life, home to the British Museum and its world-famous library, and to University College London (UCL), founded in 1826 as a secular alternative to Oxford and Cambridge. Described by T. S. Eliot, who worked at the publisher Faber and Faber's offices in Russell Square, as 'a delightfully seedy part of town', during the interwar years Bloomsbury had become a gathering place for free-thinking artists, writers and intellectuals, in particular those of the eponymous Bloomsbury Group, whose members ranged from the novelist Virginia Woolf to the economist John Maynard Keynes, and whose radical thinking and complex personal relationships had given the area a reputation for bohemian living. In a quip often, although not necessarily accurately, attributed to the American poet and wit Dorothy Parker, the Bloomsbury Group were said to have 'lived in squares, painted in circles, and loved in triangles'.

By January 1941, when this book is set, everything has changed. The British Museum is closed, its precious artefacts dispersed around the country for safekeeping, and UCL's buildings in Gower Street have suffered devastating damage in air raids. Virginia Woolf and her husband, Leonard, have joined the list of displaced local residents, forced out of their Bloomsbury home by another air raid.

Fans of the Blitz Detective books tell me how much they enjoy and appreciate the historical details, often learning things they didn't know, and I'm very grateful for this encouraging feedback. Sometimes it can be difficult to establish what was actually what, because published accounts are either contradictory on the point in question or silent. Even our much-vaunted new friend Artificial Intelligence frequently has to plead ignorance. I had particular trouble pinning down a few points concerning the wartime experience of UCL, so I'd like to thank the staff of the UCL archives for giving me access to their historical records and helping me to find answers to all my questions in one visit.

UCL must be unique among British universities in one respect, in that by the time the war started, the preserved remains of the philosopher Jeremy Bentham were still sitting on one of his own chairs in a glass case in the college library more than a century after his death. While not strictly speaking the founder of UCL, he was acknowledged in the college's annual report for 1939–1940 as its 'patron saint', and he had left instructions in his will for his body to be preserved and clothed in one of his black suits. The account given by my imaginary Professor Masterson of the restorative work done on the body and its evacuation to safer accommodation before the bombs fell is true.

Having heard that Jeremy Bentham still resides in

a glass case at UCL, I was keen to see him for myself, but the rebuilding work going on at the time of my visit meant I had trouble finding him. I'm grateful, therefore, to the passing stranger who stopped to help me, took me to him and introduced me to him, then walked me to my next destination on the site. How appropriate that while Professor Masterson was a UCL historical fiction, my kind mystery guide serendipitously proved to be a real-life UCL counterpart – so thank you, Professor Marek Ziebart.

My thanks go also to the archive staff at the British Museum for enabling me to delve into the history of its wartime evacuation and its rules on the disposal of items from its collections. The museum itself was not spared by the air raids of 1940 – its records showed that in one night alone in December of that year, at least twenty incendiary bombs fell on its premises. I'm grateful that even in the midst of such havoc the museum's governing body continued to keep meticulous records of its wartime operations and decisions, and that these have been faithfully curated for later generations to this day.

On the subject of what is real in my books and what is a confection of my own imagination, I should note that the author to whom Dorothy refers, Anthony Weymouth, was a real person, the remarkable scope of whose activities was as described by her. What Dorothy didn't know, though, is that Anthony Weymouth was only the pen name of Dr Ivo Geikie Cobb. As for why he adopted that particular pseudonym, even the omniscient AI assistants at my elbow draw an apologetic blank, but I suspect it was because his address in the 1930s was Weymouth Street, a turning off Harley Street in London. Several of his mystery novels are still in (electronic) print, and he also wrote a fascinating diary of the part of the war in which my story is set, *Plague Year*.

Experts on the operations of the wartime Ministry of Information may quibble at my apparent conflation of roles in the person of Miss Mildred Frobisher, but I can only plead that what I have written is what she said, and I cannot necessarily vouch for her accuracy or indeed veracity.

In writing this book I've been grateful for the assistance of some Human Intelligence sources of expertise. I'd like to thank Nathan Hazlehurst for checking my details about the London Auxiliary Ambulance Service, Alastair Bates for enlightening me concerning some aspects of wills, and David Love for doing the same with regard to what happens when you hit someone on the head with a poker. My thanks go also to Silvianne Aspray for checking the English of my German character, Nat Hollands for checking my Canadian English, and Rudy Mitchell for checking my American English. I have checked my own English English. Since these good people's advice is filtered through my own cranium, I note that any errors are mine, not theirs.

I'd like to thank Broo Doherty, my agent, and Susie Dunlop and her team at Allison & Busby for their continuing enthusiasm and encouragement as we share in the process of bringing the Blitz Detective stories into the world.

And finally, my deepest thanks and love to Margaret, Catherine, Pete, David and Lizzie, my literary, and life, support and advisory team.

MIKE HOLLOW was born in West Ham and grew up in Romford, Essex. He studied Russian and French at the University of Cambridge and then worked for the BBC. In 2002 he went freelance as a copywriter, journalist and editor. Mike also works as a poet and translator.

blitzdetective.com   *@MikeHollowBlitz*